Schizoid

Matthew Tait

'Tait weaves his magic once again, creating a charming, nostalgic trip back in time. A hall of meta-mirrors, the author pours himself into his fiction like never before.'
– Daniel I Russell, Shadows Award nominated author of *Retard*

'With *Schizoid*, Tait performs an intricate autopsy on the writer's soul and the act of creation itself.'
– Greg Chapman, Bram Stoker Award-nominated author of *Hollow House*

Cover Art: Greg Chapman
Editor/Layout: Shannon Gambino
ISBN 10: 0-646-99698-3
ISBN 13: 978-0-646-99698-1

First Printing: December 2018

For Shannon and The Tribe – long may we reign

TABLE OF CONTENTS

Chapter One	1
Chapter Two	11
Chapter Three	24
Chapter Four	39
Chapter Five	61
Chapter Six	80
Chapter Seven	99
Chapter Eight	110
Chapter Nine	125
Chapter Ten	133
Chapter Eleven	147
Chapter Twelve	171
Chapter Thirteen	195
Chapter Fourteen	206
Chapter Fifteen	228
Chapter Sixteen	254
Chapter Seventeen	274
Chapter Eighteen	290
Chapter Nineteen	311
Epilogue	313

ALSO BY MATTHEW TAIT

GHOSTS IN A DESERT WORLD
DARK MERIDIAN
OLEARIA
DIFFERENT MASKS: A DECADE IN THE DARK
SLANDER HALL
DAVEY RIBBON
PROVIDENCE PLACE

Chapter One

The first time Micha Tudor went to Hadley Grove, he thought the whole experience a fever dream – fallout from the stress of his sister's death when he was seventeen.

Returning a second time – on this occasion via death, itself – quelled the dream notion entirely.

***

Suicide. The eternal taboo of ill-fated man finally greeted Roger Brust at the age of twenty-seven.

The letters were scrawled on a yellow legal pad, a bulk of notes sitting adjacent to his writing laptop. When ideas failed to materialize on the machine, the legal pad would receive the brunt of his hieroglyphic scrawl composed in a drunken stupor. The sentence, penned in red cursive, had

1

all the grace and opportune eloquence of a hack.

Brows furrowed, Micha picked up the pad and studied the words, a subtle tremor running through his fingers. These days there always seemed to be a tremor – the tangible scar from another bout of drinking cheap red wine. Only two bottles, according to his nightstand, but it was enough; sufficient to produce a loose roiling of nausea in his gut – and to open the door to the first flickers of nihilistic thought … a dark accompaniment for the rest of the day.

He could not recall writing the words.

They belonged to a short story in-progress. Roger Brust was the ageing, prize-fighting protagonist of *The Farmer*, Micha's first lighthearted stab at literary fiction … or whatever it was the pretentious crowd labelled it these days. Micha preferred to think of his latest attempt merely as a departure from his usual forays – journeys into the darker spectrum of the human experience.

Like his ill-received second novel, *The Midnight Mare*.

Remember The Midnight Mare*, Micha?* the voice of his hangover quipped. *You know, that book that took over two years to complete and failed on almost every level? It was sold to a reputable small press with high expectations – only to disappear into the ether shortly thereafter, a complete tank in sales. You –*

Micha cut the voice off before it could do any more damage. Yet he knew

(unless he had another drink)

the voice would return and only get louder as the day progressed.

Roger Brust taking his own life? This was something he had never planned for the hero. Here was the sentence, spiked at the edges with ethanol fugue, yes – but somehow all the more potent for the flaw. Was this perhaps his subconscious mind trying to communicate with him? A kind of automated ghost-writing technique informing his *conscious* mind this was where the story needed to go?

That's bullshit, came the soft voice of Lila. *You're only writing about yourself, babe.*

Micha winced and scrunched up part of the legal pad.

On this occasion, like most, his girlfriend's voice was right.

Thinking about Lila brought back the nihilistic tide of thoughts – musings that were impossible to stop once they got rolling. Lila was too good for him; Lila was a sweet-natured soul in love with life, and he was a … a what? A young man with a vocation that could hardly be called a career. Saddled with a writing compulsion that – although he had seen some tangible success with his first novel – was still considered an occupational hobby by everyone in his immediate circle. As an official team (*Team Tudor!* Lila would sometimes proclaim with one happy fist pump), they had been a couple shy of two years; a time of unmistakable, unalloyed happiness. But was it enough? Life itself seemed to be a cruel game, one where you were in constant competition to hold your own against others. Despite Lila vouching her love for him on a daily basis, *drumming* it into him during his more insecure moments, he perpetually had the niggling feeling that he wasn't good enough for her or anybody else. And an existence without

Micha Tudor was probably in the best interest of not just his inner circle but for the wider world as a whole.

You've played this game many times before, Micha. It's nothing but your hangover talking – you'll be feeling better again later tonight.

Oh God, tonight … what did tonight entail? Exactly four hours standing behind the desk of a store that sold used Blu-rays and DVDs. The mere thought of it filled him with a kind of fatalistic dread that the words he'd scrawled on the legal pad had somehow failed to do. Staring into the eyes of numerous strangers over the shift, their faces like the bloated contours of fish in an aquarium, proceeded to feed the meditations of his hangover even further.

Micha glanced at his reflection in the ovoid mirror above his desk.

His facial features were a study in pain.

Part of it was just waking up, of course: his short black hair stood up in unruly fuzz; on his chin, neck, and cheeks, a three-day growth was already making inroads. But those eyes … the eyes of a person seldom lied. Hazel with flecks of green, they carried a forlorn unhappiness deemed wretched by anyone with even a miniature grasp of interpreting human emotions. Looking into them, the moment seemed to feed upon itself, and Micha experienced a wave of melancholy so profound he staggered from the mirror and fell backward onto his mattress.

I can't let anyone at work see me like this, he thought. The intimate voice of his hangover was a tired, old cadence; words uttered to himself so many times they mirrored a litany. Next up, like predictable clockwork, came the expectant reply: *I don't have a choice.*

But was that exactly true this time? Sprawled on his back, Micha's eyes alighted on his bedside nightstand and found the two bottles of red wine with a congealing dollop still remaining in the bottom of the one closest to him. Near the bottles were his Samsung tablet and a shaded vanilla lamp; beside *them* sat a small white bottle containing prescription medication. Over ninety pills of Valium to be precise. Micha had obtained half of the bottle legally from his general practitioner over a twelve-year period, a kindly middle-aged woman who didn't mind parceling out one fill of the stuff every six months or so (no more, though, not for a young man suffering acute depression). The other half he had purchased online from some dodgy overseas dispenser – although these were usually on par with their legitimate cousins.

Ninety pills, give or take. Enough to take me out of the equation for good.

Micha's eyes lingered on the bottle – all the answers to mankind's idiotic questions seemed suddenly poised, ready, and waiting. Every problem he was shackled with and every anxious thought that rained down with the stuttering regularity of a lightning storm could be expunged by that bottle. No more tremors; no more dreading the countdown to work like the countdown to something imploding. Best of all, no more feelings of inadequacy regarding Lila – she would be free to move on with her life and find somebody with a happier disposition. Each pill in that bottle seemed to carry its own tune, whispering this elegy had been his destiny all along … he only had to reach out and play the notes for himself.

Lila.

Her face rose up before him, unbidden. Not merely her face but the life they shared together: she a doctor's receptionist; he the flowering writer. Weekends spent watching movies, kissing passionately on the bed, and drinking shoddy fruit champagne until the break of dawn. His father secretly adored her, yet secretly loathed him. Her parents, immigrants from England, looked upon the starving artist with a certain brooding disdain. Friends were slim-to-nonexistent because he preferred isolation to socialization – something Lila had been trying to help him with but with little success. His complete inability to dance, despite Lila's promise to teach him. The elaborate worlds of his fiction – the only outlet in life that seemed to provide him with any kind of succor.

You can't do it straight, a voice whispered. Though Micha couldn't tell whether this was the voice of his hangover or not. *More alcohol will be required.*

Did his current funds permit the purchase of more? He had just enough left in his savings account for one final, glorious bottle of mid-range vodka.

A tub of yogurt in the fridge would provide the necessary conveyance for the ninety, crushed pills of Valium.

The booze would provide the necessary courage.

***

Years previous, Micha had purchased a book entitled *Final Exit* by Derek Humphry. The work contained dozens of painless methods for delivering oneself or a loved one into the great beyond. Ostensibly, he had purchased the book for research into one of his novellas, *Noble Place*, where a cult of people drank the Kool-Aid to reach a higher level of consciousness. Although some of the book's contents had ultimately reached the novella, purchasing *Final Exit* had always been – whether this was in the back of his mind or not – an *In Case of Emergency, Break Glass* talisman against the darkness. A calm against the storm. Knowing how to exit reality with as little pain as possible was something Micha could consult should the need one day arise.

Returned from the liquor store, fat with not one but two bottles of Stolichnaya vodka, Micha took *Final Exit* out from the dusty contents of a bottom drawer (a hidden place where Lila would never think to look), and proceeded to read pertinent passages he'd highlighted over the years. This was another mental ritual that – although he had performed it numerous times – still needed to be carefully adhered to.

Exiting the world was not something you wanted to fuck up.

No matter how much you wanted to leave it.

***

What about The Mercury Man, *Micha? Have you thought about that?*

With his hangover now somewhat eradicated after

three straight shots of vodka from the bottle's cap, its deleterious voice had gone quiet. Though in its place as calm as a convent came the voice of reason, glowering sobriety and just causes. Once enabled, he could usually get on with any given day at hand; although, beginning an inner-monologue by referencing a novel-in-progress was never a good start.

Cue the malaise of *things that would never be finished.*

In past instances of being this close to leaving the world, thinking about his writing usually brought Micha back from the brink. Incomplete novels – for anyone who was a staunch completest – were like jittering flames of hope. To leave characters' fates dangling ad infinitum would not only be a disservice to their histories but a spit in the eye of creation as a whole. *The Mercury Man,* a run-of-the mill horror tale he had begun in February, was not even a quarter completed.

Now that I'm thinking about it, voice of reason. You know what? I honestly don't give a shit about the new book.

Though expecting some sort of stalwart riposte, Micha heard no reply whatsoever.

It seemed the voice of reason had given up.

All the more reason for Micha to do the same.

***

Things were in order; things were clean.

Micha had decided long ago there would be no note left behind, no form of worthless sentiment to add to the drama. His parents would suffer temporarily; their grief would be mired in the absolution of self-pity, not the deceptive, misplaced sorrow of losing a son. His girlfriend would be somewhat scarred, if only initially, but she was born of a different ilk than he; a young woman who could rise above calamities and be stronger for their incursion.

Holding a vodka bottle in his right hand and the Valium-spiked yogurt plate in his left, a palpable sense of relief overcame Micha as he made his way toward his final resting place. He was going home, back to the blissful, formless amnesia before the advent of life. And this time, there were no riotous voices clamoring he abstain from the process. The only solid thoughts he had now were a kaleidoscope of past memories; haunting conversations shared with Lila about mortality … and the everlasting question of what came after.

You don't believe there would be some kind of cosmic repercussions for taking your own life? she had once asked him. *That rejecting the universe might piss it off at some quantum level?*

No, he'd replied emphatically, yet couldn't help laughing at the insightful way Lila shaped her phrases. *Not if you make a conscious decision to exit reality for a different one with greener pastures. I believe suicide can be like taking off a virtual reality meat-helmet and going back to the* real *reality.*

Lila had laughed right along with him, but there had been an obvious solemnity in the back of her eyes that bespoke of concern – apprehension for the man she loved. Though numerous questions must have been on the tip of her tongue

(do I have to worry about you, Micha? You're not really thinking of taking that step, are you?)

she had moved onto other subjects. Yes, Micha found himself at the mercy of a black dog named depression, but throwing scraps to that dog only caused it to hang around more often.

Front door unlocked – check. Electricity turned off – check. House cleaner than a priest on Sunday – check. Why , Micha, I believe you are ready for take-off.

Before lying down, he took a final swig of vodka from the bottle, relishing the clean and hot explosion of its digestion. Without stalling lest a moment's hesitation gave an inner voice its audience, he bolted down the laced yogurt in four long swallows, working the concoction as though it were an elixir.

More vodka chased the barbiturates.

Accompanying Micha to the pillows was a pleasant languor, which only intensified as he closed his eyes.

Behind the dark void of his eyelids, shadows chased each other like animals at play.

Some of his final thoughts were of Lila, her laugh, and how she would never get an opportunity to teach him how to dance.

The distant susurration of a briny sea joined the shadows, and thereafter, Micha Tudor slipped quietly into death.

Chapter Two

The sound of salt spray, of water jettisoned against rocks, did not recede as Micha floated on a tide of thought. That there was thought at all was a tacit revelation, surprising in its particulars. Death, the eternal taboo of ill-fated man, was rumored to quell the notion of all thought entirely.

Micha drifted. In his flight, vague outlines were slowly being illuminated in addition to the sounds: the pencil scrawl of a bird in flight, its cries conjoining the cacophony of the sea. Below, the winding impression of a concrete road, its trajectory hugging the side of a rocky cliff-face. Above the landmass, the churning clouds of an overcast sky, billowed forms merging to create a giant whole.

I know this place, Micha thought.

Moving along the highway, other signs of life folded into his awareness: a lighthouse perched on the lip of a hill like a resting gargoyle, its outer façade bleached white by

the elements. And running parallel with the sea, the timbers
and scaffolding of an artificial walkway, its stick-like
protuberances like an easily solved maze.

I know this place, he repeated to himself. And on the
heels of this thought: *I've died.*

Vague snatches of memory were seeping through now,
but they were subtle – more like grains of sand struggling
through a sieve. Some kind of final decision had been
reached in the world he'd left behind, a choice there was no
returning from. After years of thinking about this thing, he
had finally found enough courage to make it happen.

And now his soul wandered free.

Past the mountainous road, Micha glided over
additional rampant hills forming a bridgework to more
civilization. On the arteries of the streets, slow-moving cars
navigated in between tall pines and brazen redwoods. Built
into the hills, like growths of the land itself, were dozens of
lavishly built mansions, all of their windows facing
outward toward the sea. A main thoroughfare, laden with a
myriad of shops and storefronts, traversed through the
middle of it all with the undulating rise and fall of a wave.

Hadley Grove.

Heretofore a place existing solely within Micha's
imagination, there could be little doubt this was the small
metropolis, Hadley Grove – the setting for novellas,
numerous published short stories, and the main playground
for his abandoned book, *The Mercury Man*. He knew this
not just from the familiar sights, of which there were many
(everything from the shapely curves of Main Street to the
algae-green composition of the sea), but also from the

ashen color of its overripe atmosphere – a town existing in the perpetual twilight of a world darkened by winter. Hadley Grove even had a scent: an oxidized amalgamation of pine needles and ever-present sawdust, a byproduct from an old industrial mill situated on the outskirts; a place where wheat, wood, iron and cloth were routinely pulverized to make new materials. His spirit, perhaps sensing its destination was near and at the whim of other forces, suddenly took a swan dive from its higher echelons and made haste toward Main Street – a curve of road brimming with the hum of human activity.

Words and images from another life, another world, came to Micha as his progress slowed: stories of people dying in the earthen realm only to be resurrected in a heaven of their own making; mythologies when decoded meant *belief* in something was ultimately enough to bring it into being. Surely those tales were just that: the ceaseless mythologies of an evolved animal who refused to reconcile its own mortality.

And yet here I am.

Could the afterlife really be something as arbitrarily prosaic as a town named Hadley Grove? Did the universe permit such things? Admittedly, Hadley Grove had somehow always felt the more tangible of the duel worlds he inhabited. A place, although lifted directly from waking dreams, contained more substance than his material real life in Concord, New Hampshire. On occasion, Hadley Grove was filled with monsters, yes – but it was also teeming with a cast of characters who behaved very differently to Micha's human counterparts. In this world, men did not suffer the exactitudes of loneliness merely for wanting to create art. In this world, the monsters were ultimately vanquished for a period of time.

Slowing down, Micha's bodiless form could make out some of the individual people who populated the municipality. Samantha Moffat, a twenty-seven-year-old who wrote stories and moonlighted at the local library. A small and petite blond with an impeccable fashion style, Samantha was in the process of crossing Main Street, one arm firmly gripped around a coffee-colored handbag. As Micha floated past, he easily discerned her white vapor of breath as it ebbed and flowed from her mouth and nose. Wholly unaware of his presence, Samantha proceeded to mount a footpath. In her wake, a white station wagon slowly maneuvered past; its unseen occupant producing a solitary one-handed wave from the driver's side window.

Samantha smiled and waved back.

This can't be real, Micha thought. *Because I created her.*

A heroine in one of his novellas, Samantha had once battled an ancient evil raised in the tracts of a swamp just south of Hadley Grove. She'd come away victorious, of course, and had gone back to her life as a librarian, galvanized and wiser for the encounter. The source of the evil had been attributed to an ancient and malignant manuscript – a book that harbored a supernatural ability to mutate Hadley Grove's children into grotesque monstrosities.

The children.

Here were some now, carrying backpacks and walking

in the opposite direction to Samantha. Micha instantly recognized some of them (wasn't that the Goforth boy sporting a blue windbreaker and curly brown hair?) while others he was seeing for the very first time. Next to the boy with curly hair

(Charlie? I think I named him Charlie)

walked a girl with a long mane of orange hair who trudged with the lumbering gait of someone handicapped. Her friends, all of them talking raucously and emitting spit-spraying laughter, kept their pace unhurried in order to accommodate their friend. These must be the dozens of extras Micha had only ever alluded to in passing or never mentioned at all … the unseen characters existing as invisible glue, binding together all of the leading players.

Though Micha longed to linger on these characters, it seemed his spirit had other ideas. Once more ballooning upward, he rode a current of wind past the children and followed the arc of the road until coming to rest before a group of houses. Like the ones nestled in the hills, these were also of the large and luxurious variety. While Hadley Grove supported only a small population of roughly four-thousand people, its coffers and average income were brimming, a substantial wealth accumulation thanks to a local ski resort beyond the northern flank of the cove. Sleek and modern, featuring Bavarian architecture, the houses' interiors burned with soft ambient light, entire living rooms awash in the yellow glow of numerous lamps. All this despite the early morning hour.

Along a driveway he moved, past two idle station wagons and up to a bay window of the house closest.

Below Micha lay a hedge of trimmed rosebushes, their network of skeletal branches like a canvas of claws. Through the window lay more human activity: a family rousing itself from the torpor of sleep. Again, he recognized these individuals, this particular family.

In a kitchen nook pleated with yellow curtains, a young woman busied herself with bread, butter, and an array of sandwich ingredients. On a carpeted area not far from where she stood, two young girls – physically identical – were laying down on their stomachs, hunched over numerous exercise books and relaying information to each other in the offhand, extemporaneous manner characteristic of those who had once shared a womb. By a television set, a decorated Christmas tree kept a silent vigil over the children, its branches withered and the space beneath them bereft of presents.

The Bowthorpe twins, Bethany and Maddie. The Christmas tree is still up because they keep it until at least the beginning of March. Their mother's name is Penelope. Daddy died in March, fighting a fruitless war in the Middle East. They –

Although formless, Micha felt his spirit recoil; felt the ethereal stuff of his composition retreat from the window. While these were not characters to appear in any of his shorter works, the Bowthorpe family were to have somewhat of a starring role in *The Mercury Man*. Early on in the tale, all those present in the living room would perish in a car accident on Terry Peak Road, one of the two snaking highways leading up to the bluffs and out of town. With no witnesses to the crash, the triple death of this loving family would spark a catalyst fire of rumor and innuendo; intimations alluding to the mythical figure known in Hadley Grove as The Mercury Man.

Micha knew all of this intimately.

Because he'd mentally outlined their death scene only a few short weeks ago.

***

Heavy with revelation, Micha's spirit left the Bowthorpe house and soared once again beyond the telephone lines high above Main Street. Past the supermarket, the pharmacy, and the closed restaurant-portion of town, his awareness shifted back to the coastal woodlands and tracts of farming acreage to the west. It was in these turfs and rutted roads where Hadley Grove's sprawling churches were located, including one bulging brick-and-mortar cathedral perched above the town like an ominous castle. Punctuated by two needle - point steeples and a l ime-green bell tower, its apostolic architecture was more reminiscent of something from Europe. Although Micha had spent untold afternoons at his laptop describing this portion of Hadley Grove (and others), witnessing it up close in fourth-dimensional reality was something that taxed his already fevered imagination. The church, itself, was fleshy in the particulars, lent gravitas by a backbone of wind and the shimmering peak of the small bluff it rested upon. Because Micha knew what presence rested behind its walls, he struggled to resist its physical pull.

But the church wasn't going to be denied.

Only imaginary horrors lurk here, he thought. *Of which you are the architect.*

More questions arose – queries having no place in any conceivable afterlife. Surely he was immune from harm here; protected from the darker aspects of Hadley Grove? After all, this world was conceived by his own fiery ambition. While the presence lurking inside the church

(Father Natal Purson. Just say his name ... Father Purson)

carried a human face, was it not conceivable he resided here as a kind of Satan in residence? A devil ready to confront his god?

Increasing in speed the closer he got, Micha could already feel something amiss. A quality to the church that other buildings in Hadley Grove failed to possess. As if something malignant resided in the hilly embankment directly beneath its foundations; something that never deigned to brook the surface but nevertheless acted as a conduit to the gothic edifice above. Again, Micha tried to break the bonds of this airborne sojourn, but his flight was now assured.

Though he might be the original writer of the story, some higher power was moving him like a chess piece, seeking he bear witness to a tale presently encompassing Micha Tudor's own private hereafter.

***

Candle smoke greeted Micha as he floated through the

open doors of the church, a cloying miasma of honeysuckle and jasmine not usually reserved for a place of worship. Father Natal Purson, the chief pastor of the cathedral, had lit a smorgasbord of scented candles more in keeping with an ossuary. While their main presence was reserved for the Nave, hundreds were also burning in the recesses between the pews and lit up parts of the central aisle like an airport runway. Still at the whim of some unseen tether, Micha floated through the smoke and jittering candlelight as if he were the spirit of a banished saint returning home. Adjacent to either side of the wooden pews, towering windows of stained-glass depicted the mythologies of Christ in corniced-shaped friezes, six to each side. The Nave – a raised promontory that would compete with any European Basilica – supported a high-alter table dwarfed by an illustrated triptych. Although this was similarly a place Micha had described extensively in his stories, both the altar and illustrated triptych were added additions he had never written of, let alone imagined. The same could also be said of the carpet underneath, a purple wash of insignia-branded flooring.

He had also never typed a sentence regarding a glasshouse.

It stood to the right of the Nave, a see-through enclosure giving a church-going audience an intimate glimpse into the more natural aspects of God's creation: plants and ferns, some of them so large as to compete with an unseen skylight above. Intertwined throughout the fronds, Micha glimpsed a running rivulet of water, which slowly blossomed into a large-scale pond.

The glasshouse was not empty.

Father Natal Purson crouched down in the shallows of the pool.

Engaged in some kind of activity, only the black smudge of his cassocked back was visible through the glass. There could be little doubt this was the Catholic priest who commanded only a small portion of faithful adherents from the town below. Grey hair streaked with black – almost a wizard's mane – ran down both sides of his cassock like a peacock's plumage. Comparable to Samantha and the others outside, the priest seemed entirely oblivious of his audience.

Here is your antagonist, a perpetrator of nefarious deeds.

But was this really the case? In Micha's fiction, Father Natal Purson had only recently been introduced onto the stage – first in a thirty-page novella published solely as an eBook – but whose main, dark performance had yet to be committed properly to the page.

Everything was going to take place in The Mercury Man.

Gliding parallel to the triptych (a staggering set of gothic illustrations featuring Christ's realm atop one of purgatory), more of the glasshouse was revealed.

Another person shared the priest's space in the water.

The figure was lying on his back, a naked and pale male form's upper torso jutted above a shallow tide. Immersed from the waist down, the scene was evocative of baptism; a sacrament performed on a willing participant. Brooding above, Father Purson scooped small handfuls of liquid water onto the supplicant's chest area and abdomen, all the while muttering whispered entreaties. When the supplicant's head and neck came into view, Micha's spirit immobilized, hovering just beyond the partitioned glass.

Grey hair clung to the scalp of the adherent, strands of it sprouting in between bald patches red with infection. His eyes, milk-white cataracts shot through with strands of red, stared up at his savior, seeing nothing. Yet a small smile was evident below ... as if this benediction was a collaborative affair, both participants joined in shared harmony.

First perceiving the liquid of the greenhouse to be nothing more arbitrary than water, Micha noticed now a brackish hue within the element, a molten sheen containing its own strange luminescence.

Continuing to scoop palmfuls, Father Purson spread the liquid liberally over every aspect of the man's flesh, kneading it in places where the skin degenerated into course white flakes.

The Mercury Man, like most of Micha's fiction, was a largely un-plotted book. It was typically while writing them when a character's motivations and subsequent actions became clear.

Was this one of those actions? Was this particular scene – one involving Father Purson baptizing the body of an emaciated old man, whose withered skin appeared jaundiced from malnourishment – something that Micha was *going* to write? Had death somehow skipped him forward into Hadley Grove's unrecorded future? If so, then what was the purpose of this summons? To spend an eternity getting to know the characters of his addled mind? Perhaps he had been beckoned here for the pur pose of being appointed scribe.

Hadley Grove's own John the Apostle, a mouthpiece for revelations yet to pass.

***

Departing the church, Micha felt something snag on his consciousness – a thing entirely divorced from the invisible tether that moved him. Audible sounds, seemingly broadcast from above, suddenly competed with the rushing tide of the wind. At first they were monochrome; the white dirge of static through a telephone line. Then it grew to encompass whispers, a vibration with human characteristics.

The voice was female and faintly familiar.

From this high up, Micha could see the town of Hadley Grove spread out below like something dolloped on canvas. Streets corresponding to arteries; the moving dots on them like slow-moving blood cells. Ever present, tall cypresses colluded with the tops of buildings to give the impression of a rolling sea of ochre, the houses and shops, themselves, submerged in the nuclei of another world. Despite everything he'd been granted thus far (and all its ambiguity), Micha could not deny staying here would surely be a fine thing – perhaps even a *just* and fitting thing. To preside over a place of one's own making, a new home where new memories could be forged. With time, perhaps, his former inhabited world – the world of flesh and dissatisfaction – could be forgotten entirely.

And yet that familiar voice … riding coattails with clouds and demanding to be given an audience. Yes, he *did* know that voice. Knew it intimately. Once, its owner had claimed to love him without reservation. But in the end, her love had not been enough to save him. Nothing had. So why should he listen to it now?

Never left your side, Micha … I never left.

With the words came a face: green eyes atop a small nose with a smattering of freckles. Pixie features in a halo of blonde hair. Small ears similar to his own. A smile that felt like home.

Lila.

Home.

Chapter Three

White-cracked paint on a yellowed ceiling.

Beside him loomed the hanging tapestry of an intravenous machine, the sprouting network of its conduits a bridge to his body. The sound of high heels echoed down a hallway.

His tongue felt caged, a slimy slug he couldn't move, the taste around it like mothballs. Though Micha's eyes were partway open, they grasped only the outline of the IV tubing and the dark silhouette of a narrow bed. Drawing in a breath, his nose and throat constricted with the effort, beads of mucous stifling the attempt.

'Micha?'

Her voice was barely above a whisper, coming just to the left of the saline bag. Though he attempted to turn toward it, the physical act of even subtle movement was beyond his capabilities.

'Shhh. Don't move. Not yet. Just relax. You're awake,

that's all that matters.'

Tactile senses were becoming more acute, and Micha inhaled a heady scent of blossoms, the concentration of lilacs. Although flowers were not giving off the scent in this instance. This was more pungent, having the hallmarks of

(*Pacifica*)

Perfume.

Lila Owen's perfume.

She was here with him in this room. But where was *this* room? And what had transpired to bring him here?

Then Lila's face suddenly appeared, her cheeks wet with tears. Iridescent eyes that were pleased to see him but were also forlorn, heavy and lethargic with sorrow. Heavy with *grief*.

And now it all came careening back: his recent decision to end his life with a handful of Valium and a bottle of vodka. No dream, no flight of fancy but something to have actually *occurred*. A terrible and tangible action in a lifetime filled with them.

An action he had somehow survived.

In his field of vision, Lila's face abruptly twisted, contorting around the edges to become something sinister, accusing and malign. Bland yet acidic, the stale taste of vodka rose up in the back of his throat, threatening to spill out. Pain blanched throughout his esophagus, a place where hospital staff had no doubt penetrated him with tubes and solutions to retrieve the life-ending chemicals. His stomach felt like raw hide, his lungs were bagpipes composed of leather.

You had one job, Micha thought.
And the darkness swallowed him again.

***

When Micha regained consciousness for the second
time, a nurse was on hand to facilitate the transition.
Sporting round features and a harsh demeanor, she
regarded her patient with barely concealed disdain. Too
often, her expression seemed to say; this happens far too
often for my liking. Young men swallowed up in a stew of
self-pity and selfishness, their egocentric patterns a burden
on humanity as a whole. And she, a mistress of caring, was
forced to carry out repair to individuals who didn't deserve
mending.

'Do you know your name?' she asked. 'Age?'

A light was produced, and with clinical detachment,
the nurse inspected his eyes. Her bosom so close, Micha
read the nametag pinned to her side: *Radford*.

'Tudor, Micha,' he replied. 'Thirty-four. Can I please
have a glass of water?'

On his left, Lila burst into action, rummaging through
a handbag with the awkward dexterity of the sleep
deprived. 'I brought you some soda water,' she said, and
produced a small bottle which she proffered to him. 'I
knew you would want some when you woke up.'

Micha looked at her, relieved his neck felt fully
functional again. Gone was her sinister edge and
reproachful eyes; gone, too, any lingering defeatism. Her
gestures now spoke of fortitude; of a clear-and-present

mission. 'It's all right, isn't it, nurse?' she said. 'Just a little bit –'

'It's fine.'

Equally reassured the rest of his body moved, Micha reached out and took the bottle. Chilled on the surface, he watched as icy rivulets of water trickled down the side of the plastic. Though Lila's gesture was a simple one, he suddenly felt his reign of control slip for an instant. And in its wake: a sea of guilt, its tide threatening to spill over completely. This girl sitting beside his bed was beautiful and kind. And he was –

'You're back,' a voice called from the doorway.

Confident, male, full of bravado: a doctor's voice.

He strode in casually, sporting a forceful grin and clutching a chart. A white beard complemented a white gown. Horned-rimmed prescription glasses completed the ensemble of an archetype. With a wave of his hand, he invited Nurse Radford to take her leave.

'I'm Dr. Hughes,' the man said. A brief flick of his eyes toward Lila, followed by a knowing nod of sympathy. 'How are you feeling at the moment, Micha?'

Though half-a-dozen cynical responses bubbled up, Micha suppressed each and every one of them. In reply he gave a barely perceptible nod.

Dr. Hughes nodded back, still smiling but clearly not reveling in his current assignment. 'It was Lila, here, who found you just in time. You weren't answering your phone –'

'I never answer my phone.'

'You weren't answering text messages or emails,

either. Going on two days, I believe. I only have couple of important questions for you today, Micha. Have you stopped taking your medication? Your –,' he quickly consulted the chart. 'Antidepressant: Avanza? Had you begun taking something else? Were you also taking the un-prescribed Valium in the lead up to your latest … depression?'

Making eye contact was hard so Micha settled for the bedsheet. Shame, guilt, remorse … all the standard-issue emotions were there. But there was also an uncanny feeling of disappointment, of something denied. None of this would be occurring if the suggested dosage in *Final Exit* had worked …

'Nothing different,' he replied, without moving his gaze from the bedsheet. 'I was taking my Avanza. It's always helped me to sleep.'

'But you were drinking again, weren't you? Drinking, ah, more than usual?'

No point in sugar-coating any of this. 'I'd been sober for a month-and-a-half. Recently, I had a short-story sale so I celebrated. It carried on more than it was supposed to.

Doesn't it always? the returned voice of his hangover quipped. It was back. For good, it seemed. *It's your curse, Micha. And a tired mantra. The plan is always to get a little fucked-up … but you can never stop, can you? You need to slurp that shit up until every last droplet is all but gone. And then go out and slurp up some more.*

'How much would you say you've had to drink over the last week, Micha?'

Another standard question that had always riled him.

Invariably, his rejoinder usually consisted of: all of it, whatever was available. Yet the quacks always wanted a precise amount. The truth was, Micha had no real idea … and the only way to tally an exact body count was to total the empty bottles lying in his recycling bin or piled on his desk.

About to voice this detail, Micha felt a wave of relief when the doctor held up his hand, a gesture of restraint. Whatever he saw in Micha's expression was all the information needed.

'We can come back to all that later, if you'd like,' he said, and Micha heard a small exhale of relief from Lila. 'Right now, the important thing is for you to get physically better. Currently, you're on a dosage of 30 milligrams of Lorazepam that will help with the withdrawal symptoms. I've given you something else for abdominal pain. You're blood pressure and body temperature are a little high for my liking, but that should significantly decrease over the next forty-eight hours. I see here on your chart that you've been hospitalized before for alcohol withdrawal-related seizures?'

This time Micha's response came in the form of a grimace as past memories threatened to rise up. Responding to his visible pain, he felt the hand of Lila engulf his own … and squeeze. He squeezed right back, letting out a long sigh.

'Then you know we have a duty of care here, Micha. Seventy-two hours is the legal amount of time I have to keep you hospitalized after something like this. A security guard is stationed right outside this door. We also have in-house counsellors on hand should you require their services or feel the need to speak to anybody.' Dr. Hughes's brows furrowed as he considered something unpleasant but necessary. 'We also have a resident priest in this medical center ... if that's the kind of counsel you think might be appropriate to your situation.'

At the mention of a *priest*, Micha felt his grip on Lila tighten even more, clenching the knuckles so hard he felt her recoil and try to pull away. His chest pain, mellowed since awakening, began to flare up once again. The plastic bottle of his soda water crinkled under added pressure from his palm.

Priest ... Father Purson. Hadley Grove.

With the word acting as a facilitator, everything abruptly came crashing back: his mind's journey to a town called Hadley Grove and his observations of the people who resided there. Although he recalled all of it; every small subtlety, had any of it been real? Or had his neurons, starved for life-sustaining oxygen, granted him a final vision of something that could only be conjured by the mind?

'What's wrong?' Lila asked, alarmed at the swift onset of his apprehension. She swiveled toward Dr. Hughes. 'Doctor ... could Micha and I be alone for a little while? I think we need some privacy.'

Though reluctant in his expression, Dr. Hughes, nevertheless, acquiesced, stepping back and pulling the curtain shut in the process.

***

'I'm okay,' Micha said. 'I just need a second.'

Unscrewing the soda-water bottle, he proceeded to swallow, holding it with fingers that still trembled. Three large gulps took care of the contents.

Carbonated water had never tasted so sweet.

'For a second there …'

'I looked like I was going to freak out?'

'Yeah.'

Writ large over her eyes, an unspoken question. Did he want to talk about it? Was he capable? Over the course of their relationship, there was little they *didn't* share; everything from their real-world fears to night terrors. Surely this important thing didn't warrant holding back …

Micha wanted to. He wanted to spill all of it, right there and then: his spirit had wandered over a place so palpable and concrete he had felt the salt-spray of its ocean and inhaled its clement wind. But it was too much. And too soon. Other, more clinical questions trumped the revelation. How long had he been dying before she found him? What had prompted her to come over to the house when going days without talking or texting was sometimes par for the course? In between mouthfuls of soda water, he asked these questions and more. He asked them because that's what you did after a failed suicide attempt.

'Just a feeling,' Lila said. When she spoke, her eyes moved away, and Micha knew immediately she was lying. 'And your Facebook post from the night before. It was so … cryptic.'

Again this was nothing out of the ordinary. Micha's posts, even when he was feeling sanguine, were almost always cryptically bent.

Or so he had been told.

'Your car was in the driveway, and even though I know you like to walk sometimes, I could tell you were home because the hall's window shades were down.' The ghost of a smile crept through, a throwback to happier dialogues. 'You pull them down when you're home because you don't want anybody to *know* you're home. I called out a few times, rang the doorbell, but discovered the door unlocked. I could smell the vodka as soon as I walked in, and I *knew*. I slapped you a few times, turned you over and tried to get you to bring something up. Then I called the ambulance. You had a faint pulse, but your face and neck had turned completely blue. The paramedics got you breathing again. They said you had been under for probably fifteen minutes. Micha, your skin was *blue*. You were dead.'

Tears came again, but they were subdued. A heaped pile of tissues on the bedside cart and collected in the wastebasket gave evidence many had already been shed. Although expecting a fresh wave of culpability, Micha discovered his well of guilt was dwindling somewhat.

Because Lila was lying.

She hadn't been there to check up on him, concerned about his welfare.

She had come over to the house to break up with him.

***

The next few days entailed nothing but rest, and

Micha's body purging itself of alcohol, sweat, and prescription medication. Ironically, he was still being given small doses of diazepam by Nurse Radford who, after three days, still refused to make eye contact or indulge in even rudimentary forms of small talk. Though Lila brought some battered paperbacks from his book collection, the act of reading seemed like a foreign skill he was never equipped with in the first place. Tomes he had once cherished (*Everville* by Clive Barker, *Dune* by Frank Herbert, and others), now felt about as meaningless and throwaway as something assigned to him in high-school English class. They were nothing but lies, flummery; a nonsensical spiral of words by men and women he would never deign to meet. By day, Micha sat stonily and stared at the upraised television mounted to his bed; by night, he endured wave upon wave of nausea and depression, only succumbing to sleep when the diazepam finally did the work it was supposed to. Of his parents or relatives, there was no sign … though Micha had the suspicion Lila had never called them, knowing their presence might act as a catalyst to upset him further. Messages from his boss at *Movie Maniacs*, reams of them, took up a large portion of his unanswered emails and text messages, but he ignored them all. The day job, now void, felt as hollow and insignificant as the paperback books adorning his bedside.

True to his word, Dr. Hughes gave Micha permission to leave the hospital after three days … although he had one final and unexpected piece of news.

'I've arranged for you to see someone, Micha – a specialist in his field and someone who happens to be a good friend of mine.' Sensing Micha's dissent, he held up one finger as if scolding a med student. 'Just hear me out. You've described a lifetime of anxiety and depression. Despite a variety of different medications and on-and-off behavioral therapy sessions, you have responded very little to the proscribed help. I believe this is because you've never received a proper diagnosis.'

Cutting through the malaise, they were words Micha had never heard from a doctor's mouth. At least pertaining to his personal situation. Against his better judgment, Micha's eyes rose from the bedsheet and met Hughes's.

He continued, 'All too often medical professionals look at an alcohol addiction as the source of the depression, when in my belief, it's just a symptom – a symptom of something else going on entirely.' He smiled, then paused. 'Micha … you don't like labels very much, do you?'

Either Hughes was reading his mind or he'd done some homework. 'No,' Micha stated. 'I don't. Bipolar disorder was thrown about a few years ago but quickly retracted. Because I don't have highs. Borderline, obsessive-compulsive disorder, I've heard of that, too. None of them fit. After a while, I began looking at mental illness as a kind of pseudoscience.'

Hughes was nodding as if he anticipated all of this. 'Quite common for a person of your intellect, Micha. I've seen individuals lose faith in the system simply because they carry through life never getting the proper help they require. Micha, I believe very strongly this new doctor can help you. Of course, patients don't always heed my advice … but at this stage in your life, what have you got to lose?'

And there it was: the good doctor ejecting just a snippet of forceful suggestion. Or, put more succinctly: tough love served on a platter. Micha was a young man who had decided nothing – not even the girl who came to visit him each day to sit by his hospital bed – was worth sticking around for. Nevertheless, she and Hughes had gone ahead and saved his life, anyway. At the absolute nadir of one's existence, what *did* he have to lose by taking one more stab at getting better? Rock bottom, as the alkies sometimes liked to profess, existed for a reason.

Micha asked, 'So what's this quack's name then?'

Smiling, Dr. Hughes reached into a coat pocket and produced a business card.

***

On the two other occasions Micha had received hospital treatment after a bout of depression and subsequent alcohol abuse, coming home had felt like a small victory: his books and personal space were a fortress against those dual maladies. Having dodged death's bullet, he could begin a process of laying down new beginnings and starting afresh. His two-bedroom townhouse, while far from the Taj Mahal or a five-star getaway, often felt like an unwavering avenue of retreat where, though alone, its snug confines ensured he would never succumb to loneliness.

Not so this time.

Now it was all too easy to envision his house filled with ghosts, the memories of sadness and depression circumnavigating the walls with the wild abandon of demons. Chosen as Micha's final necropolis, his bedroom presently had the appeal of a funeral home.

'You'll be okay,' Lila said beside him. Tasked with driving him home, she stared at the road ahead with a fixed agility of concentration. 'I did some food shopping yesterday and loaded up the freezer – everything you like, including lasagna. I also bought a few DVDs. Nothing too full on, of course. Some old episodes of *The Office*. Some *South Park*. Stuff like that.'

Since becoming aware his girlfriend was in the process of ending their relationship – a notion living in the land of mere conjecture and brought into being by her body language – Micha had chosen to stay silent on the subject. Just as he had chosen to remain silent concerning

(Hadley Grove. I went to Hadley Grove)

his near-death experience. These things, while important, needed to be examined under the cold light of an abstemiousness mind … not one occluded by the rationale of post-mortem living.

'Thank you,' he replied. And couldn't muster any other pleasantries. While the word 'awkward' could certainly be applied to their exchanges in the aftermath of Micha's survival, it somehow went beyond even that. Truth of their predicament lay like an unseen miasma that could be felt but not articulated with words.

We're not going to survive this, was the unspoken axiom. *Things are too far gone – things have changed between us forever.*

Five minutes later, they were pulling into Micha's driveway.

***

As it turned out, his anxiety was somewhat misplaced. The house, while cloaked in shadows and smelling a tad clammy, was only a house. Evidence everywhere proclaimed this was the domicile of a loner (no family portraits on mantelpieces; no pet pictures adorning the fridge), it could also be said the environment was home to someone who enjoyed unrestricted freedom – freedom from debt, responsibility, and the perpetual obligations that entailed raising a household of children.

In the bedroom, Lila found his manuscript.

'Is this new?' she asked, not looking at him but staring at the cover sheet, the tips of her eyebrows bent in the beginnings of a frown.

'Sort of. I hadn't mentioned it before?'

She went quiet, backtracking their year together. 'No,' she said finally. 'I would have remembered a title like *The Mercury Man*. What's it about if I may ask?'

Why, it's about a fictitious town called Hadley Grove, he thought. *And a monster that calls itself The Mercury Man ...*

'You know I don't really discuss ongoing projects.' Almost daintily, he stepped forward and rescued the manuscript from under her nose. 'I don't want to jinx myself.'

Almost immediately the absurdity of this struck him. He had just attempted suicide. Did things like jinxes and silly superstitions really figure into the equation anymore or any of the old dogmas he had lived by, for that matter? All of them now seemed trivial and utterly inconsequential. From Lila's expression, she thought so, too.

'When I'm done, you'll be the first to read it,' he said, somehow managing a smile that felt crooked on his face. 'At least now the story will have an ending.'

Lila attempted to smile, too. For a second it held … and then crumpled under the weight of what was essentially a tasteless and inappropriate comment.

Dear God. I've changed her by my actions. Her perception of life has changed, and it's all my goddamn fault.

Suddenly he needed her gone, not only from the house but from his very existence, before any more damage could be inflicted. Of course, this had been his motivation all along – removing himself from her life by removing himself from the world – but attempting to articulate this coherently was something neither the writer nor lover in him was capable of doing.

Instead, he said, 'I have the new doctor's details. First thing tomorrow morning, I'll make an appointment. Let's see if Hughes is right about a different diagnosis.'

As a form of farewell, both of them settled for a perfunctory hug. Though just as awkward as their recent verbal interactions, Micha was grateful to hold her one last time.

Chapter Four

A shaft of unexpected sunlight roused Micha from sleep.

Though the harsh brightness was suggestive of a hospital environment, he knew this could not be so because they'd discharged him. A terrible thing had happened … but he had lived to fight another day.

And now he was home again.

Blinking away a fog of fugue, Micha felt a pressure beneath his back that was not his bed. Yes … he remembered now. After a brief attempt to doze on his queen-sized mattress, Micha had retired to the lounge room's sofa to watch Lila's proscribed movies in the hope they would usher him into some semblance of sleep.

The pressure underneath his back had the hard texture of cement.

Above, the daylight filtered down through a layer of clouds.

I'm not on the sofa – I'm not even inside.

The revelation prompted him to push his body into an upright position. As he did so, Micha became aware he had been sleeping or had passed out in an alleyway. Not far from his body, crates containing goods were piled around a green doorway; trash and recycle bins nearby added to the flotsam. There were other things he noted immediately: the shouting voice of a woman barking out orders from within a building and the smell of cooking grease; but these were eclipsed by the figure standing not three feet away, staring at him.

A cowboy? he thought. And following on from this, a dozen different questions surfaced as to the how and why a person found himself sleeping in a dirty alleyway. Had he blacked out again after another drinking spree? Had he –

The cowboy stepped forward … only Micha wasn't so sure it *was* a cowboy. Donned within something like a black cape, a haggard and wrinkle-strewn face peered out at him from under the brim of a weathered wide-brimmed hat. Through the undergarments of his cape

(yes, it's a him *all right, no doubt about that)*

Micha could make out the bony protrusions of an ancient body. Despite the almost theatrical appearance, something about the man felt almost familiar.

'Hello?' Micha inquired. 'What's … where am I?'

The words felt ridiculous on his tongue, but Micha had no other avenue of introduction. As he spoke, the man took another quick step forward, revealing eyes that until now had been hidden under the shadow of the wide hat.

Silver eyes.

As if coins were cocooned within the sockets.

Micha took a step back, flailing both arms and almost tripping over.

Though the stranger did not speak, he kept his quicksilver gaze steady, a wordless exchange taking place, nonetheless.

He's curious about me, Micha thought. *And just as surprised.*

Curiosity aside, there was something else in that steely gaze – a strange species of judgment; a weight of being *marked* and perceived by something powerful.

Breaking the moment, the sound of a door banging open. Turning around, Micha saw a middle-aged woman – presumably the owner of the voice – framed in a doorway and holding a bag of trash. A cigarette sat crookedly in the corner of her mouth. She stared at Micha, her look every bit as perplexed as the arrival of the young man in front of her.

The caped apparition had vanished.

One moment, he'd been standing close enough for Micha to catch an undercurrent of his scent. The next, nothing. Not so much as a swish of cloak rounding a corner.

You imagined him. As you're probably imagining –

'Can I help you?' asked the woman. Her cigarette, dangling precariously from her lips, felt strange to Micha's eyes. *Nobody* smoked in public places anymore, least of all in eating establishments. Which, evidenced by the chargrilled smells wafting through the snot-green doorway, seemed to be the case.

'I said, can I help you?' she repeated, moving closer.

And then, as a shaft of sunlight hit her bosom, Micha saw it: her uniform shirt. Or, more specifically, the *business* name sewed into the left breast: *The Grove Gourmet*.

Sudden vertigo threatened to push Micha to the ground once again.

Like the town of Hadley Grove, itself, *The Grove Gourmet* was an entirely fictitious place of Micha's own imagining – a coffee shop and bistro where locals congregated on weekends and after work. Staffed by a husband and wife team, *The Grove Gourmet* had its address halfway up Hadley Grove's main thoroughfare, the archetypal small-town mom-and-pop store found in anywhere, USA. Though Micha considered the brief possibility of coincidence, he quickly discarded it when the woman was joined by a man at her side, his weathered features as startlingly familiar as any character Micha had ever committed to fiction.

'What's going on here?' the man asked. Like the woman, he also sported a grease-smeared shirt. 'Who is this young man? Is everything okay?'

Surprising even himself, Micha found his voice. 'Everything's okay,' he said. 'Say … did either of you happen to notice a strange man here just now with me? He wore a black cape, and …'

And there was nothing else to say. Because the owners of *The Gourmet Grove* were staring at *him* like he was the strange one, their eyes lingering on the lower portion of his body.

His feet were currently bereft of any shoes.

Micha wore the same attire he'd gone to bed in the

previous night: a long sleeve jumper and tracksuit pants.
Underneath the pants, he could feel no underwear grazing
his cock. The jumper hung loosely on his frame, one size
too big after his recent brush with death and the hospital
stay's liquid diet.

Death was my entry point the first time ...

And the second time? It seemed falling asleep was
another doorway into the town of Hadley Grove.

The woman, a tad impatient, said, 'You look like
you've had a rough night. Should I call someone for you,
son?'

A brief glance at her husband, the subtle roll of her
eyes. *Her name is Harriet*, Micha thought. *Harriet Wilson
and her husband is Edward. They've been stewards
here for over ten years. If you don't say something soon,
they'll be calling someone, all right. Though it won't be
anyone you know. It'll be someone driving a black and
white cruiser with a flashing bubble on top ...*

Micha smiled and made a tipping motion toward his
mouth with one hand. 'Out celebrating last night, and I got
carried away,' he said. Only now did he notice a twinkling
Christmas decoration stenciled on the other side of the door
and seized on it. 'End-of-year office parties. You know
how it goes.'

At the mention of *Christmas*, he could see the Wilsons
visibly relax. Christmas was big in Hadley Grove. The
Wilsons' coffee shop even had a float in the end-of-year
Magic Cave street parade. Micha had alluded to the float in
his novella: *Mary Stall's Monday*.

'I'll see myself home,' Micha said. 'I'm sorry to have

bothered you.'

Reassured by his justification or not, Micha could sense Harriet and her husband wrestling with the predicament. Their town was small, and in a pint-sized metropolis almost all of the day-to-day faces were passingly recognizable; Micha's was not. Micha was a shoeless stranger standing in their doorway and grinning at them like someone a few screws short of a hardware store.

Yet, I'm also their fucking God. How about the irony in that!

Behind the Wilsons, someone – possibly one of their cooks – shouted out Edward's name. Sensing his moment, Micha turned around and proceeded across twelve feet of concrete littered with dirt and cigarette butts, toward Main Street.

When he turned back around, the snot-green door of *The Gourmet Grove* was closed.

***

Too preoccupied to fully inspect his environment upon awakening, Micha attempted to do so now. His anxiety – a stark and menacing passenger in everyday waking life – was now threatening to implode. What he needed (what he *always* seemed to need), was a drink.

Just one, he thought as the whirring engines of cars in the street beyond began to make themselves heard. *Just one sip of strong spirits to take away the edge. I think coming to an imaginary place probably entitles me to one.*

The cars, visible now, were a slow moving herd, and

Micha almost shrunk back into the alleyway again. Simply being noticed a second time was a basis for retreating, but Micha had not counted on another overriding factor that had only been hinted at.

Vehicles from another era populated Main Street, Hadley Grove.

While no expert on automobiles (or being a grease-monkey, for that matter), Micha, nevertheless, recognized some of the models. There were Buicks and Chevrolets trundling along; there were Ford Broncos and LTDs. Resting in a row of slanting parking spaces nearby sat a black Pontiac Firebird, its shining hood decorated with the splayed wings of its emblem. A white Cadillac purred along like a boat misplaced from its moorings, slowing down as it approached Micha's side and searched for a parking spot.

From a shop's interior, Micha heard the blare of a saxophone followed by the sound of percussion with a synth undercurrent. As the song built through its harmonica-laden verses, the band's signature sound became unmistakable.

Micha was listening to the rocking strains of *Huey Lewis and the News* piped through a radio's speakers, a band whose radio presence peaked during the Eighties.

On the sidewalk, a young couple strode toward him, a man and woman linked at the fingers. Pink sunglasses adorned the woman. Her hair, a spiky-red matrix offset by bangles, bobbed around a fluorescent halter top.

The man sported a thick mullet with curls ending roughly where his pectorals began.

Walking past, they glared at him; the woman doing a double-take as he followed their hostile expressions.

Underneath the cacophony of sights and sounds, barely audible, Micha could feel the voice of reason trying to break through. *None of this is real!* it insisted. *It can't be!* And underneath *that* voice, struggling to rise above all the layers of denial, some other voice insisted it knew the reason he appeared to be trapped in some version of America's past …

All the stories taking place in Hadley Grove were set during the last century.

Yes, they were. Either during the Eighties when cell phones did not exist, or at the tail end of the Nineties when the Internet was just a moat in the mainstream's eye. Exactly why he had done this was somewhat of a mystery. Although his inner critic vouched an earlier time period was a gateway toward supplementary suspense, a more pragmatic part of his writer's brain merely felt the Eighties to be a far more suitable backdrop for Hadley Grove as a town. While the municipality, itself, wasn't exactly a Norman Rockwell painting, its overall visual aesthetic was still in keeping with a decade more predisposed to innocence.

It's not just the cars and music … the world smells different, too.

This was a thing often broached in time-travel literature, Micha mused. In film, too, come to think of it. As the protagonists adapt to their new surroundings, invariably, it's the *smell* of a year that's often approached first: the reek of unwashed humanity if one is thrust backward; the stink of some colossal dystopian machine if one travels forward. What Micha inhaled now was somewhere in a land between: a heady mixture of gasoline and plastic, but lurking beneath all that was a whiff like purple chewing gum – as if capitalism had a scent.

A car backfired, and Micha jumped. A horn blared, followed by someone shouting … and suddenly yielding to a full-blown panic attack while standing on the footpath of an imaginary Main Street didn't feel like such a far-fetched notion.

Just get a fucking grip. Keep your cool. Pretty soon you'll wake up in the real world again.

Other pedestrians were coming closer, these ones every bit as intimidating as the Eighties couple. On the left, a family of three walked, the mother pushing a stroller and wearing a big fuck-you frown upon her face. On Micha's right, a big man with silver hair strode purposefully toward him, wearing a navy-blue duty jacket embroidered with a woolen collar. And hitching up his matching uniformed pants: a large belt that also served as a gun and flashlight holster. The man's stern gaze, while currently fixed on a shop window, would soon be meeting Micha's the second he turned around.

That's Brandon Delgado. The Sherriff.

A character Micha had written about extensively in the past (and who was to feature predominately in *The Mercury Man*), police officer Brandon Delgado was not an individual you wanted to meet – even casually. Brandon was a man with a closet full of skeletons so big he shamed your average fictitious psychopath; shamed even the prominent ones like Norman Bates, whose Freudian mother fixations had served as minor inspiration when Micha had first committed the character's name to paper on an old-fashioned Olivetti typewriter.

Without stopping to check for traffic, Micha scurried across Main Street.

He did not look back.

***

A flashing neon sign bearing the words Delta Bronze greeted Micha as he mounted the adjacent footpath. Another sign, this one an old-fashioned wall-mounted blackboard, proclaimed the chalked words: *THIS MONTH! STOMP 'N HOLLAR FEATURING HADLEY GROVE'S OWN MARY LAMONT! TIX $2.50 AT THE DOOR. CIDER SCHOONERS ON THE CHEAP!*

In Micha's fabricated version of Hadley Grove, no such bar called Delta Bronze existed. At least, not one he remembered writing. The same thing could not be applied to Mary Lamont and her band, however. Ms. Lamont, a former prostitute turned country singer with a heart of gold, was a reoccurring cast member in at least three novellas and one of Lila's favorite characters. Or so she had professed.

That feeling of drugged vertigo, not felt since the alleyway, began to make headway again, this time blurring the straight lines of the Delta Bronze into dreamscape shadows. If he were to fall over or faint now –

'Going to stand out there gawking all day?' a voice

inquired. 'Why don't you come in and have a drink?'

Without Micha noticing, a woman's head had appeared through the bar's door. She was smiling at him ... that kind of country smile you read about, wrote about, but seldom in life had visited upon you. Her eyes, a kind of glistering brown that were almost black, contained the same kind of dazzling welcome. Dimples, each one as pronounced as the other, were centered on cheeks so startlingly white they were like ceramic.

Despite himself, Micha smiled right back. Gradually, his panic began to recede. Through the window, he observed her hand flicking a sign over, this one from *Closed* to *Open*. Still smiling, she motioned with her other hand for him to enter Delta Bronze.

***

It was dim inside, the air astringent with the smell of hops.

'I'm Sara,' said the woman, still busying herself by opening blinds. As daylight seeped in, it did little to assuage the dingy interior. All bars everywhere, Micha noted, were like this. Even imaginary ones, it seemed.

'Sara Childs. And you are?'

'Not from around here,' Micha replied absently.

There was a hiccup of genuine laughter, and Micha felt himself at ease even more. 'I gathered that. It's why I invited you in. You don't just look lost, mister. You look like you're hiding from someone, maybe.' Another brusque laugh, the lilt of it in keeping with her smile.

He coughed. 'Micha Tudor.'

'Sorry?'

'My name … it's Micha.'

Sara, in the process of switching on a jukebox by its power outlet, paused in her labor. 'Micha? Gosh that's so … *original*. You don't often hear names like that nowadays. My ex-husband Brody told me that he wanted to name our first-born *Ronald*. No way, I said. No son of mine is going to carry the same name as a burger clown as well as that *clown* who's running the country.'

'It's Hebrew,' Micha said, as if that explained everything. He coughed again, embarrassed, and slowly pivoted his butt onto a stool. The drink coasters on the bar featured a Basset Hound with large brown eyes and equally large ears.

From the jukebox, soft music wafted over. Belinda Carlisle singing *The Ballad of Lucy Jordan*.

Sudden nostalgia gripped him, so sweet and persuasive it was like a dollop of water. Though just a boy, Micha had been *alive* when this song and Belinda Carlisle were reigning supreme. If Hadley Grove existed as a factual town just south of the New Hampshire border, then the *real* Micha Tudor was only a two-hour drive away, perhaps riding his bike or even watching Belinda Carlisle ham it up with a microphone through a small color TV screen …

'What can I get you?' Sara asked, entering through the bar's drawbridge and flicking on more light switches in her wake. 'First one's on the house.'

She talks, Micha thought. *Like a woman in a book.*

'I'm supposed to have quit drinking,' Micha replied,

surprising even himself.

'As of?'

'About twenty-four hours ago.'

Sara blew out a puff of air. 'I've heard that one before.'

They both chuckled. Micha said, 'I'll take a Guinness, then, please. If you have it.'

'Wouldn't be any kind of bar if we didn't.'

Pouring, Sara eyed him behind a frosted glass. 'It's true, isn't it? You really are miles away from home?'

Whatever she saw in his troubled expression must have been answer enough.

'I watched you through the window, crossing Main Street just now,' she said. 'It's weird, but my first thought was that I *knew* you from somewhere. Knew you like you were family. But that can't be right, can it? We've only just met.'

As the beer's clouded head reached its zenith, Sara let go of the tap and grinned. 'Ha! Perfection. I have that down to a science if I do say so myself.' With only a centimeter or so of perfectly rounded froth at the top of the glass, it appeared she did. As they waited for the Guinness to settle, she said, 'Then I saw you had no shoes on. Which automatically disqualifies you from entering, by the way.'

Micha glanced down at his toes, wiggling them. All ten were smudged with dirt. 'It does? What made you change your mind?'

'Like I said, it looked like you were in trouble.'

And all at once, Micha felt like unloading. Not all of it

– not even part of it – but enough for him to get his bearings. If he was clinically insane (and this was definitely a plausible possibility), then he could do worse than have this kind and beautiful woman as an attentive ear.

'It's true,' he admitted. 'I went to sleep last night in a different town and woke up in Hadley Grove.'

Though Sara didn't laugh this time, a corner of her mouth tilted upward in wry amusement. Then she handed the Guinness over, and Micha took two long swallows, bypassing the froth to get to its meaty interior.

It tasted real. It tasted *better* than real.

He said, 'If all of this is just pretend, I'm not sure I want to go back to what isn't.'

'Steady on there. None of this is *real* you say? And what town *did* you go to sleep in?'

'Concord.'

On the jukebox, Belinda Carlisle had been replaced by Madonna's *Crazy For You*. Another upsurge of nostalgia followed … though this was caused more by the scant scent of perfume emanating from the woman across the bar. 'I'm dreaming it all, I must be. Because before today, Hadley Grove was only a place I ever visited in my dreams.'

Sara's look of droll humor turned to sly suspicion. 'In your dreams, huh? If that's some kind of line, I'm here to say it's one of the worst I've ever heard.' She grinned. 'And I work in a *bar*.'

'Is the place yours?' he asked, hoping to subtly divert attention away from the subject of his arrival.

'Every brick of it,' she said, sounding proud. 'Originally bought and paid for by my ex, but I bought him out when he moved on. My daughter, Alexa, goes to the local middle school, and she *brags* about living in the apartment above a bar. She was also the one who came up with the name for this pretty place.'

'Alexa?' he asked. 'That's lovely. Even more original than Micha.'

Sara beamed. 'A name *I* came up with for a pretty person.'

Their gazes locked, and in that brief instant before Micha looked away again, he felt an unmistakable upsurge of attraction … a flush of heat and a quickening of the heartbeat. Embarrassed (because he was sure she had felt something, too), he reached for his drink again and downed what remained of the glass in four long swallows.

'Hadley Grove is real,' Sara assured him. 'We may not be as picturesque as the town by Lake Winnipesaukee but we have our attractions. During the winter, Eagle Mountain House, that's a ski resort, opens its doors to some of the most elite in the state.' Sara caught his expression. 'What? You know this already, Mr. Tudor? Am I boring you?'

Having already pictured the resort hundreds of times in his head, Micha merely gave Sara a sheepish nod, an invitation to proceed.

'Churches, too. The prettiest ones you'll see this side of the state line. In fact, if you tilt your head just right on a clear day, you can see the giant Catholic one out past Terry Peak Road. Some folks say it's just shy of creepy, like something you'd find in a movie. But Alexa and I think it's beautiful. A gothic wonder. Of course, Father Purson only has his services one day a week, but we like to drive up there when …'

There might have been more, but Micha barely heard the rest.

All of a sudden he was back in a harness of flight, hovering over Hadley Grove's ominous church, buffeted by ocean winds and feeling the presence lurking within. Was Father Purson up there right now, brooding within his glasshouse? And who was that other unknown man by his side, keeping him company? Despite Micha feeling completely at ease with Sara Childs, he shivered. Hazards loomed in Hadley Grove, of which Brandon Delgado and Father Natal Purson were only offshoots of a much darker and broader puzzle.

Sara was looking at him curiously. 'What? What did I say?'

'Nothing,' he replied. Sudden revelation struck; a get-out-of-jail free card. 'The truth is I've been talking in riddles, Sara. Well, more like metaphors. You might say it's a trick of the trade.'

'Trade?'

'I'm a writer,' he said simply. And felt no guilt at the sentiment. It was the truth, after all. 'About a year ago, I decided my next book was going to be set in Hadley Grove. So I travelled here pretty much on a whim, driving all through the night. Yesterday I stopped in Hivesville, and today I arrived at my destination. You could say this is a research trip.'

Sara's eyes brightened. Her expression, a strange dance between seduction and mirth, took on an even more animated air. 'That still doesn't explain the lack of shoes.'

He laughed, feeling the small amount of imbibed beer doing its work. 'No, it doesn't, does it? Let's just say Hivesville has a few bars of its own – and know how to treat an out-of-towner who writes thrillers. I must've caught a cab late last night after tying one on.'

'A thriller writer who travels to Hadley Grove to research his next book – sounds like the plot of a movie. No, wait, you're just like Tom Hanks in *Splash*. Getting loaded and chasing a dream. Alexa and I saw that one at The Palace just before Easter.' Sara was pouring another beer, seemingly on auto-pilot to the task. 'Although … a girl like me can only *dream* of looking like Darryl Hannah.'

It took Micha a full thirty seconds to realize what Sara was referring to: Ron Howard's seminal Eighties' flick featuring a New York yuppie in a romantic tryst with a mermaid. When had that been released? '84? Or was it '85? Which meant he had arrived smack-bang in the middle of the Eighties, a time of general prosperity all round. Somewhere out there, John Candy was alive and well and enjoying *Splash*'s success. Hell, even horror authors could eke out a decent living, thanks to a certain behemoth living up in Maine.

Careful. Thinking any of this is real is dangerous thinking, Micha.

'Daryl has nothing on you,' he said, and though he meant every word of it, added, 'Which sounds like another lame flirty line. Do you have something like a swear jar for these occasions? Also, I can't pay for that second beer you're about to pass over.'

Sara merely smiled. 'Think of it as a sponsorship. You write me up as a charming character in *The Horror of Hadley Grove*, and I'll keep supplying the Guinness.'

'Now that's a title worthy of distinction,' he said. 'I can almost see the movie posters now.'

A fitting title or not, Micha could feel those initial primal dregs of anxiety returning. Because he could *see* that movie poster a little too clearly in the particulars, and the word *horror* was marked with a blood-flecked font. If his time in Hadley Grove was temporary, he would do well to test its limits and ascertain what (if any) laws governed its borders.

Or even if borders exist, a strange voice whispered. *Have you thought about that? About what lies beyond the town?*

As Micha gulped the last of his glass, he said, 'It was a pleasure to meet you, Sara.' Already he could see lines of disappointment on her brow. 'I can't thank you enough for your hospitality, but I should head back to Hivesville and see that my car is still accounted for. After last night, it could be towed or impounded, for all I know. And I should probably buy some shoes.'

Behind them, the front door swung inward for the first time since Micha's entrance, letting in a huge plume of wind. Turning around, Micha saw a bald, elderly man stride in, holding a cane and grimacing with his movements. Though this was not a character he could immediately place, Micha still felt self-conscious … as if he had been caught in the act of doing something he shouldn't.

'Of course,' Sara said from behind the bar. Her

intimate tone had vanished, replaced by one of professional courtesy. 'We'll see you again, won't we, Mr. Tudor?'

'You can bet on it,' he said, and put on a smile that felt forced. 'And next time I'll bring my wallet, that I promise.'

Exiting, he kept expecting the old stranger to glance down at his feet, but the bald man only had eyes for his face, a study in concerned concentration. Either the man was on the verge of giving him the evil eye, or the residents of Hadley Grove distrusted newcomers on sight. Before he could speak, Micha had found the bustle of Main Street once more.

***

The smell hit him once again, a tang like cheap perfume. And like a statement of contradiction: a grime-smeared footpath weathered by the elements. The Eighties, while being far more pleasant on the nose, had a somewhat dirty veneer to its exterior environment. In front, station wagons and pickup trucks trundled unhurriedly past two sets of pedestrian lights. Across the road and to the right (something Micha had missed while standing on the opposite side), a giant marquee poster advertising the film *Back To The Future* served as a theatre's awning.

Must be The Palace where Splash *was showing just last Easter.*

Curiosity – thus far held in check by anxiety – was slowly overtaking Micha's baser instinct. While the downed beers were no doubt semi-responsible, his child-like fascination simply felt the urge to *explore this*. Sure, he'd been alive and kicking in 1985, but only as a small boy, somewhat blind to the enchantments of the decade. What would it feel like to drive one of those cars or perhaps take a girl

(Sara – admit it, you're thinking of Sara)

on a date somewhere? As Micha ogled the pedestrians, it was blindingly obvious none of them were staring into the maw of a smart phone, tablet, or any other modern contraption. They were like blank slates, unspoiled by the twenty-first century's collective, nihilistic outlook.

You're getting ahead of yourself, good buddy. Remember, this is your *version of 1985. Not some rose-tinted real-life version.*

Yes, it was … and this was a good reason to get moving again. Those same pedestrians, while not occluded by a screen, were turning their attentions elsewhere. Namely, to Micha Tudor: a shoeless man from another world, garbed in bedclothes and already two pints down before lunch.

***

A twisting thoroughfare of side streets brought Micha into land less populated by houses. For the most part, he'd gone unnoticed, skipping from shrub to tree and back to shrub again with the furtive movements of a prowler. With every street he passed, Micha kept reminding himself he was inside a world of his own creation (much like a tiny creature caged within a snow globe), but this did little to assuage his agitation every time a car blasted by or a door banged open. In every practical sense, this was a real world with real people, its inhabitants just as likely to cry foul or haul him away as the ones in the tiny, ocean state where he made his real home. Although failing to garner much attention at the moment, there was still the strange cowboy man to worry about; he who had worn a cape and stared at Micha with quicksilver eyes and the same kind of surprise a landowner might give to the arrival of something feral. Although it occurred to Micha such a wildcard citizen might potentially provide some answers to Hadley Grove's existence, he'd had the aura of a man who would shoot first and answer questions later.

Which rules out meeting him again or seeking him out. In fact, I'd better just –

About a hundred yards from a water tower, the man appeared again.

After jumping a roadside fence, Micha breasted a small, nondescript hill, walking in a rough diagonal line that would (hopefully) take him to the outer limits of town and away from civilization, altogether. With his head to the ground and walking briskly, seeing both water tower and man emerge together was like coming across an island oasis in a sea of dunes.

The cowboy man still wore his cape.

Grey hair billowed around a black collar.

Micha was too far away to see his face clearly or read his expression, and for this one small thing, he was grateful.

He stopped walking; as he did so, the man advanced.

On the road he'd left behind, the reassuring sound of a

car engine could be heard and the subtle change of gears as it climbed to a higher altitude. Changing direction, Micha began a slow trot back in its general direction, building into a powerwalk and not deigning a backward glance. When both car and its shadowed occupants were close enough to see

(an Audi. Is that an Audi? Have I seen that car before?)

Micha began to wave his arms, hoping the driver would interpret his hailing as a sign of distress. She did. Slowing down as he came toward the fence, Micha could just make out the jostling forms of other, smaller passengers in the back, their faces pressed up against the glass in a shared show of curiosity.

The fence loomed, and Micha straddled its barrier with both arms, leaping over it with only minimal effort. Another quick, panicked glance behind him revealed the caped man still followed, his black visage significantly closer despite the fact he strode with the casual finesse of a silver-screen antagonist.

The passenger door of the Audi was flung open, and Micha jumped in. During this period, it took almost a full five seconds to register and recognize the face sitting behind the wheel and the two behind her.

Not enough time to slam the door or alter his chosen method of escape.

Chapter Five

Micha's first appointment with Dr. Halbrook was scheduled on a Tuesday, just over a week since returning home from the hospital. Expectantly, a sullen period had followed as Micha adapted to life at home after an authentic suicide attempt. With his part-time job at the movie store now annulled, certain sections of his family had stepped in, attempting to fill the void.

'You're still writing, aren't you, Micha?' his brother Justin asked him over the phone on his second day at home. Justin lived in New Jersey with his large family. He was a church-goer with a full-time job which, in their parents' eyes, blessed him in perpetuity. 'Keep doing that until you find something else. Lila said you're going to be speaking with a new doctor.'

'You've spoken to Lila?' he asked, incredulous. Since dropping him home from the hospital, she had gone completely silent. Though it wasn't something he begrudged her for. He had, in a manner, both anticipated and encouraged it. But she was speaking to other members of his family … ?

'Briefly,' Justin replied, sounding embarrassed. There was a pause as he cupped his phone and shouted something at one of his children. 'She knew you were going to be alone all week. She mentioned the doctor. You should make an appointment today.'

And there it was: Justin's confession. He hadn't called out of any compassionate gesture on his part. He'd called because Lila had asked him to. 'I'll get on it,' he said, and swiped the call closed before his brother could say anything further.

Dr. Halbrook's office was located on the eastside of Concord, and on the day of his appointment, Micha decided to catch a bus. Though driving was an option, finding a parking spot in the city without paying for it was always a hellish affair. Sometimes, Micha enjoyed public transport – the ease of being able to zone out and daydream while somebody else took over the wheel, navigating the human herd. Justin didn't understand it; neither did his parents. They considered public transport beneath them. This predilection was just another eccentricity in a long line marking him out as a black sheep of the family. No doubt, this would be something worth mentioning to the good doctor … among other things, of course.

But do we dare mention Hadley Grove? Is that a rabbit hole you're prepared to go down?

Entering Halbrook's building, he wasn't entirely sure. In the past when put under the spotlight of a psychiatrist's

care, he had decided honesty was oftentimes the best
policy, frequently divulging things he hardly dared admit to
his conscious self. And where had this approach gotten
him? Usually nothing but skeptical looks with a prognosis
of increased medication, the only kind of assistance
specialists seemed capable of offering these days. Got a
mental malady nobody understands? Let me fill out this
prescription pad with my impenetrable scrawl so your
disorder can be glazed over with an additional addiction ...

Keep the cynicism in check, Lila's voice whispered to
him. *At least for your first session?*

To this, he didn't reply. Talking back to the voices
inside of your head (while only minutes away from meeting
your shrink), could potentially be construed as crazy.

***

'So you don't actually have a phone, Micha?'

When Halbrook spoke, his patterned necktie moved in
symphony with his throat, the flowers adorning it rising
with the ebb and flow of a psychedelic arrangement.
Though at first Micha found the visual somewhat off-
putting, Halbrook's soft and intelligent voice had an
eloquent cadence that frittered away all external
distractions. Many mental health professionals carried the
hallmark, of course – but Halbrook had it down to a
science.

'Yes, I do have a phone,' Micha replied. 'Technically
speaking. A pre-paid one.'

'But you never buy credit for it?'

'No – I do everything by email.'

A few jots on the good doctor's notepad, another tried-and-true habit of a head shrink. 'What about to speak to Lila?'

'If we needed to talk, we did everything over Skype, Facebook, or email.'

'And the same thing goes for the other aspects of your life? For everything related to writing, publishing and, ah … your part time job?'

'Everything.'

'Would you say that's … eccentric in this day and age?'

Micha fidgeted. Yes, he did think it somewhat eccentric never to talk on the phone unless it was absolutely necessary. Other people had often pointed this out. But Micha had only ever considered it a quirk. A small oddity, no doubt, common among many introverts on the planet.

Dr. Halbrook, a good looking man in his forties with designer stubble, smiled across at him. 'I'm not saying that it is, Micha. I just wanted to know how *you* felt about it.'

'It's sometimes difficult,' Micha admitted. 'It's not like you can email absolutely everyone. But for the most part, I get by.'

They'd been talking for around thirty minutes with Micha sitting directly opposite in a comfy blue recliner, Halbrook getting into the meat of his personality. All by-the-numbers stuff that was familiar during the introduction process. Although the man was somewhat fixated on …

'Besides your girlfriend, Lila … is there anybody else outside of your family close to you? Any friends from school or the university? Is there anybody in your life you would consider a close friend?'

Micha frowned. Although on the cusp of replying in the affirmative, the question was an ambiguous one in the modern age. Did one count their social-media friends as close associates – taking into account you conversed with them on a daily basis? Though ephemeral, close ties were often forged this way. On some occasions, Micha would even meet these friends (like Grayson Ross, another scribbler), if one of them happened to be passing through Concord or going to a writing convention in the general area.

Micha said, 'I guess you're talking about bona-fide flesh-and-blood acquaintances?'

Halbrook crossed one of his legs over the other. 'The world is a different place, Micha. A lot of us today, me included, keep the ones we share intimate secrets with inside our phones. But in this instance, yes – I'm talking about friends in the real world. Is there anybody you can think of that fits that category? Do you seek out relationships with people that aren't online? Are you even interested in them?'

Micha's eyes had found the carpeted floor rug beneath his shoes, and there they lingered. Admitting you were a loner wasn't an easy thing to do – even if you sometimes prided yourself on being part of the misanthropic tribe. 'No,' Micha said finally. 'I suppose I'm not. Having a girlfriend, a single partner, has been enough for me in recent years.'

'Would you say you find the experience of being

around others … exhausting?'

Micha laughed. 'Who doesn't?'

Halbrook grinned and jotted down more notes. Finally he said, 'That's something we'll come back to a little later. I just want to talk some more about your family. Your sister, Rebecca, she …'

'Died when I was seventeen,' Micha said.

'And she was only … ?'

'Twelve. She was hit by a car while the family was on vacation in Maine. I wasn't there – had decided to spend the summer at a friend's house, basically couch surfing. I didn't go on many vacations with Mom or Dad or the other siblings. And I think they wanted it that way, too.'

'That must have been a pretty horrific time in your life.'

'It was,' Micha agreed. 'But it's not something I feel overly sorry for myself about. Trauma is a constant thing in the world, occurring daily. I know this. What happened to Rebecca was … horrific. In fact, I'd use the word macabre. Because it wasn't painless, and she didn't die instantly. But even back then, I was conscious of how the world works – how bad things often happen to good people.' Micha paused, realizing he sounded a touch … ostentatious. Almost juvenile. They were lines he'd delivered more than once and had the aura of repetition. But they were *true* words, for better or worse. 'It was a terrible time, sure – it still is. My mother will never properly heal. But the events weren't a catalyst to spiral into depression or alcohol addiction.'

'The roots were there beforehand?'

Though Halbrook framed the sentence as a question, the tone was more in league with a statement. The doctor was building to something – perhaps a diagnosis that was plainly obvious to him and the reason Hughes in the hospital had referred him here.

'Around the age of twelve,' Micha said. 'That's when Mom took me to see my first therapist. I think she knew something was terribly wrong, could sense it ran much deeper than typical adolescent melancholy. Truth is, I think she was trying to nip it in the bud before it settled in for good.'

Halbrook lifted his eyes from the pad, looked at Micha directly. 'And what did that long-ago therapist say?'

'That it *was* typical adolescent melancholy. That it was totally natural for a twelve-year-old to think of himself as the center of the universe. And pretty much ever since, this has been the general consensus among my family. That I'm a self-centered person and inward looking. That I live in my own fantasy world. Let me tell you, hearing those words when you're just a teenager is harsh, but when you're *still* hearing them in your thirties, it's even harsher. Kind of like a death sentence, or an admittance that there is no help for you and never will be. Ultimately, going to those doctors had an adverse effect on me because I felt even *worse* after I left those rooms than I did going into them.'

'And was that a …' Halbrook was twirling his one crossed leg in addition to his pen. '… pattern that repeated itself over the years? Is that why you stopped going to therapy for your anxiety?'

Micha nodded in quick bursts. 'Pretty much.'

'Yet you kept taking medication?'

'Provided by a general practitioner. Have they ever helped me? No, not really. I can't say that they have. But they weren't giving me any negative side effects, either. So I thought it couldn't hurt to keep taking them. Mainly to appease Lila. To make her feel content that I was *doing* something to combat this mental illness.'

For a while the doctor had eyes only for his notes. Then he said, 'You self-diagnosed as having Asperger's or ASD just a few years back?'

Micha described doing just that: how his personal research into mental illness had led him to believe he exhibited similar traits associated with Asperger's – the difficulty with real-life social interactions; Lila pointing out he would sometimes avoid eye contact when in close proximity to others. However, having explored the diagnosis with one psychiatrist, it was ultimately ruled out. And the reason? During Micha's interview he had displayed regular eye contact throughout the examination, and also exhibited a warm and caring disposition … a component that was (apparently) lacking in genuine individuals existing on the autism spectrum.

'I can say with honesty you are those things, Micha,' Dr. Halbrook said. 'You are also articulate and intelligent. I'm a little surprised, though. When engaged in your personal exploration of behavioral and cognitive disorders, you never stumbled across the personality disorder SPD?' Seeing Micha's stony expression, Halbrook elaborated. 'SPD, more commonly known as schizoid personality disorder. It's a class of ailment classified by a lack of interest in social relationships, among other things.'

Micha thought. He supposed he had previously heard the word *schizoid* used in some kind of vocabulary – but not its core criteria. Of course, the word, itself, resonated with *schizophrenia*, a much-maligned term if there ever was one. Though Halbrook assured him they were related by only the most tenuous of threads and not to be confused with each other.

'Micha, during this interview I've seen you describe significant life experiences with little to no emotion. What I would call 'reduced affect display.' You also talk about your recent suicide attempt as though it were of no more consequence and as trivial as stubbing your toe. This is definitive emotional coldness and apathy. With your own published novels and a penchant to immerse yourself in both film and literature, you demonstrate a rich, elaborate, and exclusively internal fantasy world. You are also somewhat impoverished in forming intimate attachments with others, including people in your own family. Over the course of this careful examination, and from what Dr. Hughes first indicated to me in his original referral, I believe you fulfil the criteria for schizoid personality disorder.'

For a moment there was only silence, Micha weighing Halbrook's words as their import struggled to catch up with his intellect. In their earlier interaction, he'd stated to Dr. Hughes his distaste of labels, that many forms of mental illness were poorly understood and constituted a many-branded tapestry of pseudoscience. Of course, this was only a personal philosophy. Something derived from his years of riding the express train called anxiety. Ultimately, though – he was no authority. And certainly no expert. Perhaps it had taken until now to finally meet someone who was …

Halbrook glanced at his watch, a clinical gesticulation. 'Micha, we need to wrap things up for today. But I thank you for being so forthcoming with me. I'm going to pass on some literature regarding SPD, and how ongoing cognitive behavioral therapy is usually the best course of action after initial diagnosis. Dr. Hughes will also receive a letter.'

'So … another booking then?' Micha asked absently.

'A week from now, if the front desk can swing it. We have a lot of ground to cover from here on out. Next week, I'd like to talk to you about Hadley Grove.'

***

Though Micha was tempted on the ride home to pore through Halbrook's sheaf of SPD related literature, he resisted the impulse, knowing he would do the core of his personal research in front of a computer. Instead, he gazed out at the cars and buildings flying by as though seeing everything under the gauze of new eyes; as if the network of trees, winding roads, and human beings were only miniatures paraded on a set – paper-mache models on a larger scale. None of it seemed remotely real.

Certain words from Halbrook came back to haunt him.

You demonstrate a rich, elaborate, and exclusively internal fantasy world.

No argument there. It's what all people of the creative

stripe did on a daily basis. However … what Halbrook had alluded to with this statement had nothing to do with writing stories – or creating fiction for entertainment's sake. No, this smacked of creating imaginary worlds to *escape* reality.

Worlds like Hadley Grove.

Awakening from his brush with death, Micha had surmised his experience was something akin to an NDE – more commonly known as a *near-death experience.* The kind of thing hundreds of people around the globe postulated about in literature, movies, and daytime television talk shows. In lieu of being given a ticket to Hell (something extolled by certain brands of Christianity with regards to suicide), Micha had instead been shown an afterlife of his own making, the imagination given musculature and wings to fly. Afterward, in the dark glow of being revived, a sliver of that afterlife had somehow carried over into the waking world, permitting Micha to travel there when the walls were thin. At least, this was the abridged version h e had laid out to Halbrook in their initial introduction to each other. Sitting on the therapy couch this time around, Micha had wanted everything (no matter how fantastical it sounded), t o be laid out bare.

Yet the theory no longer held sustainable weight. Because …

Because I demonstrate a rich, elaborate, and exclusively internal fantasy world. One that feels every bit as real as this one.

And there was the rub. Hadley Grove was now an explainable happenstance, one brought into being by the malady of a classifiable personality disorder.

But what if it's not?

Exiting the bus and making his way toward home, this one-sentence litany beat an incessant rhyme until Micha felt dizzy with it.

But what if it's not?

***

Back on his laptop, it wasn't Google Micha immediately pulled up but the single-spaced Word document entitled *The Mercury Man*. He supposed any normal person, having been subjected to probable hallucinations, would have made this unfinished novel their first port of call. Not so for Micha Stephen Tudor, though – he who was prone to a wild superstitious nature.

Only four days had passed since his last fugue state. Taking a peek at *The Mercury Man* (even a subtle one) could constitute another boarding pass into the world of Hadley Grove. Returning was perhaps inevitable, but Micha wanted to be duly prepped and prepared if and when the curtain call came again.

Perhaps the book *is where you should have been looking all along. Perhaps it's the most important tool to understanding what is happening to you ...*

In the cold light of day, it was hard to argue with this logic. It's what he should have done from the very beginning, of course. But Micha's health and imagination had fought against the idea. He –

Scrolling through the document, his hand froze over

the mouse. Although partway through the first couple of pages, it was not words that claimed his attention so completely but numbers in the bottom left-hand corner. Numbers detailing a word count. When had he last worked on *The Mercury Man?* Just a week or so before his suicide attempt, give or take a few days. This was during a prolific period of cold sobriety and general well-being … before he'd relapsed and picked up a bottle again. Micha didn't keep a word-count diary for this particular project, but his memory was usually good enough to recall the overall evolution of any book in progress.

A few weeks ago, the number count on *The Mercury Man* had stood at a paltry fifteen-thousand words. Barely enough framework or adequate structure to properly introduce his cast.

Now the word count hovered at an astonishing forty-two thousand.

It's a mistake, Micha thought. *It has to be. I've conjoined the document with something else.*

But scrolling even further, he discovered this wasn't the case at all. Fresh text had been added after page twenty-one.

A continuation of *The Mercury Man.*

More story.

Micha read, and what he saw in those initial lines reflected some of the events to have taken place when *he* was present in the town of Hadley Grove. A male protagonist named Mason, suffering amnesia, had awakened in a dirty alleyway. After being moved on by some locals, Mason was introduced to a character by the name of Sara Childs – one owner and proprietor of Delta Bronze, a local bar on Main Street.

Staring at the screen, slack-jawed, Micha felt heat rush to his cheeks; he then felt his balls contract and expand again. A tremor – one that had nothing to do with booze-shakes – had gripped all five fingers of his mouse hand. What was this? What was he looking at? The composition of someone else who had crept into his bedroom while he was away? Despite the sheer improbability of such a thing, what immediately came to mind was the fable of Goldilocks who had snuck into a den of bears and unwittingly violated their sanctuary. Had his own Goldilocks sat in this chair and tapped away at his newest creation, becoming an allegorical and literal ghost-writer in the process?

No – what happened here has nothing to do with someone else. This is you, Micha – every word of it. Or are you too scared to admit this to yourself?

Of course he was. Acknowledging Micha Tudor was the sole author here was paramount to a species of insanity, one that made a thing like schizoid personality disorder seem rather tame. What was the word given to people who experienced massive blackouts

(crazy ... there's no other word for it)

without the aid of drugs or booze? Also, this was no garden-variety suppression of consciousness, either – but a vacant fugue period where Micha had physically worked on a novel. Reading, his eyes pored over prose and text every bit as vivid and articulate as anything he'd ever written. By somehow accessing his unconscious mind, Micha had granted himself an untapped wealth of creative potential, constructing paragraphs riddled with an ease of traction he had seldom found this side of the waking veil.

When did I do all this then? Sleeping? Perhaps, instead of my mind visiting the town of Hadley Grove, I was simply sitting here, typing. It would go a long way to explaining everything ...

With the cursor held steadily on the down arrow, the document was quickly coming to its end. Mason, having run afoul of a mysterious caped figure with quicksilver eyes, was now attempting to escape.

And who should decide to pick him up? Why, it was a single mother named Penelope Bowthorpe, the resident of Hadley Grove who drove a black Audi. In the backseat, her twin daughters, Bethany and Madison, had their faces pressed up against the glass as they pulled over to offer assistance to the stranger who had hailed them ...

***

As the Audi rounded a corner, the headlights of another car filled the windshield, a collision imminent. Shouting something, Micha reached over and instinctively wrenched the wheel back toward his body.

Losing her own grip for only a fraction of a second, Penelope's hands and feet reacted accordingly, turning the wheel and hitting the brakes in tandem. For a moment, the oncoming bonnet disappeared, replaced by rotating farmland and road. Then a small shower of dirt rained down as the Audi narrowly avoided impact and shuddered to a halt.

In the backseat, two young girls *whooshed* with relief.

In the review mirror, Micha saw the other car speeding away, its brake lights like beacons.

'Oh my *God*,' said the woman in the driver's seat. A hand went from the steering wheel to her mouth. There it rested, shaking. 'That lunatic didn't even stop for a *second*. Girls, is everything okay back there?'

It took Micha perhaps fifteen seconds to process his new environment.

He had returned.

Returned to Hadley Grove.

Like the flipped pages of a book, he had arrived at almost the exact moment he'd departed, swallowed up by the Bowthorpe's Audi while retreating from the caped, silver-eyed hallucination. Seeing the familiar family – whose inner lives he had borne witness to while in spirit – had brought on a moment of unadulterated panic; a kind of fear far beyond anything the mysterious old man had evoked.

Because Micha lived inside his novel once again.

And shared space with characters who were going to occupy *The Mercury Man*.

Here they all were: the Bowthorpe family consisting of Penelope, Bethany, and Maddie; the family who had picked him up from the roadside after he'd hailed them down. Had they also seen the cowboy man stalking him from the water tower?

Her seatbelt cast aside, Penelope maneuvered herself into a kneeling position, the anorak jacket she sported a bulky impediment delaying the moment she could reach out and touch her daughters. Finally she did so, patting down their cheeks and heads of hair while murmuring entreaties. The sisters, while almost identical in features, had different hairstyles. Madison, a bob of brown like the head of a mop. Bethany, longer locks with an auburn cast. Their jackets, while not anoraks, were nonetheless vintage.

Just in case you have forgotten, Micha: Hadley Grove exists in the vacuum of the 1980s.

Having seen to their well-being, Penelope glanced over at him. *What prompted me to pull over and give aid to a stranger?* her look said. Then her sight cleared, and she spoke, 'Are *you* okay, mister? If you hadn't pulled the wheel when you did … I'd hate to think what might've happened.'

Neither do I, Micha thought incoherently. *Because I haven't written this part yet.*

He uttered no such thing, of course. But when he *did* speak, what spilled out was just as unexpected as anything else to have recently occurred: 'Can you take me to a phone in town, please?' he asked. 'I need to speak with Sara Childs.'

***

Easing her Audi through intersections, Penelope drove not only with the deftness of a local familiar with the town's geography but of someone well-versed in the mechanics of what Micha's father would have coined a *Shitmobile*. Of course, that particular kind of parlance for an old vehicle was not applicable in the reality Micha existed in … a time when its odometer would have read somewhere just north of three hundred fifty thousand miles. The Audi, while having a polished gleam to its dashboard components, also contained a hint of that unmistakable *new car* smell underneath the scent of the family it carried around.

'Did you get the license plate number?' came a voice from the backseat. Madison, Micha reminded himself. 'When there's an accident, Mrs. Files says you should always take down the plate number of the other car.'

'There was *no* accident,' replied the voice of Bethany, sounding a touch exasperated. 'Does our car *look* messed up? That was a *clean* getaway.'

Through the rearview mirror Micha observed Madison making a face at her sister. For the briefest of moments, her eyes alighted on his … and he quickly looked away toward the road once again.

Soon Bevin Street and the Bowthorpe's house came into view.

In the double driveway, a cream-colored Ford Bronco sat in the vacant space.

Daddy's car, Micha thought. *The one who died. What did I name him? Eric? Eli? The Bronco's been in the driveway since the day he left – for some reason she can't touch it, can't so much as hop in and turn the key. Out of everything of his she's kept, somehow that ugly vehicle is the hardest part of him to let go …*

Micha glanced down at his feet … and was astonished to find sneakers covering them. Also proper corduroy pants this time. A plain black jumper rested on the top portion of his body – the same ensemble he'd put on back in the real world, a last-minute provision against the coming storm of his return to this fictitious town.

I've got to remember that. You come in just as you leave.

The duel worlds were meshing together and refunding memories of his other existence. There was his appointment with Dr. Halbrook and the man's revelatory diagnosis. Now the manuscript was writing itself. After powering down his laptop for the night, Micha had retired to his mattress fully clothed, having a distinct gut-instinct that a return was perhaps imminent and simply gone to sleep.

Guiding the Audi into the driveway, he heard what may have been a small sigh of dismay from the driver – audible pain from the visual cue of the Bronco.

Hearing it, Micha was aroused by one burning question: why this family in particular? What role did the Bowthorpes – and more importantly, *himself* – have to play in the story of *The Mercury Man*?

Chapter Six

Making his way from the bowels of the church and into the upper levels, Father Natal Purson reflected on what a tedious journey it had become – an expedition fraught with uncountable stairs that were beginning to try his physical strength. Walking them as a young man with Daddy Orobas had entailed no such travails, of course … although back then, no auto-immune disease named arthritis festered within his bones. And no varicose veins bulged from behind his knees, either. Daddy Orobas had sometimes carried him, guiding young Natal up ancient serpentine risers older than all the years of Hadley Grove, itself.

Briefly, he ruminated on the possibility of installing a motorized lift.

Never, he thought, rounding the final bend of the final staircase and extinguishing a hand-held candle. *Brother Malphas would never allow such a luxury.*

No, he wouldn't. But Natal could daydream every now and again, couldn't he? There was no sin in daydreaming.

Speaking of Malphas: his brother was probably daydreaming right now, too, buoyant in a mercury pool, as oblivious to the real world as the dozens of saint statues ornamenting their church; although, his mind was never idle and often engaged in numerous tasks beyond even Natal's limited ability to grasp. Though twin brothers who'd once shared a womb, their differences were sometimes vast.

One could say he has returned *to a womb, in a fashion. A womb engineered by his brother, Natal.*

Smirking at this astute observation, Natal walked one of the narrow corridors that led him to his brother. In these passageways, evenly spaced walled-mounted torches were arranged, a throwback to more gentile times. Although their outer façades were aesthetically archaic (each individual sconce containing a medieval chandelier), the technology they used to harness light was not. Contained within wooden frameworks, LED bulbs encased in glass flame pillars threw out just enough light to keep the corridors bathed in a soft glow. Malphas, who shunned most ultraviolet light due in part to his linage, allowed Natal only the barest minimum of illumination to coalesce inside their personal passageways. Of course, the basilica of the Nave, itself – an open space reserved for their devout faithful – adhered to no such rules. In that contained space of pews, alter, and chancel, the natural light of the sun was given free rein to play, providing the illusion the brothers were normal men of the cloth; honest and upright clergymen who cared deeply about the plight of Hadley Grove and all of its citizens.

Those same citizens knew of Malphas only peripherally, and they were seldom granted sight of him. Mentally and physically handicapped, Malphas had been regulated to the shadows for decades, Father Natal Purson his sole caregiver …

A ruse narrative currently serving their needs.

To reveal any of the truth wouldn't be conducive to their overall plan for the town. Sheep did not possess the capacity to understand their shepherd. And make no mistake: both he and his brother were possessed of a birthright that *qualified* them as shepherds of the human flock and were beholden to certain abilities far removed from anything humans layed claim to. For the time being, Malphas had to remain completely unseen, soaking in his pools of mercury so their great, symbiotic work could continue unhindered by the world at large.

His pools.

Here they were now, the converted glasshouse set apart from the Nave; a small portion of the church which nonetheless appeared imposing from outside. While access could be granted through this particular staircase, Malphas used the mercury pools as a conduit, paddling between the glasshouse and his personal quarters with the same aplomb an aquatic creature might apply to a similar environment. Suffering the exactitudes of the flesh like other mortal men, the pools provided Malphas a means to move around with adroitness and only a minimal amount of help from Natal. The passageways, like arteries of quicksilver veins, carried its amalgam burden around and kept him buoyant.

Descending the staircase, Natal quieted his footsteps, timing their arrival on the balustrades. He did not want Malphas aroused by his presence.

Too late, he thought. *He already knows I'm here.*

As Natal stepped over the last riser, the pool came into view, a shallow depression of silver liquid and artificial greenery. Natal knew Malphas was aware of him not by his physical presence, but by the subtle telepathic link the brothers shared. Words, carried on a tide of thought, were making themselves known: Malphas was presently busy and did not want to be disturbed. Couldn't Natal leave him alone in solitude for the time being?

Instead of replying, Natal ventured further into the glasshouse, fumes of mercury wafting up from the pool's surface and colliding with his flesh. Immune from their carcinogenic properties, the subtle quicksilver tide ebbed at his feet.

No, what he had to tell his brother couldn't wait.

Not at such a crucial time.

***

Although a stranger shared their kitchen, neither Madison nor Bethany seemed perturbed by Micha's presence. Quite the opposite: the girls ran in circles around the living room and back again with the same wild abandon they might have shown on a playground. Penelope, still visibly shaken by their near-miss on Terry Peak Road, busied herself preparing coffee while Micha sat perched nearby on a bar stool. Ordinarily, an acute form of social-anxiety might have prevented Micha from speaking at all … but Hadley Grove was no ordinary world.

'I can't explain it,' Penelope was saying. 'When I saw you coming toward us, I felt I recognized you from somewhere. Actually it was more than that … you felt like somebody I knew.'

Sara's words from Delta Bronze came floating back: *My first thought was that I knew you from somewhere. Knew you like you were family.*

Here the same thing was transpiring: Hadley Grove's characters feeling an inexplicable familiarity with the writer.

'Did you see anyone with me?' Micha asked, hoping to unravel the mystery of his own mysterious stranger. 'Behind me, I mean? Was there anybody chasing me?'

For a moment, Penelope stopped midstride and looked perplexed … as if listening to an inner voice. Then she said, 'Chasing? No, I didn't see anybody. I thought something had happened, and you wanted a ride back to town.'

As the electric kettle began to whistle, his host reached over and unhooked its cord from the wall. This was the moment Micha *properly* noticed it, and everything surrounding it. From the Formica-topped island counter, to the old rotary-dial phone, to the kitchen blinds with ears of corn stitched into them. Everything (the wallpaper, the floor tiles, even a fan sitting in the corner) like set-pieces from an Eighties sitcom. Penelope's fridge (a giant white utilitarian monolith), even had a Felix wall clock mounted on the freezer door.

For small-town folk, stopping for strangers was no big deal. And stopping for strangers during the *Eighties* did not so much as register as a blip on the big-deal radar. Penelope and other characters in this story might be drawn to their creator for reasons unknown to even them, but the motives for picking him up from the side of the road were arbitrary in this era.

Pouring coffee, Penelope asked him, 'With everything going on in town at the moment, the recent deaths we've had … it felt like the right thing to do. *Was* somebody chasing you, Mr. Tudor? Were you running away from something or somebody?'

In Micha's head, a light went off. *The recent deaths.* Had they begun already in this three-dimensional version of Hadley Grove? If so, why hadn't Sara Childs mentioned as much? As a working trope, Micha had employed the motif in many of his small-town horror stories, a gamut of deaths invariably paving the way to the big bad monster causing them. You could say it was *Horror Writing 101*. What Micha found frustrating about this entire scenario was his own disturbing lack of knowledge. Because *The Mercury Man* had never received anything like an outline or even a basic treatment. For better or worse, he was as much a passenger in this story as the characters, themselves.

'I thought I was hallucinating,' he said, hoping some sort of description would elicit more information. 'But there was a man wearing a black cape standing by the water tower. He wore some sort of cap, like a cowboy's. He was old, almost ancient, but seemed somehow nimble and quick on his feet.'

Micha's portrayal must have touched on something …
if only delicately because Penelope's single-minded look
bordered on alarm.

She said, 'Oh my God - you've *seen him?*'

***

'Malphas … can you hear me?'

Wreathed in the mercury pool's steam, his brother's
fragile body twitched. From where Natal stood looking
down, both the cleft of his bulbous belly and knees were
visible. Bleached white by age in addition to the element,
the belly appeared fish-like. Below his torso, Malphas's
knees were like the protruding stumps of a knuckled
branch. Only his brother's head gave any indication of the
sentience attached, bobbing in the swirl of liquid like a
malnourished mask.

Nothing – no reply, audible or otherwise. Coated by a
thin film of silver, Malphas's eyes stared vacantly into
nothing.

'I wouldn't be here if it wasn't important,' Natal said.
'I know you're … indisposed with certain tasks. But
Sherriff Delgado sends us news.'

A subtle tick of the lips. Or was that Natal's
imagination?

'Mr. Delgado informs us the Moffat girl is causing no
serious complications and urges us to stay away.'

Submerged, Malphas's long hair spread out from his
skull like fertile kelp, large portions of it indistinguishable

from the solution. This somatic characteristic, a lone carry-on from the genes of their father, Orobas, was one of the few physical things distinguishing the brothers. Shaved entirely bald from a scalpel, Natal's own head lay covered in a black Biretta he seldom removed.

Still nothing, and Natal was about to speak up again when a single silver bubble rose up from his brother's lips. There it lingered for a moment, a pearlescent reflection, before popping. Jaws working like ancient gears, Malphas managed to whisper one word, a sound so faint it might have been a mumble.

'*Madison.*'

***

From the living room (a room Micha had hovered over as nothing but spirit not long ago), cartoons and the sounds of girls' laughter could be heard. At Micha's mention of the caped stranger, Penelope had quickly excused herself to check in on them, telling him to go ahead and use her phone while she did so. That now familiar rush of nostalgia (not felt since his time in Sara's bar) enveloped him again. Just how many afternoons had he experienced similar to this one, splayed out on a floor rug while Pepe Le Pew seduced a cat and his own mother made hot coffee in the kitchen … dozens, if not hundreds. And it had taken an average middle-class family of his own creation to reawaken those memories.

When the screams began, Micha's line of sight into the lounge room was cutoff, the sliding door partially open, but its glass façade not entirely folded back. Micha *heard* but could not see what at first he assumed was one of the girls injuring themselves.

But then the chorus of voices swelled to include every member of Penelope's little tribe, a shrieking more in league with being attacked.

From his small stool, Micha bolted upright and sprinted into the adjacent room.

He was presented with a scene every bit as unforeseen as it was terrifying – a tableau of horror so pronounced it made his fiction domestic by comparison.

***

Natal knew of the young Bowthorpe girl, one half of a greater whole. Though the Hadley Grove family had once been part of the Purson congregation, they had stopped attending mass the very week Penelope became widowed. The event had also served as a catalyst to bring the family unit to the close attention of Natal and Malphas … who saw in them three bright and burning potential souls to be consigned into the Hall of Portals. Initially, Malphas had wanted to draw upon the sisters' life-force post-haste, seeing their existence in Hadley Grove as providence; mirrors of the dark twins who roamed (and swam) these sepulchre hallways. But Natal had urged restraint in the matter. Yes, providence surely did have a hand in this – and yes, Madison and Bethany would eventually be added to the Hall of Portals. Nonetheless, the Bowthorpes sudden disappearance (especially in the aftermath of the husband's demise) would only arouse unwanted suspicions and probes that even Sherriff Delgado could not hope to shield them from. No, it was better for the brothers to bide their time and wait – to seize upon the moment when it was properly presented. If they needed any evidence at all what repercussions could come into play when *not* showing proper restraint, they only had to reflect back on the events of the previous winter in the dark swamps to the south. During that showdown, they had been lucky to escape not only with their lives, but also with their vestments and hierarchal standing intact.

So what is Malphas doing right now, pursuing the girl?

But the more important question here was*: If he has decided to go against my wishes, what can I possibly do about it?*

Below, Malphas's cracked lips broke open into a stalwart grin, his prune cheeks bulging with a smile that was unmistakably predatory. Witnessing it, there could be little doubt his brother was *not* participating in any arbitrary Hadley Grove mission, scoping out further peoples in the hope of securing additional candidates for their bourgeoning collection. No, this time Malphas was summoning the creature he only brought into being on very rare occasions; a creature who, by slow degrees, had morphed into the boogeyman of the town below.

***

Screaming, Madison Bowthorpe cowered at the foot of

an apparition towering above her.

Eight-feet tall, a chrome figure with four gesticulating arms and a barbed head writhed and contorted, its frontal anatomy in flux. From an abdomen sprouted spiky protuberances of two silver legs; their chitinous muscles bright enough for Micha to see the girl's small body reflected back on their surface. To his left, Penelope and Bethany also cowered ... but they were not in the creature's immediate line of sight – which consisted of two elongated eyes like wicks of burning candle flame.

A silver and chrome giant with madness in its gaze had suddenly appeared in the mundane environment of a living room.

The Mercury Man. The monster of Hadley Grove.

Nowhere, neither in previous stories nor in the uncompleted manuscript, had Micha made allusions to a creature such as this one. Yet there could be little doubt it was the titular character whose namesake provided the title. Alerted to Micha's presence, it brokered him with fixed and giddy attention, the amber eyes deforming and brightening in league with the changes affecting its body. Stepping forward, Micha motioned Madison away, back toward her sibling and mother, though never taking his eyes off the threat.

***

Beyond hearing, beyond even the parameters of the physical world, Malphas's eyes flickered open once again. Opaque, they looked on at something his brother could only guess at, jittering with the rapid-eye-movement of a dreamer.

For a brief moment, Natal considered simply reaching down and waking Malphas … but he fought the urge, knowing that such an interruption could possibly hurt or even injure his brother. When conjuring extensions of their shared will out there in the real world – Malphas often used the word *golem* to describe this corporeal summoning – they, themselves, were impervious to harm. Or so Natal had believed. But calling on the silver serpent was another kind of anthropomorphic calling altogether. If Natal severed the link with Malphas still inhabiting the creature, there was no forecasting the potential damage wrought.

And if he gets carried away, there'll be hell to pay.

Torn between what was necessary and his allegiance to Malphas, Natal Purson could only stare on at the silver water and wait.

***

A kind of heat issued from the creature, as though the air was filled with the charged particles before a storm. Frozen in place, Micha could only regard the thing, hoping its attention failed to revert back to the family.

Bare moments before its arrival, Penelope had spoken of a *him*, taking Micha's description of a caped man as the mythical figure terrorizing her town. But this was no caped figure with silver eyes … this was something from another state: one whose borders broached Hell, perhaps.

Rooted to the carpet, its anatomy continued to shift,

fresh thorny protuberances budding along its neck, arm projections, and leg joints. Beneath the amber eyes, an opening formed; from the opening, a steel tongue lashed out, working around the newly formed orifice with the sinuous motion of a coiled snake.

It's trying to scare me, Micha thought in dumb wonder. *That seems to be its entire purpose – to induce fear by its form.*

Though such a thing was absurd ... because ...

How can I possibly be scared of my own creation?

Not all that long ago – say, when meeting the owner of a local bar, for instance – embracing the concept of Hadley Grove as pure illusion (a mere byproduct of his schizoid personality disorder), was something Micha could have grudgingly accepted. But how could he now? How *could* he when heat from this Mercury Man was singeing filaments of hair on his lower arms and wrists? How could one discount or brush aside the reality of a monster whose spiked body resonated with a sharp and metallic scent only something existing in the physical world could hope to provoke?

***

Father Natal Purson finally decided enough was enough.

In the process of reaching down to interrupt his brother, Natal was shocked when Malphas abruptly shrank back from his touch ... and then jerked awake, his normally placid eyes coming alive with streaks of molten red. Brief moments of thrashing ensued as though Malphas's lower anatomy struggled to hold onto something large and

(*the girl ... he's taken the girl. Can it really be her?*)

wriggling.

Then Malphas disappeared underneath the surface of his pool, bubbles of mercury and filaments of grey hair leaving a foamy wake from his departure.

***

There was a bright flash from the entity – like close lightning glimpsed through a window. Though shielding both eyes in the crook of his elbow, the light was enough to induce a corona of burning afterimage behind Micha's closed eyelids. Opening them up once again, he saw the creature had vanished.

No ... not quite. An acrid plume of smoke lay over the living room, staining the walls a sepia grey. Soot and silver ash hung like a miasma over the coffee table, couches, and curtains. In the immediate place it had stood, the carpet appeared crisped, a cast of indented impressions left behind like supernatural scorch marks.

Still fearful, Micha, nevertheless, felt an upsurge of giant relief: the Mercury Man had disappeared back into whatever nowhere it had crawled out of, its sudden appearance perhaps no more than a cautionary warning or show of strength.

With new knowledge to work with, Micha might just be able to –

Wailing came from behind – the sound lost. As the air

cleared, Micha could now make out Penelope's partial shadow, a cut out against the gloom. And below her, still cowering, the up thrust of her daughter's hair and soot-stained clothing.

Daughter.

Only one.

Of course, the possibility remained Madison had simply run into the kitchen – or off to another part of the house. But the look on Penelope's addled face told him all he needed to know: her daughter had been snatched; abducted by the thing that hijacked their living room. The flash of blinding light was the wake of its sudden exit, yes – but it had *also* been a kind of shockwave emanating from its extracted pound of flesh.

As this realization dawned, Micha felt a now-familiar vertigo signifying his own departure was imminent – the same shift of perspective he'd experienced as Penelope's Audi had pulled up beside him in what felt like a lifetime ago.

In the street outside, sirens arose – the warble of multiple vehicles alerted to the scene. Another chapter was closing, and Micha felt no nearer to discovering the real antagonist of Hadley Grove, or the true meaning (if any) behind his presence here.

Before things shrank away completely, there was time to wonder if a certain Sherriff would be among the cavalry coming this way …

***

Malphas *seethed* at the interruption.

He'd been close, so very close to procuring *both* girls – but some strange and enigmatic thing, *person*, had waylaid him at the last possible moment. Not Natal. His brother's annoying interference was sometimes expected and easily assuaged. No, the menace came directly from the unforeseen wildcard – the young man who had sprung up without warning in the dirty alleyway beside *The Gourmet Grove*.

First alerted to the unknown presence by sense, alone, Malphas had scoured the matrix of his town like a carrion bird seeking prey. His first instinct, to consult the shade of Orobas in the catacombs below, had been tempting – but so too was the allure of locating the anomaly on his own. He was king here; he was protector. And he would be the one to root out any glitches in the banquet of souls comprising Hadley Grove. For the journey, he had assumed one of his favorite forms: the nomadic Wanderer, a golem inspired in part by the ancient races of old to have populated this region of the world during the days of Orobas's reign. Garbed in a seraphic black cape and wide-brimmed hat, the Wanderer often took to the streets of Hadley Grove, completely unseen by its peoples yet moving among them as one of their own. Through midnight streets he walked, and through the daylight hours, too, seizing up their malleable souls as a farmer might his herd of cattle for potential slaughter.

It had not taken Malphas long to locate the foreign enigma.

With the sun distilling the last frost of the morning and

Main Street quickly filling up with citizens, Malphas had *felt* the man before laying eyes upon him: a crucible of energy saturated with a stink of the unknown. Whatever it was, it did not live inside the limits of his town. Moreover, Malphas had been uncertain as to whether it resided in *this* world, altogether. Its signature, alien in the particulars, lent itself more to something summoned from inside the bowels of their Church – and whose appetite raged on a different spectrum.

When Malphas found the man lying unconscious on the ground – a flesh and blood *man* as opposed to some kind of spirit adversary – he didn't know whether to feel disgusted or outright amused. If Natal was to discover his misgivings were tied to a human who barely straddled manhood, Malphas would be secretly mocked. The encounter, strange as it was, became even stranger when the man awoke, stood up, and *registered* the golem of Malphas staring down at him. That the foreigner could see him at all was unsettling … but it was also proof positive the newcomer did not belong here.

Unused to the initial scrutiny of any living being in Hadley Grove while golem-guised, Malphas quickly fled the scene; but not before marking the man with his silver-eyed stare. Back inside the mercury pools and his golem discarded, Malphas had *rallied* at the encounter, refusing to inform Natal until he had at least a soupçon of knowledge pertaining to the threat. And promising himself a swift and brutal confrontation when and if the enigma decided to reappear in the town of Hadley Grove again.

That was my mistake. I should have informed Natal.

And reappear, it had – quickly after their initial
encounter, no less. This time, the man had been wandering
the hills on the outer limits of town, seemingly on the cusp
of trying to flee it. Upon seeing the nomadic Wanderer, it
was the *man's* turn to flee … running right into the arms of
a family who had been marked by the brothers some time
ago. Such a twist, one as wholly unanticipated as the threat,
himself, had not factored into his thinking at all. Just how
did the enigma know the widow Penelope and her children?
More importantly, how had he *summoned* them at the
precise moment Malphas began giving him chase?

Infuriated beyond telling, Malphas had followed the
family home, shedding the Wanderer in the process.
Although Natal had urged restraint in acquiring the twins
for their collection, Malphas could delay the moment no
longer. Of course, it would require using his most prized
golem, the silver serpent – a significant risk in broad
daylight. But the time had come to secure the precious
cargo of the girls' flesh before the stranger could interpose
further.

In the aftermath of the encounter, only one girl-child
lay screaming and gasping for breath in the shallow end of
their regular water pool, the place where all potential
candidates were amassed. And it would soon be up to Natal
to claim her from the water and see that she lived.

Having lingered too long here already, Malphas could
feel the burning sensation of natural water against his skin,
grinding through his pores like acid. Submerging himself,
he kicked away from the girl, and soon his buoyant flesh
once again found the closest artery of mercury running

through the walls, a blessed compound of relief to his ancient bones.

Chapter Seven

On the morning of the 7th of June, Micha awoke and checked his Facebook account: only one gleaming red notification inside the messages icon held sway. Usually a steadfast social media commentator on any given day, Micha and Facebook had not been on good terms since his return from hospital. In fact, his posts during this period were sporadic *non-sequiturs* pertaining to nothing of any relevance. No book promotions; no personal anecdotes; no comedic videos lampooning a political figure. Lila, knowing his predilection for solitude, had also kept her distance. Yet here was one message from the woman he had not spoken to for over a week.

Hey you – I know you haven't been on Facebook at all lately, but thought I would write anyway. Please know I'm not ignoring you or giving you the silent treatment, I'm simply letting you have time to yourself during your adjustment period back home. I know you better than you think, Micha Tudor – and I know this is what you would prefer. The last thing I want to do right now is hinder your recovery, and let's face it: serious talk on top of everything else would only exacerbate our anxiety. You only need to know that I love you ... and will always be here for you, no matter what happens between us. So rest up, and rest well. I'll be here waiting for you as your friend when you come out on the other side. xxx

Micha stared at the screen for several minutes before deleting the conversation in its entirety.

***

Almost a week had passed since Micha's last jaunt into the imaginary world of Hadley Grove with more time spent adjusting to the real one. His rational expectations (that the whole experience would once again take on the hallmarks of a vivid dream) were negated with every passing day. If anything, gallivanting around fantasyland felt *more* real and more authentic in its minutiae than it had during his recuperation phase in hospital. Put simply: Hadley Grove was a bona-fide memory, filed away within his subconscious mind as something to have physically happened; the drama every bit as factual as time spent with Lila in *this* world. Even the varied supernatural elements of the excursion, of coming face-to-face with a towering quicksilver entity with limbs of steel and fire for eyes, had branded themselves into Micha's awareness as recollection.

The Quicksilver Man. The Mercury Man.

Waking up the next morning, Micha *sprung* from his mattress, sure in the knowledge more pages had been added to the burgeoning manuscript – that his time away had been recorded as fresh chapters to the novel in-progress. But on this occasion, there was nothing. Not so much as a supplementary scrawl added to either the document or the physical pages of the A4 crème paper his printer had decided recently to shit out like magic. Micha thought, in that secret part of himself he barely acknowledged, this would be how his story panned out: man newly diagnosed with a personality disorder succumbs to strange fugue states. During these departures from reality, a brilliant new novel comes into being – an outstanding work of art that (although the author has no memory of composing it), finally has enough successful clout to put him back inside the 'prolific' circle of the tribal world that sometimes comprised independent dark fiction.

There's your elaborate and exclusive fantasy world right there, Micha. A penchant to believe in dumb miracles.

Dark fiction: a world he hadn't thought about in a while. How was it going in the virtual reality ether of writers, artists, and storytellers? How many Twitter tirades and publishing success stories on Facebook had he missed out on since becoming a full-time hermit and crazy person? Like anything else in life, probably not all that much. Things, while *not* seeming static and patterned-orientated when you were inside them, appeared to be just that when you were on the outside looking in. People (and in particular, their politics) seldom changed. And neither,

Micha was willing to bet, did the often hilarious and all-consuming world of publishing dark and speculative fiction.

No new novel – beside the one writing itself – and no short stories to speak of, either. If any other person had been sharing his space these past few weeks, they would be apt to call him lazy.

I have been reading, though. There's that.

Yes, he had. And not just the usual suspects of Clive Barker and Robert McCammon, either – whose words were as much a part of his being as breathing. In addition to his regular heroes, Micha had been gorging over his own horror stories with a fine-toothed comb.

The novellas dealing with Hadley Grove, for instance.

There were four of them at last count; two of them dealing with Natal Purson as the antagonist, a Lovecraftian-type demon in human form whose church acted as an enormous front for wicked deeds performed in the ossuary hidden below. The offshoot of a higher demonic power (scouring the manuscript he came across the name of Orobas); Natal would sometimes procure the souls of chosen victims in order to resurrect the long-dead infernal deity who had originally sired him into being. The Catholic church, brooding on the bluffs above Hadley Grove, operated as a giant gateway under construction; the catacombs underneath a labyrinthine metropolis of hellish architecture in league with some of Dante's darkest dreams. In essence, Natal's church was like a machine that required flesh *and* spirit to grease the cogs of its underworld edifice. Natal, acting under the auspices of a genuine and caring

Father of the cloth, was slowly feeding both willing and unwilling human participants into this macabre instrument of resurrection. While some of these souls came from his own Sunday flock, others were rounded up from the town of Hadley Grove, Natal's bequeathed supernatural abilities giving him the skill to sniff out individual lives like an unseen god. Of course, there were those living below who had some knowledge of Natal's overbearing gifts (relatives of the missing, for instance), and occasionally worked to thwart the demon from his upraised lair.

Although great fodder for storytelling, Micha saw none of these plot elements as anything approaching original. Demons brooding from above had all been done before, by many great authors. The trick (for any writer of horror fiction), was to try and dig something original out of the sand – throw in some memorable characters and choreograph them around exquisite paragraphs that would (god-willing) go on to live in the readers' imagination long after they had finished the tale. At least, that had been Micha's ambition while composing *Most Of All*, a seventy-five page novella originally published in an anthology called *Evil Empire – Tales From Below*.

The big question remained: was Father Purson the mysterious Mercury Man? And if not Father Purson, then who? And what exactly *was* this silver serpent, anyway? Although there were more than a few bad eggs in the landscape of Hadley Grove, only the demonic Father had the supernatural clout to produce such a being. When Micha returned to the town, he would have to make it his business to investigate the old man up on the hill … and his church.

A voice spoke up then – one that (while having a similar tone to the voice of depression), was more like its distant cousin:

You do realize what you're thinking, don't you, Micha? You've just begun ruminating about returning to a made-up world you wrote about in one of your horror stories. About stepping into the pages of a goddamn book. That kind of thinking doesn't even qualify you for schizoid personality disorder – it qualifies you for a padded room and a straightjacket.

Maybe so … but at least Micha was not alone in the endeavor; at least this time he was seeking out some kind of help.

***

His second appointment with Halbrook took place early the next day, and again, Micha took the bus. This time, he almost enjoyed the journey. On some days, the world and its people *didn't* look or feel like a giant model set; on some days, the world seemed almost … pleasant.

Is that some kind of positive affirmation, Micha? An optimistic thought? I'd forgotten what they were. Perhaps Halbrook slipped you some kind of meds without you being aware.

Through the bus's side window, Micha spotted the ghostly reflection of a smile. Yes, he could admit (even to himself) that today he felt good. Though his imminent appointment with the good doctor was perhaps partially responsible for the good vibe – or not. Sometimes a person didn't need a reason to feel good.

Some days just being alive was enough.

***

'And how've you been sleeping this week?' Halbrook was asking. 'Everything okay there?'

'Actually, that's what I wanted to talk to you about. What happens to me when I sleep.'

Crossing his legs for the second or third time, the left side of Halbrook's face twitched in what was unmistakable amusement – body language that demonstrated: *as a doctor, I'm going to enjoy this.*

'What *happens* to you?' Halbrook asked. 'Are we talking about sleepwalking here or something of similar ilk?'

'Something like that.'

Micha paused, going over just what he would divulge and how. Halbrook was going to get part of the story … just not all of it.

Micha said, 'We've talked a little about Hadley Grove? The small town in New Hampshire?'

The doctor's eyes found his notes, lingered on certain paragraphs. 'Yes. The town you first saw in a dream after your sister died?'

'I said it was a dream … but at the time it was much more than that. When I slipped away on my bed that afternoon, I swooped over Hadley Grove like a bird. I remember seeing not only the way its streets were laid out, but the way it *smelled*. Like the smell of winter here, but much sharper and more acute. And I could hear the town, too. Hear kids playing in their backyards with their pets – hear the growl of lawnmowers and birds pin-wheeling over the ocean. The Atlantic … I saw that sea as clearly as I see you sitting in front of me.'

'But you convinced yourself, otherwise?'

Micha nodded. 'Who wouldn't do that? Persuade themselves it was a dream? After all, I was lying down on the bed when it happened – dozing off with a Dean Koontz paperback on my stomach, if I recall correctly. Despite the strange nature of the encounter, that's the rational conclusion I reached at the time.'

'And what …' Halbrook's eyes travelled up to the ceiling, weighing his next words like navigating a puddle. 'What are you saying, Micha? That there was a little more to it all than a boy who was reading too much Dean Koontz on a lazy weekend and fell asleep?'

Micha took a deep breath, assessing his next words as carefully as Halbrook's. 'Yes. Because I've been back there.'

Showing no signs of surprise, the doctor nodded. Looking at his pad, he jotted down some more notes.

'I know what you're thinking. Hell, I've been thinking it, too. One of the schizoid's main criteria is the ability to immerse yourself in an internal fantasy world. And that's pretty much what I've been doing my whole life, when I look at things closely. But that time felt infinitely different – something almost supernatural in its effects. And if not supernatural, then it was just a very complex coping mechanism my brain produced.'

'And now you've experienced another emotional catastrophe … something on par with the death of your sister.'

Surprised to hear a giggle escape his throat, Micha said, 'Yes, that's true, isn't it? This time it was coming face-to-face with my own death, my own mortality. I suppose, in a way, Hadley Grove was due for an encore performance.'

Halbrook said, 'So you do admit … that this fantasy town is most likely a psychological coping mechanism – albeit a very involved one?'

'Yes, I can admit that. But it could *also* be something much more – like an adjacent reality making itself known to me when I'm vulnerable. Lila and I, we used have debates about that kind of thing. Inside a dream, one is usually not aware he is dreaming, is he? So is *that* reality any less material than this one? For me, the question then becomes a moot point because the *results* are the same either way. Be it a dream world I'm inhabiting, or another level of existence, everything becomes a collision of catharsis, the kind of therapy that could potentially shame regular psychoanalysis.' Micha grinned. 'No offense, of course.'

This time Halbrook laughed – a short cackle. 'You'll get no argument from me there, Micha. You mentioned at the beginning that when it happened this time … you went back to Hadley Grove during a normal period of sleep?'

From the beginning of his collusions with Halbrook, it had been on the tip of Micha's tongue to inform him that death had been his boarding pass (at least on that first occasion). Yet for now, he chose to keep the revelation a secret.

Just admit it to yourself: Halbrook looks like the kind of man who could have proficient knowledge in the area of near-death experiences. Delving into the enigma too deeply and too quickly could stymie the thing altogether ...

Micha cleared his throat. 'Not long after that first session with you, actually. When I go under, I feel completely conscious the whole time – yet when I come back, when I *wake*, I feel refreshed ... as if awakening from a normal five-hour sleep cycle.'

'Interesting. I have another patient who describes something similar. What happened this time around?'

Another abbreviated version of events followed: Micha thrust back into the aromatic world of a different era, one containing different cars and clothing styles; he described conversing with the owner of a prominent drinking establishment and subsequently being welcomed into the house of a local family.

Micha decided to make no mention of a monster made of mercury.

'And how close does this version compare to the one you've written about in your stories?' Halbrook asked.

For a moment, the directness of the question caught Micha off-guard; it was something (even while *reading* the stories), he'd given only a cursory thought to. He said, 'Everything's there and accounted for – the nuts and bolts of it, I mean. Shops and houses are where they are supposed to be. Even the streets are laid out according to how I originally imagined them.' Pausing, Micha thought back to the characters he'd seen that were never committed to paper; he thought about the gentle morning light arrayed on the hood ornaments of cars.

'But there are subtle differences, too. Like it's all taking place on a slightly different time track. Or it's a version, almost a simulacrum, where another author has taken a stab at the same literary world.'

Chapter Eight

Sara Childs glanced up at the wall-mounted clock above the tavern's television set for the tenth time in ten minutes, hoping each occasion she did so would somehow speed up the time. Of course, almost everyone knew clock-spying had the *opposite* effect, with the larger hand seeming to retract *backward* every time she pulled her gaze toward it.

Only another twenty minutes until midnight, she thought. *At least everyone's cleared out.*

Or had they? A quick survey beyond the wooden balustrade of the bar revealed a singular drooping head only one seat cushion away from the jukebox, his short and curling grey hair wreathed in a white cloud of cigarette smoke. Sitting on the table directly below the head was a straight double-shot of untouched amber whiskey.

Sherriff Brandon Delgado, she thought in a kind of resigned dread. *I don't even remember him coming in.*

Such a thing wasn't uncommon during peak hour – a time when she, Joe Foster, and Rachel Warner were serving, on average, one customer per minute. Saturday nights at Delta Bronze (those happy hours between six and seven) were a raucous affair, every face seeming to blend into a monstrous one. Failing to recognize someone – even a familiar someone – had always been part and parcel with owning and working a bar.

Sara eyed the wall clock again.

Its large hand had not moved.

Sara knew the Sherriff would be putting in an appearance, of course – just not this swiftly and certainly not at this hour of the night. Mr. Tudor had only been living above the bar for two days, time enough to become the focal point of gossip not just within Hadley Grove but the counties surrounding it. Arriving at the same time of Madison Bowthorpe's disappearance, he had become a suspicious person-of-interest concerning her whereabouts. Which in itself wasn't surprising, really. Not in the least. Because until just a few short days ago, nobody (including Sara Childs) had ever heard of a writer named Micha Tudor.

Across the tavern, alerted to Sara's presence as if by the power of her gaze, Delgado looked up from his whiskey and zeroed in on her position behind the bar. On his cheeks he wore a crooked smile, one that revealed bulging teeth so bright they were like glowing pieces of chewing gum. In the reflected halogen light of the jukebox, Brandon's bloodshot eyes regarded her playfully.

He's completely wasted, she thought. *And still in his*

uniform. Why the hell did I tell Joe and Rachel they could go home early?

For the same reason she'd wanted to close up early and get some alone time with her new tenant, Micha Tudor. To talk with him a little.

Which was exactly what the only customer left in her tavern wanted to do: get up close and personal with the mysterious new stranger. Perhaps even cart him away, if the action was within his powers. And not even to a jail cell. No, sir. Delgado was the kind of man who would do his interrogating inside the confines of a personal cargo van … or perhaps on the outskirts of an everglade swamp. Despite claims to the contrary, witch hunts often took place inside small municipalities. Sara knew this for a fact. Just as she *also* knew that if it wasn't for her good-self intervening the other afternoon, Micha Tudor might have been strung-up from a nearby tree the afternoon the police and neighbors had pulled into the driveway of the Bowthorpe residence.

Mercury Man sighting be damned, she thought. *A visitor like Micha Tudor has all the earmarks of a perfect patsy.*

Slowly, Brandon stood up. Expecting the man to make a straight b-line for the bar, he surprised Sara by walking over to the jukebox. Though no song had broadcast from its speakers for well over an hour, it appeared the good Sherriff was about to remedy that situation. Bending over the glass, he perused the selection like some kind of strange connoisseur. Then, without preamble, he slotted multiple coins into the contraption and made his selection. After a muted silence of nothing but static, the sudden strains of Elvis Presley erupted from the speakers below – the King crooning his rendition of *Run On*.

'You know what I'd *like* to hear?' came the voice of Brandon Delgado from across the room. Even over the sound of the music, his voice was perfectly audible and attuned to its drunken frequency. 'One of these days, that is? I'd like to hear Johnny fucking *Cash* do a version of this big bad momma. A voice like that with lyrics like these would be *badass*, that's what I think. What do you think, sugar?'

Hunched over and facing away, Delgado waggled his ass, cocking it left and right according to the beat. Also beating in time: his police-issued pistol holstered to his side. Tipping over even further, he regarded his reflection in the jukebox's plate-glass window, angling his grey-stubbled chin to-and-fro like a caged bird in contemplation. Soon the lyrics he'd alluded to filled up the tavern with their precise, eerie nonchalance.

> *You Can Run For A Long Time ...*
> *Run On For A Long Time ...*
> *But Sooner Or Later, God is Gonna Cut You Down ...*

Despite the indoor heating, Sara shivered. Somehow imagining Johnny Cash singing those words made them even more ominous.

Look at me, I'm like a deer caught in a pair of fucking headlights.

Midstride, she'd halted and hadn't budged an inch

since spying the man across the room. With a force of will, she picked up a yellow dishrag from the countertop and proceeded to wring it as the good Sherriff sidled his way over.

'Isn't it customary …' he asked her, 'for those in the bartender trade to *smile* when serving their clientele? I know that's a fucking lost art in a hive like *New York City*. But over here, pretty lady, we *smile* for the cameras when booze is the barter being exchanged.'

'What'll it be then?' she replied in a whispered falsetto. 'Just so you know, we close in fifteen.'

Another furtive glance at the clock.

This time it *had* moved closer to twelve.

On his journey over, Brandon had not deviated once from his little jive, swaying his hips and rolling his fists like a boxer preparing to sucker-punch something.

In a booze-marinated echo, he sang, '*Sooner or later, God is gonna cut … you … down!*'

One additional verse of the song, and he was standing right in front of her with all ten fingers splayed against the wood, his wrists bent so far forward his knuckles were white. This close, the bloodshot in the whites of Brandon's eyeballs were like tributaries glimpsed from the window of a plane, huge fault lines crisscrossing mother earth. He said, 'Sara, I've been working on the police force in Hadley Grove for fifteen years. And I've been *living* here since I was pissing in the sandpits of Hadley Primary. Did it not once cross your city-cuckold mind that I might be somewhat *aware* of what time Delta Bronze closes up shop?'

By its inflection, the question was rhetorical. Yet Sara managed not only a meek reply, but the crack of something vaguely resembling a smile.

'Force of habit.'

'Not that it matters,' he told her, pretending not to hear. 'I'm here on official police business, after all. But I think you knew that, didn't you? That's why you're wound up tighter than a girdle on a Baptist minister's wife.'

And what would the state police think of you being soused on official police business? Sara thought but did not utter. Because that particular question didn't even skate the rhetoric line – only a moot one. The higher-ups probably wouldn't think anything of the Sherriff being shitfaced ... because small-town law here had always been a law unto itself.

From inside the crease of his uniform jacket, Brandon produced a pack of Marlboros. As Elvis Presley closed his last verse singing *Run On*, the deputy sparked one with a match procured directly from one of the books adorning Sara's line of clean ashtrays. 'With compliments,' he mumbled around the cigarette, reading from the packaging. 'The fuck you say? Sara, do you know what I'm *really* doing here tonight? Besides drinking your ass-tasting whiskey, that is? You do, don't you?'

Sara nodded wordlessly. She then went about the ritual of pouring her customer another ass-tasting whiskey.

'It's that woebegone you've got secreted away upstairs,' he said. At the mention of *woebegone*, Brandon's eyes brimmed. 'This individual – this *perp* – was placed not all that far from the Bowthorpe residence when little

Maddie went AWOL the other day. Tonight ... why, tonight, I'd like to go up those stairs and have a little word with him.'

With no replacement for Elvis on the jukebox, the bar had fallen into a sullen silence. Even the dishwashers out back had completed their work for the night. The double shot-glass filled, Sara slid it over toward her customer.

She said, 'You can speak with him tomorrow morning, after he's rested up some. Tonight, I had him cleaning some of the bigger stock pots we do by hand. When he'd finished those, he went ahead and cleaned some spare rooms. At the moment , he's sleeping – and free men are entitled to their sleep, aren't they , Sherriff? You can come back and speak with him tomorrow , if it suits you.'

Delgado's eyes had become slits; they moved with the lackadaisical grace of a cat. Without first consulting his wallet, he upended his drink, grimaced, and shook both shoulders before slamming the glass back down again. 'Thought you might say something like that,' he muttered. Then, adopting an almost bored cadence, continued. 'Ms. Childs, these are very dangerous times. A person of serial killer ilk, what the pundits out there have dubbed the Mercury Man, has been stalking our good citizens for months now, terrorizing people in their homes, out on the street, and sometimes taking lives in the process.'

Delgado paused to sniff, rubbing one hand across his stubbled jowl. 'Despite dressing up in a goddamn silver suit like a fucking clown, nobody has been able to lay a claw on him, let alone get near enough to actually *catch* him. Rumor has it this madman is, shall we say, of *supernatural* persuasion; we all know that's just the reaction of a scared people – a people that don't know their elbows from their assholes when it comes to things they don't understand.'

Sara said, 'You mean, like all those trials they had over in Salem hundreds of years ago?'

Unreconciled to being mocked, Brandon pumped his chubby head up and down in an emphatic swoop, wiping his nose again in the process. 'That's goddamn right, lassie. *Just* like that. Folks screaming about angels, devils, witchcraft, and every damn demon under the sun when all the while it's only ever been *men* who wear the true face of evil. Wouldn't you agree to that?'

Sara, thinking of how Delgado had once shot and killed a homeless man on the snowy grounds of Eagle Mountain House, slowly nodded in turn.

'And that's just what this Mercury Man thing is – a fucking *man*. A flesh-and-blood man who's now about the business of kidnapping people in addition to slaughtering them.'

'Penelope doesn't believe –'

'*Hush* now, Ms. Childs. Don't breathe another goddamn word. Right now, I don't give a tin-shit what Penelope do-gooder Bowthorpe believes or not. Right now, all I care about is the man who has recently arrived in town. A man who, for all we know, could well be the psycho everybody is talking about.'

A long pause ensued as the policeman took another drag of his cigarette, blowing it back across the bar in Sara's direction. Then, so quietly it bordered on a whisper, he added, 'A man you've inexplicably decided to provide safe harbor to.'

'*Mom?*'

The voice came from behind her, through the curtained partition separating the kitchen from the bar, and Sara felt her feet elevate onto her tiptoes. Completely under the spell of the man talking, she had thought about little else … including her daughter sleeping upstairs. Wearing nothing but a long *Madonna* emblazoned t-shirt and rubbing sleep from her eyes, Alexa came partway through the partition before stopping completely again – halted midstride as inexorably as Sara at the sight of the police officer.

For a moment there was a mutable silence – the drawn-out kind appropriate to a duel, perhaps – as Delgado and Alexa regarded each other across a fog of cigarette smoke.

A joker in the deck he didn't suspect, she thought. *It's stumped him.*

'Back to bed, sweetheart,' she called over to her daughter. 'Mr. Delgado was just leaving. I'll be up there in a minute, after I've shut down the lights and done the till.'

With only the dark shadow of Alexa's long hair and t-shirt visible in the gloom, her expression was lost in shadows. Though it was obvious from her rigid posture, her eyes had not left Brandon's – no doubt issuing him with the kind of challenge she frequently did to others who decided to infringe on their territory. *Girl's got more than moxie*, Rachel Warner had once declared after Alexa had persuaded a drunk to make haste from the premises. *She's got a fire in her belly to rival her namesake in that show* Dallas.

It was an analogy Sara could live with (comparing

Alexa to a fictional character brought to life by Joan Collings). New York, while being unkind to her daughter in circumstance, had instead decided to play fair when it came to smarts – instilling in the girl a deep sense of self-assuredness. And did Brandon Delgado across the bar perceive any of it? Without question. It was written in every nick and groove of a face suddenly turned cold.

Delgado's eyes loitered on the face in the shadows for the moment, weighed his options, and then seemed to decide harassing the young barkeep and her guest upstairs could wait until another day. Before turning around, however, he picked up the contents of his glass and downed what remained in one prolonged swallow. During which, those red-rimmed cat's eyes remained open.

And they never left Sarah's face.

***

Afflicted with a personality disorder, one that put him at a distance from the human tribe, Micha was somewhat fallow to the ordinary conduct of that tribe; of being in the thick of their colognes and perfumes; of trying to read their facial expressions and body language. In the world of Concord, he could excuse himself from other people merely by retreating to another place – a physical place to be alone, or simply a place inside his imagination. This was an easy thing to do when the regular attachments of the human world had always been restricted.

Not so in Hadley Grove, though.

Living inside the small town once again, Micha had

interacted with dozens of people; he waded among their mannerisms as though placed smack-bang in the thick of a movie. With no option to retreat anywhere (either physically or figuratively), he was at the mercy of the cast of characters – some of whom regarded him with animosity, if not outright hostility; others looked upon him with the same species of kindness people like Sara Childs and Penelope Bowthorpe had.

Two worlds were warring with each other; worlds that went far beyond what was real and what comprised make-believe.

And no line existed dividing either of them.

***

He'd been lucky to escape.

Thrust back into the precise moment he'd vacated (with the sounds of sirens warbling and the sudden retraction of the silver entity), Micha had bolted from the lounge room, crossing the very air where moments before a little girl sat shrieking. Through the kitchen, he sprang out the backdoor, almost colliding with a swing set. Wholly aware his actions were cowardly (hell, throw in criminal), there was no going back. Taking on this story – however insane that sounded inside his own head – had to be accomplished in a manner befitting the predicament. And that meant keeping his body away from harm. If there existed an unseen architect pulling the strings here, then any action on his part was probably futile. However, he would not be cowed so easily while still in control of his own faculties, if not the advents surrounding him.

Because I'm the fucking writer here.

Micha had been in the process of leap-frogging the back fence when the first vehicles pulled into the driveway, a red firetruck sounding like a behemoth, its top just visible through the skeletal fingers of a tree. Landing in a patch of sand on the neighboring side, he had been struck by the absolute cartoonish nature of the moment. Even Micha's Mercury Man, a capricious creature that looked like an oversized special-effect, had cartoonish elements to it despite scaring the absolute bejesus out of him.

Sudden pain quelled all notions of humor when his upper right leg was encased in a white fire of agony.

What happens to you if you die here? a voice – one he could've done entirely without – whispered. *You can get injured, no doubt about that now. So the big question is: can you die in your own dream, Micha?*

Nothing felt damaged, and Micha managed to hobble a few steps away from his landing spot. He stood for a while until the soreness abated and his calves began circulating blood again. Through the fence, there was a raised cacophony of shouts followed by the sound of more cars slamming their doors. Just what would Penelope be telling them, these people aroused by screaming and smoke? That an eight-foot tall demon had decided to take her daughter? Or that a hitchhiker had made off with her, instead? Having never fully developed Penelope's character in any novella, there was no clear way to know for sure. He would just have to trust his own instinct – which currently entailed making hay toward safer pastures.

Returned to black tarmac once again, Micha slowly made his way toward Main Street … back toward a tavern whose pretty owner, with only one brief greeting, had already begun to capture his heart.

***

A faint knock heralded Sara's arrival, followed by an inch of light as the bedroom door pressed inward. First two fingers appeared, then three. Following the dark outline of a face, Sara's large brown eyes were like liquid in the murk.

'I just had a visitor,' she said, somewhat curtly. 'I'm sorry, I should've known he was coming –'

Micha sat upright on his small bed. 'How could you have known he was coming?'

'Because we knew he would, sooner or later. I just didn't think he would wait until Saturday night at closing time.'

Micha, having once written about Delgado locking a suspected criminal inside his root cellar for an entire week, had known the timing would be just his style.

'And?'

'And he was drunk. My plan was to get him drunker, if you can believe that. I wanted him tipsy enough to fall on his ass. But Alexa saved the day, God bless her. He saw her and decided to split.'

Micha let out a relieved breath, unaware he had been holding one in. Leaning over to the left, he switched on a cheap desk lamp that had been one of his sole companions for the past two nights sleeping above Sara's bar. Perhaps sensing it as an invitation, she stepped fully into the room and gently closed the door.

'Did he say anything about ..?' Micha let the question hang.

'Penelope? No, I didn't let him get that far. But he didn't mention anything about her story changing, either, if that's what you mean. She claims not to have a clue who you are. Brandon assumes she's covering for you.' A small, mischievous smile broke across Sara's cheeks. 'Just like I am, I suppose.'

For a moment Micha did nothing but study that smile in the dim light, the way Sara's right dimple creased in the center of her cheek like a bullseye. Not for the first time, he felt a pang in his chest like coming home to a thing that was both familiar and good.

She caught his own small smile. 'It's not funny, you know. You still haven't given me a good reason why I should be doing so.'

'Because,' he replied in a flat and even voice. 'I'm going to need your help figuring this thing out. I haven't hurt anyone, Sara. You have to believe that.'

'You mean … figuring out what you really saw that day?'

He nodded, fighting a sudden urge to reach into the desk of drawers under the lamp and bring out the legal pad inside – a pad containing the beginnings of what he hoped would be something approaching a dossier. Though unaware of exactly *what* he was compiling in this room, Sara had glimpsed him hovering over the pad enough times recently to put two and two together. Micha, a writer from another city, had now come into physical contact with a creature who had been mythologized as a kind of silver ghost. Arriving back at Sara's bar just a few short hours after escaping his brush with the creature (a little bruised and broken from his leapfrog over the fence), Micha had described seeing the entity: a quicksilver giant whose potent life-force seemed to visibly shift the air around it; a wraith able to influence the physical world and produce harm.

This time, he had made no mention of a cowboy with silver suns for eyes.

Sara had believed him; she believed him because dozens of others in Hadley Grove had also seen the being on several occasions. Some of them reported it to local authorities. Some, more often than not, shared the news over the phone, in the markets on Main Street, or even gossiped about it over a few jugs of beer in this very watering hole.

Something strange had indeed arrived in their small town, a thing whose presence was inexplicable and – for the moment – unexplainable.

'You can stay here for a while,' Sara told him. 'Alexa doesn't mind at all. In fact …' Here Sara tipped her head, a coy movement in lieu of a full-blown wink. 'She told me she actually *likes* you. Those were her exact words. I may not know you very well, but trust me, if you've earned my daughter's seal of approval, then you've got mine all the way.'

Chapter Nine

Although regular mass was scheduled only a few short hours away, Father Natal Purson was far from ready. By this time on any usual given Sunday, Natal would be locked away in the sacristy of his private chamber, diligently rehearsing portions of his newest sermon by the wick of candlelight. Inside the Nave, thick rivulets of incense would already be sweetening the air and making delicate patterns of smoke among the pews, each burning stick of jasmine and honeysuckle a small signpost to usher in the faithful with their bouquet.

Instead, Natal traversed the hallways of the dead on his way to the shade of Orobas.

Usually a place of tranquility, recent events concerning his brother, Malphas, had turned these antechambers into a raging tempest hive of activity, each slab of dark sarcophagus lining the wall luminous with an agitated spirit … agitated, no doubt, by the fresh innocence they perceived above. In addition to their light being prevalent, their voices were, too – echoing throughout the giant ossuary like a parade snatched from paradise. Upon seeing the shadow of Natal's cloak pass by, their voices climbed louder still. Jeers, catcalls, and laments rebounded off the crumbling stone to become a singular mournful din. With quick, precise steps, Natal walked faster on the cement, hoping none of their eyes (or whatever passed for their sight) could fix on him long enough to recognize him.

With Malphas attending to the girl, I've been given this slim window of opportunity.

Despite his hurried trot, Natal felt himself shiver. Though he and Malphas were born of the same cloth (and womb), thinking of his brother lording over the little one during Natal's absence was somewhat unsavory.

Any more unsavory than what you plan to do with the girl?

Grimacing at both his physical exertions and the question posed, Natal quickened his stride even more, finally rounding the last pillar that gave way to the very beating heart of their building: the Hall of Portals, where the shade of Orobas could be accessed.

Once through the hallways of the dead, the clamoring voices ceased – a vacuum of sound every bit as ominous as their clamor.

***

Hundreds of years ago, the Hall of Portals had been built for other purposes: the ancient stones hewn to withstand the deluge of anything the natural world could bring to bear. Though architects during Orobas's reign could not have foreseen the current great work taking place, their ambition to keep out the world above, nonetheless, had the same desired effect: lay the groundwork of a seamless and impenetrable moat of stone so that anyone who chose to use this space could do so knowing its bricks were unbreakable and its circular walls impassable. While the moat's height was impressive – at least fifty furlongs from base to tip – its width was even more so: an ovoid space, a distance unperceived by a human's naked eye. Leading to it, across a chasm that fell away into the interior, lay the Hall of Portals's sole access point: a thin stone bridge broaching away from the church's antechambers like a needle radiating from an eye.

Though Natal had traversed this particular path hundreds of times, his long cassock whispering along the cobblestones, no amount of practice could ever induce familiarity. While the cement had always provided its own illumination, the void to either side of the bridge detailed a saturated darkness so acute it appeared composed of another substance altogether. Keeping his eyes trained forward, and with vertigo acting as a constant and beneficial companion, Natal was able to navigate the final distance, bringing him to the cusp of the Hall of Portals.

Not an appropriate name, he thought, and deigned to strain his head partially over the lip. *Poetic, yes – but not appropriate. This is a well ... its sheer vastness defying adequate description.*

Below the hem of Natal's cassock, just over the edge, a

phosphorescent indigo light not dissimilar to those fashioned by the antechambers created a misted halo of radiance ... before giving way to a riot of form and color. These shapes, like quixotic puzzle pieces randomly brokering for space, both warred and devoured each other, giving way to even newer forms and shapes in the process. Though Natal had only the vaguest notion they were sentient, this seemed to matter little. What *did* matter were the massive physical objects extending along the walls of the structure, itself: black archways of steel; each individual one separated by only the slimmest of margins, their entire length running from the top of the well into the unseen depths below.

Portals.

Presently sealed, each of these items were a monolith unto themselves, walled-off partitions acting as the nexus of Natal and Malphas's current great work. Having come into being not long after the demise of Orobas's corporeal self, they were the product of that departure: their father continuing *his* work long after returning to the world below.

And more were coming into being with every passing day.

And with every passing human soul we harvest, Natal thought, *power of which I only have a rudimentary understanding.*

He did not fully comprehend the Hall of Portals ... not yet. But one did not have to comprehend an edifice to usher in its purpose. All one needed was the proper instruction – teachings which came from the shade of Orobas, himself.

Though not the spirit of their father, in essence, enough of his energy remained behind for the brothers to seek counsel should the need arise.

Sensing his presence, the myriad forms below quickened their movements, an erratic dance of something approximating order to the chaos of color. By degrees, the scraps of puzzle pieces were lifted on a tide of indigo air, starting as scrawls before slowly coalescing into a shadow more or less recognizable as that of a man with a dragon's head.

Orobas, his dark energy placated by time, moved along the ions of air before rising up in a malformed cloud to greet the figure of Natal standing below with one arm raised to shield his eyes against the radiance.

***

Words carried on the tide of air, but Natal knew it would be some time before he could make proper sense of them. The shade, a strange maelstrom of something unknitting then reknitting, continued to shift between man, dragon, and scrawl.

Finally, a simple statement, devoid of anything except a kind of programmed personality: *News, my son.*

'Malphas …' Natal said, and let the word hang for a moment. 'My brother continues to be overeager. He has recently acquired a child.'

The shade spasmed into rivulets of matter like black magma. When it spoke, only a rudimentary mouth could be perceived inside the haphazard dragon's head.

Innocence ... too soon.

'Yes, Father. That is why I come to you today. I'm afraid I'm torn, not knowing if we should proceed with her invocation into the Hall of Portals. These are unpredictable times. Something strange – an anomaly has come into our midst.'

I've felt it.

This statement from the writhing shape, almost nonchalant in the particulars, sent Natal reeling. Still partially shielding his sight, he braced his toes forward just enough to maintain a proper balance. As though fueled by the words, themselves, the puzzle pieces of man-dragon became darker still, some individual fragments conjoined to form an unmistakable torso.

'You ... have?' Natal managed.

I'm talking to the shade of Orobas, Natal thought. *Not my real father. How is it this energy has been able to stretch its fingers into our world so readily?*

But Natal knew the answer to this question as surely as he knew why his brother required the element of mercury to stay alive and function. With every new portal added into this hall, the edifice was amassing in strength, the lines between multiple worlds becoming more solvent. So it stood to reason his father's shade was feeding upon this strength, his presence growing ever brighter with the invocation of each new soul.

Something ... unnatural. Yet it could be Providence.

Natal waited, hoping for more. But the shade sat poised within its own extremis, filigrees of shadow still warring upon the revelation.

'Shall we proceed with the girl's invocation?' Natal asked. 'Should we continue with more acquisitions?'

The shadow quelled itself enough to be the black outline of a man again. Then: *Nothing ... must stop ... the portals. Perhaps she is also meant for the fire – a final ingredient.*

Again Natal hoped for more elucidation, but the shade's import had a ring of finality to it. And its answer was plain: the brothers were to continue with their work, no matter the arrival of the anomaly; no matter that Malphas's golem had recently acquired a piece of innocence named Madison Bowthorpe whose absence could potentially jeopardize their whole endeavor. Perhaps the shade knew Hadley Grove had enough human acolytes aiding the brothers – and in some cases working directly for them (like the Sherriff) – that any danger, no matter how capricious, could not circumvent what was now inexorably in motion within the Hall of Portals.

And that is their opening, Natal thought, with a trace of something like unease. *New worlds beginning to spill out into this one, Orobas's ambition finally fulfilled.*

Above, the shade had fractured enough to communicate their time together had closed, the man-dragon now a clotted mass of puzzle pieces once again. Despite Natal receiving only a rudimentary portion of information desired (certainly not enough to waylay his tenuous unease), for now it would have to be enough. A mass was scheduled, and Natal needed to hurry back through the antechambers and once again meet his obligations to the faithful.

Hopefully the devout would not sense this growing disquiet.

Or catch scent of his time in the Hall of Portals.

Chapter Ten

Those afflicted with Schizoid Personality Disorder are able to demonstrate a rich, elaborate, and exclusively internal fantasy world.

As Micha readied himself for another day, the sentence beat a fixed and frequent tattoo inside his skull.

Rich and elaborate doesn't begin to describe it, he thought. *This is the ultimate VR experience – one I may never return from.*

Though the thought was disturbing in its implication (was Micha sleeping away in his Concord bed, pissing and shitting himself as days flew by?), his overall disquiet was waylaid by the sights and textures of living in a territory of illusion. Yes, there existed a strong likelihood his physical self was wasting away in another world – but that world had always been polluted and choked full of weeds. On the other hand, a driving internal fantasy world had the capacity to be a virtual paradise … in spite of the monsters inhabiting the illusion.

If one could simply award it a level of acceptance.

Micha was up to the task.

In Hadley Grove, it was December 8th 1985, a sunny Sunday afternoon and only one week having passed since Brandon Delgado's whistle-stop tour and hasty exit of Delta Bronze. Since then, there had been no sign of the Sherriff, or anybody else that might have wished Micha harm. His new allies, Sara and Alexa, had not only afforded him a safe harbor to stay but also played the part of tour guides in what was now shaping up to be an extended vacation inside the vacuum of 1980s America. *Small* town America, yes – but somehow all the more potent for the locale. Here, in this tavern, no one carried a smart phone or electronic tablet; no one so much as held a laptop. Best of all, people didn't seem to carry anxiety-ridden stares like a burden of shell-casings, the byproduct of a future swimming with things like twenty-four hour cable news television.

On the morning after escaping a visit from the nefarious police officer, Micha had been keen to pay a visit to the other antagonist in this story, Father Purson, who lived inside his castle on the bluffs. While both Sara and Alexa were not overly religious per se, they still made the trip up to the church on occasion; small-town customs and pastimes soaked into everyday habit were hard to scrap. Sara had agreed amiably enough (although she had appeared confused by his enthusiasm to check out a local church that only participated in good things). Once outside, however, Micha swiftly changed his mind. Couldn't they, instead, visit the Magic Mountain amusement park where bumper cars, cotton candy, and indoor discoes were the order of the day? Or how about a simple visit to the Palace, where *Back to the Future* was still in season and would be for the foreseeable future? Sara, again displaying that casual acceptance of Micha's presence despite him being an out-of-town stranger, agreed to this as well. Alexa would help mind the bar with Rachel Warner while they were away.

Nowhere was it written that two outings constituted a date, but from Sara's slightly coy smile as she agreed for the second time, Micha could ascertain it was an unspoken edict they were both settling on.

***

A place only suggested in Micha's stories, Magic Mountain rose up in a dirty mound of addled brown brick with two separate waterslides intersecting the building like giant white intestines. Though the waterslides were predictably idle for the season, everything else, including a giant carousel and dozens of arcade games, were fair game for anyone willing to trade honest money for issued tokens. Also in the mix: sky-cycles and engine-powered bumper boats floating in a pool of water like mobile doughnuts.

Sara Childs, her shoulder-length blonde hair tied and donned in a fluorescent green t-shirt and black miniskirt, looked beautiful. Exchanging tokens at the main gate with Micha standing beside her, she asked him, 'Have you ever set one of your stories in an amusement park? Like a haunted one?'

'Yes,' he replied absently. 'Two, actually. Well, it wasn't so much a theme park but more a haunted museum.'

As the booth attendee (a middle-aged grizzled man sporting a fat cigar) slid over their gold tokens, Sara remarked, 'Not the same thing at all. Consider this a field trip then. More research for *The Horror of Hadley Grove*.'

Micha grinned. 'Then we ought to come back at night, don't you think? Sneak inside when nobody sees and nobody knows?'

'Are you suggesting we do something illegal? We can't have that now the whole town knows where you're staying.'

Sara had barely completed her sentence before Micha noticed another young couple hovering behind them, both engrossed in the act of ogling with a fixed, suspicious attention. The man (wearing a Mr. T tee-shirt and a bushy black moustache), reserved his core attention for Micha, sizing him up like an outfit in a dress window. Just another extra on the stage of Hadley Grove … and certainly not one Micha had ever described.

'Hey, buddy,' Micha said as both he and Sara swept past them taking their leave. 'The Seventies wants its facial hair back.'

In the wake of a confused stare, Sara swatted him with one balled fist. 'That was mean,' she said, though trying (unsuccessfully) to keep her own grin in check.

Into Magic Mountain they walked, and in doing so, Micha felt his hand unconsciously reach out and take the hand of the girl walking beside him. As the smells of cotton candy filled his nose and the cheers of children filled his ears, he had just enough time to recognize the day outside was sunny and crisp, the sky above Magic Mountain a perfect and dazzling reflection of the blue Atlantic beyond a wall of cliffs. In the realm of story, Hadley Grove had always existed in the perpetual twilight of an ashen winter, a gothic background to gothic events.

Not so now, though, Micha thought, and felt Sara's hand clasp his own in return. *The rules are changing. Now that I'm living them and not writing them – perhaps they'll change for good.*

***

Drawn to the arcade games (Micha hadn't laid eyes on a real one in years), he was surprised to feel the tug of Sara's hand leading him away … leading him toward the theme park's basement disco which was separated by a stringy curtain of multi-colored crepe-paper that rippled with each person who walked through. Inside, he could hear the thump of music – Belinda Carlisle again – this time singing about rain during the summer …

And dancing, of course.

'No,' Micha said, though his voice was quiet, resigned. 'You know I can't …'

'Dance?' Sara chided. 'Of course, you can. Everyone can. You just need the proper instructor.'

Through the partition, there was a hint of glitter and strobe lights with a bouncing interplay of shadow accompanying them. 'And some Dutch courage, perhaps? They sell drinks inside, you know. Alexa sees them as competition, but I don't. If Scot Thomas is working today, he makes the most *amazing* screwdrivers this side of the Hudson. Come on, chickadee.'

Before Micha could voice a second objection, they were walking through the curtain, the beat of the stereo doubling as thick streamers fanned his face like kelp. In addition to ceiling-adored mirror balls, a smoke machine was also working its magic somewhere near a mounded platform – a raised dais where a dreadlocked disco jockey capped in a Rastafarian beret was manhandling vinyl like he was juggling cocktails. Glancing up at the newcomers, he favored Micha with a grin that was both jovial and all-knowing.

'Perfect,' Sara said. 'Place is hardly packed at all. Guess everyone is parked on a couch somewhere and watching the Patriots today.'

His date was correct: perhaps six other clientele littered the dancefloor, with four others cozied up to the bar. As Belinda Carlisle built up to another rousing and anthemic chorus, the lone man standing behind the bar (Scot, Micha presumed), waved them over with a casual arm. Sara, beaming and giddy with both the atmosphere and music, hustled Micha over to some waiting stools.

'God, I *love* this song,' she said, speaking directly to Scot. He wore a spotless black shirt with a dainty white bowtie. His cropped bleached-blonde hair completed the get-up. 'I could never imagine getting sick of it in a million years. Scot, this is Micha. Micha, meet Scot. Both of us would like a screwdriver, please.'

'Isn't she *divine*,' Scot said, a mild lisp accentuating a deep baritone voice. 'And the looks to match that angelic singing. A total babe, in other words. Heaven really is a place on earth when Belinda knocks it out of the park.'

Sara giggled; Micha could only smile dumbly. Because once again he was taken slightly aback by Eighties' vernacular. Although *total babe* and addressing someone's looks were perhaps the status quo in this period, somehow the thought of being so brazen in Micha's PC world of the Obama-era wouldn't slide so easily. Across the bar, Scot the bartender smiled back at him with good-natured aplomb (perhaps even a hint of flirtatiousness, the lisp giving leeway where perhaps his sexual proclivities lay). Thankfully it was a smile completely bereft of the distrust other strangers had shown him.

'The secret to good vodka,' Scot told them, bending down under the counter and picking up glasses. 'Is to build everything in a Collins glass. Don't be a cheapskate when it comes to the brand – I always prefer citrus vodka – and always use the freshly squeezed orange stuff. A simple syrup for sweetener completes the beverage. That, and a shaving of dry cucumber. Of course, some of the Neanderthals in Sara's dive wouldn't appreciate such artistry, but here in the Magic Cave, we go all the way.'

As the duo watched, Scot proceeded to make haste with this process, maneuvering around his tight space with the practiced ease of a professional. Micha, taking it as an opportunity to scan their surroundings again, saw the disco indeed held such a title, with *The Magic Cave* stenciled in giant oblong letters over the crepe-adorned doorway.

'Straws, please,' Sara said.

Grinning, Scot obliged this last request; subtly shaking his head in the disappointed manner of *Just how did I forget that?* Sliding his glass toward him, Micha experienced a brief wave of all-too-familiar anxiety, the cucumber-adorned glass like an ill-omen from some half-remembered other life.

Surely you can't be thinking about drinking again, Micha? Did you forget what happens to you when you do?

He pushed the thought aside. That was another Micha, altogether, one whose habits and foibles were no longer pertinent ... not in this reality, anyway – a reality where a shining soul with blonde hair still gripped his arm and glittered mirror balls hung from the ceiling.

***

With Belinda Carlisle giving way to the Australian band INXS (and Micha two Scot-concocted screwdrivers down), he suddenly knew it was time. Another urgent jerk on the side of his arm told him so.

'Come *on*,' said Sara. 'This is totally rocking.'

Rocking, it was; Micha could distinctly remember listing to *New Sensation* as a ten-year-old kid, staying up past his allocated bedtime with a red Sony Walkman jacked into his ears while his older brother snored away across the other side of the bedroom.

There were other dancers on the floor now, the Sunday Magic Mountain crowd thickening considerably. As he and

Sara jimmied their way into the center of the dance floor, each couple parted for them like a proverbial sea, as if sensing one of them had, once upon a time, been crowned king or queen of some bygone prom. Before finding their place, Sara was already moving with the languid strokes of someone well-versed in many forms of the two-step shuffle. Micha, despite playing the electric guitar from a young age (while also having an above-average pedigree of musical knowledge), could only shake his head up and down like some species of ageing head-banger. And still feeling somewhat self-conscious, his trepidation was slowly tempered by Sara's evolving strut.

'Like this,' she said, and took one of his hands. It was sweaty but felt wonderful … as if a tangible current of benign energy was being passed from her palm to his. 'It's all in the hips, really. It's where you feel the bass … and you just let it all radiate out from there.'

I've got a new SENSATION! Michael Hutchinson sang, and as Micha moved his hips, he began to realize there was wisdom to Sara's words. The hips, while being a person's center of gravity, also acted like its compass point … ball-bearings in sockets only needing a proper melodic adjustment. And once you struck up a bit of rhythm (in addition to self-confidence), everything kind of flowed outward from there; elbows and joints joining in the medley as though contagious to the hips' desires.

Careful, he thought. *You don't want to –*

A brief teetering moment ensued, and he almost overbalanced. But Sara was there, holding both of his hands, grinning back at him with a kind of prideful adoration no one (not even Lila), had ever afforded him in that other world.

'That's it!' she cried, still encased in her own faultless gyrations. 'Didn't I tell you this was the most fun ever?'

She did. And Micha had been doubtful. Just as he had been doubtful any of this was real or actually happening.

If anything could ever feel this real forever, he thought absently, a snatch of another song coming to him, this one by a band from his era – a band who wouldn't come onto the music scene and make their own mark for another decade or so. Not exactly music you could shake your booty to … but Micha thought that from this day onward, he could probably make do with what Sara had shown him.

From now on, he would dance to anything.

***

The sky-cycles were next, and following *them*, Micha finally got his wish to pony up to some arcade games. Pinball machines, too – each one lined up next to the other like serried ranks of neon coffins fresh from a showroom floor. Among the procession and catching Micha's eye immediately was a pinball machine with Michael Jackson's *Thriller* as the motif; its bumpers, targets, and even flippers adorned with silver-spun glitter and zombie-illustrated mayhem. The back glass featured a vertical graphic of the King of Pop, himself, lovingly surrounded by a horde of the undead. Underneath the top glass – among switches, gates, and stoppers – secondary flippers were arrayed like claws. Micha, moving like a man in a dream, inserted three gold tokens into a coin-slot underneath and watched in wide-eyed amazement as the whole thing powered up further still, its programmed musical score giving way to a kind of Las Vegas slot-machine version of *Beat It*.

'Brody used to avoid this one,' Sara said, standing beside Micha with her left shoulder brushed up against his. 'If you want the God's honest truth, the man was a racist piece of shit – a typical hillbilly. Of course, that part I found out *after* I married him. Oh look, triple-point score. Look at little Mikey go.'

Little Mikey was a bobble-head Michael Jackson smack bang in the middle of the neon madness, this particular one his *Moonwalker* incarnation. Micha's silver pinball, having nailed successive bumpers, had activated him into dancing his patterned moves in a stationary twist. The pinball, in that lackadaisical slow-motion movement pertinent to pinballs everywhere, hovered for long seconds before falling down again into the snapping jaws of Micha's waiting flippers.

'I imagine he's got nothing on my neighbor,' Micha said, wishing – not for the first time – Sara's ex-husband was someone whose background he knew; someone he'd written of in the past. 'A man older than God that walks with a cane. His mailbox is right next to mine, one of those communal ones. And of course, *his* is stamped with a whole bunch of those ominous no junk-mail stickers, the type with devil horns on them. Sometimes, when letter carriers deposit mail who aren't, shall we say, of Caucasian persuasion, he physically *chases* them down the street, brandishing that cane of his and threatening them. His colorful language and intimidation are so foul I've actually had to call the cops a few times.'

'You're kidding?' Sara said, smiling. 'Bet you've whacked *that* in one of your stories, huh?'

'Not yet,' Micha admitted. 'But I reckon it's only a matter of time.'

For a while, there was only silence between the pair with the sounds of the pinball machine's flippers and Michael Jackson singing about demons closing in on every side more than enough to stifle any arising awkwardness. But Micha felt there *was* some … and it revolved around the mysteries between them. So far, he hadn't produced any convincing evidence of his vocation as a writer. He *also* hadn't passed on any concrete details concerning the place across the border he chose to call home, or divulged details about family that might be curious as to his whereabouts this past week. Despite feeling like the rules of normal social interaction were variable in this story environment (and that Micha Tudor had certain free passes being its author), he similarly had a sneaky suspicion the variables here only went so far. And that sooner or later, normal behavioral protocols would resume. Sara Childs of Hadley Grove would want to know most if not everything about his life. That was if he wanted to continue sharing space with both her and Alexa.

And *especially* if he ever expected to kiss her.

***

As it turned out, that moment came sooner than either

of them expected. After finishing with the arcade games and depleting all but one of their pooled tokens, Sara suggested a final amusement for the day: a ride on Magic Mountain's sole Ferris wheel – a contraption whose ominous white framework was barely glimpsed above the main attractions like a slumbering and skeletal beast.

'It's tiny compared to some of the others in surrounding towns,' Sara told him, sounding as she spoke like some incumbent tour guide. 'But it's positioned near the ocean for the best possible view. When we reach the apex, we'll be able to see everything.'

She was right. While their wheel carriage was small and befitted with a cheap Plexiglas exterior, it did provide the kind of scenic view Micha had not observed since

(since the day you died and flew over this town)

time spent cooped up in his man-cave and roaming the wilds of his imagination. Perhaps having perceived romance before they boarded, their young female attendant killed the engine just as it mounted the very summit, each wheel carriage below them jostling with the vacuum of a passenger-less rudder. It was …

'Perfect,' Micha said. 'So picturesque and perfect, it's almost a cliché.'

'Must you ruin the moment?' Sara said, and Micha felt her elbow playfully nudge him in the side. 'Look, over there.'

Micha followed the curve of her finger and found it circling Delta Bronze, the top windows spangled in sunlight and reflecting the day. Almost against his own volition, his eyes travelled further away, up the curve of

Main Street where the hills met a wide array of low-hanging clouds. Moving his neck a tad further, he could almost see …

Suddenly Sara's lips were on his own, sweet, moist and full of purpose. Responding in kind, he lifted up his right hand and cupped her chin, steadying her face to be able to receive everything such a kiss offered. Though a cold wind blew through the carriage (inevitable being up so high), Micha was compl etely unaware of it.

In the same way he was unaware of anything else existing beyond this perfect physical moment.

Chapter Eleven

A universal law, libraries often closed early on
a Sunday. Hadley Grove's sole outlet of books, periodicals,
and copy machines had never, strictly speaking, adhered to
any regular modus operandi of a functioning small-town
library. And Samantha Mulgrave Moffat, now in her third
year holding the title of administrator's assistant, had been
the lone arbiter ushering in the unorthodox policy of
staying open. Because Sunday, in addition to being the
Lord's Day, was also the only day she could devote entirely
to working on a novel of her own. The library, with its
myriad of research materials at easy disposal, acted as the
perfect backdrop for such an undertaking. After suggesting
to Mr. Benford to extend opening hours until midnight back
in January, the head-administrator had practically *leaped*
upon the idea, seeing in these protracted hours more time to
hang around the library (time in which to ogle her) and also
give some of the local university students more occasion to

get their work accomplished on the weekends. Thus, the library's resources would be open season for throngs of the elderly on weekdays: a cabal of society within Hadley Grove who treated this building with more holy aplomb than they showed Father Purson's edifice brooding on the cliffs.

Father Purson.

That the priest was the subject of her work-in-progress was something Samantha Moffat would not have divulged to anybody – certainly not to Mr. Benford or anyone else (including her best friend, Trudi Whitaker), even if she had been poked and prodded with torture devices for the information. Although keeping her project entirely clandestine proved somewhat challenging – considering the bulk of her work took place inside the library – Samantha somehow managed to accomplish the task with little or no interference.

Because no one suspects a plucky librarian to be unearthing the sinister machinations currently taking place inside of Hadley Grove.

Of course, *plucky librarian* was only the tip of the iceberg when it came to how others in this burg perceived her. *Spirited virgin* could potentially be another. One might also add 'boring, wannabe writer' to the list of similes – Although, this last was probably stretching it. Samantha could roll with all of the punches; and more easily enough, they were opinions one could tune out completely when you were none of those things.

And when they served as adequate camouflage to keep you under the radar.

Despite beginning her manuscript only weeks previous, Samantha's *real* adventures started well before setting pen to paper; a time when she had witnessed first-hand the mysterious and enigmatic presence stalking the streets of her town. Back then, the presence had been nothing as arbitrary as a quicksilver monster; nor was it anything as prosaic as a person of serial-killer ilk. No, the creature carried the shape of a normal man – a man garbed in the vestments of a saint, no less, carrying around with him a book possessed of singular power. After coming across his actions purely by accident in the tracts of swamp past the quarries of Hadley Grove, Samantha was subsequently thrust into a supernatural nightmare of strange and varying dimensions, one where the normal rules of physical reality were no longer pertinent.

In other words, the stuff of books.

Glancing around at them now (all seven thousand twenty-four of them, meticulously arranged and catalogued) from her position behind a nook set back in the encyclopedia section, Samantha felt a queer sense of sudden foreboding. And why shouldn't she? Ordinarily, on any other given day, this part of the library was filled with hushed voices, curious people, and the lazy, somewhat narcotizing hum of wall-heaters. Now there was nothing to see but the frozen silhouettes of a seemingly endless parade of library shelves, their shadowed backs like monoliths set in stone. Mr. Benford, having departed some forty-five minutes earlier, made her the sole occupant of Hadley Grove's town library.

Unless someone came in while I was working?

A quick glance down at her wristwatch confirmed it was just after midnight – four minutes past, precisely. If anybody had wandered in while she sat here scribbling, Samantha would have heard the sliding glass doors opening in admittance. Barring that, they would have rung the silver bell behind the receptionist's desk. God knew enough people delighted in doing *that*, even when the hired help was entirely visible.

In any case, it was finally time to close up shop for the night.

Standing and stretching, Samantha heard her tendons creak in protest, her whole body having been at the mercy of an ill-advised posture for the better part of three hours. The curse of the reading class, no doubt (or literature class, if you wanted to be picky about it), and one of the main reasons she chose to *walk* the distance from her home to the library and back again for each of her allocated shifts. Exercise, while not exactly a shining characteristic of the reading class, could still be something adhered to if one simply gave into small sacrifices. So Samantha walked whenever she could, *wherever* she could, while her red Datsun sedan sat idle in a driveway more than seven blocks from the library.

Samantha walked, even though she knew the streets were no longer safe.

And she walked at night, completely aware that evil sometimes scoured the land.

For God's sake, why? Trudi had asked her once after they had ordered drinks one Saturday evening at Delta Bronze. *Are you asking to be defiled in a dark alleyway one*

*of these nights walking home? What about the local
nutcase who goes around wearing a silver suit? And don't
tell me it's research for your novel, either. Because putting
a bullseye on your back doesn't make you merely crazy,
Sam; it makes you some kind of a sadist.*

In the safety of the bar, Samantha chuckled as if a
strange part of her delighted in the label. It added a fiery
dimension to her persona, mitigating the *plucky librarian*
brand; an alter-ego existing beneath her innocent exterior.
By wearing the banner of *scribe*, Samantha Mulgrave
Moffat was more an intrepid reporter willing to die for the
elusive scoop – a diligent observer who put *story* before her
own personal safety. Of course, the truth was a little more
ambiguous – for there was certainly a part of her that *was*
afraid of encountering the priest again. And if not him, then
a portion of the power he carried around with him … power
she had unwittingly witnessed up close; a malevolent
energy twisted for an unfathomable purpose; a dark design
only her sleuthing could potentially unravel.

At least that's what I'm hoping for.

Now she looked down at the manuscript, multiple
sheaves of A4 paper appearing to wither under the bulk of
her own limp ambition. Some days, those handwritten
pages felt like small wads of victory; on others (like
tonight, for instance), they appeared feeble. Just what on
earth could an exposé *book* about Hadley Grove's dark
history possibly hope to accomplish or validate? If
anything, these confessions and interviews would open her
up to all sorts of damning denunciations; attacks that would
see her not only fired from the library but reserved one of

those padded cells still in operation inside the sanatorium known as Shadow Park Penitentiary.

'Or it could bring a monster out of his hiding place, once and for all,' she told the empty library. 'All it will take is the proper proof.'

Did her accumulated interviews into Father Natal Purson and his ageless church constitute proof? No, not yet, they didn't ... but they would. In time, she would have all the proof she needed and more that Natal and his disabled brother were custodians of a Catholic palace operating as nothing more than a smokescreen for something outwardly benign yet inwardly monstrous.

***

Beyond the external glass doors, moths flitted about the parking lot's sodium-vapor lamps like a wake of fireflies, luminous bodies swan-diving in kamikaze arcs to collide with the caustic voltage drawing them in. After switching off the inner lights and activating the library's central alarm system, Samantha stood completely shiftless in the front foyer, staring at the moths, somewhat hypnotized ... knowing she had perhaps ninety seconds to fully exit the building before the alarm activated.

Every night for over a month, she left this building shortly after midnight, knowing it was a slim jaunt back to her two-bedroom beachfront apartment. Sure in the knowledge that many people were still up – their own dwellings facing the sea and her visible safety all but assured. She was left with only the most rudimentary trace of anxiety; what would be considered germane to one's survival. And yet here she was, still standing in the building, a tight wellspring of fear making inroads into her stomach at the thought of venturing outside. Any second now …

Samantha made a mad dash through the glass doors, sliding her key through the double lock and twisting it clockwise with perhaps seconds to spare before the alarm tripped. The moths, alerted by her presence, became more excited still, the vapor lamps brightening as dozens of the creatures leaped from their surfaces only to be pulled back again.

Why tonight? Samantha thought, her breath jerking out rapidly in time with a thudding heart. *What's so different about tonight? I feel like I'm going to pee myself.*

For one, the black satchel looped around her right arm. Inside lay her manuscript, all two hundred forty-four handwritten pages of it, chronicling the history of Natal and Malphas's church. Up until now, she had kept the thing under lock-and-key in the bottom drawer of her work desk, there to while away the hours until the busy portion of any evening was over. But something (call it a sixth sense or plain paranoia) had propelled her to give it a new home. Say, in the wall-safe sitting behind a framed picture of Margret Atwood hanging above her couch in the living room, for instance. There it would be safe from either Mr. Benford's prying nature or anybody else curious about her nighttime shenanigans. Paranoia or not, Samantha had recently unearthed secrets concerning the brothers that warranted a safer place for them.

But is that all? Why do I suddenly have a feeling that something's not right?

Past the carpark, Samantha could hear the distant susurration of night surf, the calming boom of water smashing against rock. Always, this elegy had soothed her, one of the foremost reasons she had originally decided to purchase land by the sea. Hadley Grove, contained within a nebulous and ragged cove, was like a byproduct of the ocean, itself; her formations, hills, and bluffs only offspring of something far vaster in scope. And while the churning tides could always be counted upon to lull her into a sanctum of peace and security, tonight those same booms felt ominous, a warning heralding danger should she decide to proceed.

Not like I can call anybody. Time to get moving.

Hesitantly, Samantha did so, skirting on tiptoes past the vapor lamps and accumulated city of moths. When distanced from their glare, she hurried even further to the footpath, thanking the fates that Mr. Benford had acquiesced on her request to wear sneakers to work. Though balking at the idea at first (Randall Benford was an older breed of boss who favored secretaries looking like secretaries), he had finally approved when learning skimpy shorts would sometimes be part of the bargain.

'And feel free to get changed here if you need to,' he had said, allowing a blush to creep into his features. 'I let Allison do that on her basketball nights.'

Wearing shorts for small favors was one thing – taking her clothes off at work was another. Samantha riposted the comment with a polite question concerning the well-being of his wife and children at home.

Afterward, attire during working hours had never been raised in any capacity again.

The library, while technically sitting on Esplanade Lane, now lay completely shrouded behind a gauze of night. Beside the streetlamps and the street, itself, there was nothing to see but the stark outline of small bungalows on the other side, their rooftops shielding her from a direct view of the Atlantic. On this night, unlike others, no illumination from windows or living rooms flooded front yards or driveways. Idle cars, parked along the serpentine street, failed to give off even a modicum of reflected light. Esplanade Lane, while a bustling vein of pedestrians and cars during daylight hours, now looked as closed and deserted as an empty stage set.

Get moving, Sam – get home.

Walking timidly at first, Samantha edged crosswise over the street where narrow lanes bisected houses leading down to the sea. Although common sense dictated she stay on her usual route, Samantha's new instinct was to get closer to the surf; its reassuring tumult and the beachfront houses were a more comforting idea than navigating the uphill footpath. As her eyes became more dark adapted, the shadow-skeleton of wild grasses, sand, and paths etched out by logs became a visible anchor.

Within two minutes, she found a clear trail from the moonlight reflected off of the waves.

Finally.

Instead of feeling calmed, however, the sight of all that rioting surf only seemed to harbinger more foreboding –

the smells of seaweed and salt, in addition to the oil-black largesse of the tide – were all cautionary co-conspirators, as ominous as light-hugging moths. Something, or *someone*, was out here watching her discomfort and had most assuredly been doing so from the start.

Hugging her satchel against her midsection, Samantha scanned the jagged teeth of rocks rising from the breakers further along the shore; she peered at the bulk of houses lining the cove. Besides these constants, there was nothing to *see*.

She was alone on the beach.

Alone but trying to intrude: thoughts of her time in the swamp, an environment as far removed from this one as another planet. On that night, she'd witnessed a ritual of sorts, and a procession of children lined up like minions of a Pied Piper. Father Natal had been there as well, clutching his malignant book, urging the children ever onward as –

Suddenly her decision to walk home (not just tonight but *every* night) seemed not only foolish but downright *irrational*. What the hell had she been thinking, doing these commutes solo? Her friend, Trudi, was right … Samantha wasn't only tempting danger with this kind of recklessness, she was giving it a goddamn invitation and putting down the welcome mat. Psychotics and sex fiends were everywhere in America, and never more prevalent than in the good year of 1985.

And we can't forget about local supernatural nasties like the Mercury Man, either …

At the thought, something glimmered nearby; something inside the churning waves set apart from the dappled moonlight. Instinctively, Samantha placed one sneaker forward in the sand, then another, attempting to get a fix on a source of light growing brighter by the second. Having been raised on a steady diet of supernatural fiction during her time working at the library, suddenly the thought of a UFO barreling over the waves didn't seem all that implausible. In fact, as the silver light

(*yes, it's silver, alright. A quicksilver glow*)

broke away from the surface of the water and began to take shape, first elongating into a disk then brokering out to become more like a ball, only a word like *alien* seemed applicable to this oddity. First, it was twenty feet from the shoreline … now only five. As its luster grew, so did its circumference, bulging outward, as if becoming mutinous by its own incandescent energy. A piece of it broke free.

Two lights.

Close enough to see the silver balls cast no shadow, Samantha began to backtrack, walking steadily, never taking her eyes off them for an instant. Although they appeared products of both the sea and night, there was no mistaking where their intent lay and who their target audience was.

As aware as she was of the lights, they, too, were aware of her.

Growing in intensity as they approached, the left orb sprouted outgrowths akin to limbs, fluorescent appendages finding purchase on the sand. The right one quickly followed, each addition like a flowering stamen adjoined to a petal. Sleek, industrial, and continuously shifting into even darker shades of silver, the oddities moved with the stated precision of pursuers, gravitating left and right so their intended quarry had no means of evasion. Still backtracking, Samantha slipped and fell, landing on her rump after gaining no more than a few feet to any potential safety.

Terror seized her.

Before, the hallucinatory quality of the night had lent itself to a species of make-believe, as though she were being guided by events beyond her control. Yes, her misgivings were both real and ripe, but they were fears for the most part regulated to her headspace. Now, something with physical characteristics slinked over the sand, terror grown able-bodied.

It's really him, she thought. *The Mercury Man has come to gobble me up.*

The luminosities, having narrowed their path, began to amend once again, anatomies shifting into a riot of form. Frameworks of light gave way to the musculature of biological flesh, scraps of peristaltic limbs, and twisting bone arrangements. On her back, Samantha pedaled both feet furiously, still not averting her eyes lest the enigma use her inattention to zero in quicker.

By degrees, the flesh shapes were being driven into definition: rounded limbs and trunks, each one an unstable height of at least four feet. In addition to limbs, there were also garments of clothing in the fray.

Slowly, Samantha perceived what was taking shape: the very same monstrosities she'd glimpsed in the swamp; children whose faces were a scarred and disfigured map of protruding teeth, calloused lesions, and vulpine eyes etched with silver light. On that occasion, only boys were among the malformed; on this one, children of both sexes – each garbed in an outfit of dirty denim overalls, snatches of the cloth somehow wedded into the meat of their torsos. With moonlight acting as the chief illumination, Samantha perceived a dark delight stitched into their blistered, grinning mouths.

They were happy to see her suffering.

And would be happy to inflict more.

In the extremis of the moment, she had completely forgotten about her satchel and the bulk it contained. A measly weapon, but it would somehow have to do.

Brandishing the strap in a claw-like grip as tight as any talon, Samantha prepared to launch a defense ... or die trying.

***

Having taken the golem forms of children from the bitch's memory, Malphas advanced upon the stricken woman. Though eager to be done with the task, he hoped to prolong her torment further, a lesson to any other would-be adversary who decided to pry into Malphas and Natal's private ambitions. In their previous encounter, she had bested them ... but not before Malphas had marked her and sworn revenge.

Through a golem, Malphas extended a sharp metallic limb and pierced the bitch's left leg, slicing through her skin, arteries, and bone; essentially pinioning her body to the sand. Repeating the act with her right leg, this time through the soft webbing of her ankle, Malphas brought down enough force on this occasion to elicit a deluge of screams that momentarily drowned out the sounds of the surf. Such bliss, these laments. If only the brothers could play with *all* their quarry in such a protracted manner, a natural ballet of predator and prey, wringing from their flesh copious amounts of blood in addition to the secret soul-stuff they procured.

***

Never experiencing this level of physical suffering before, Samantha quickly folded under the hate-filled eyes of the child-things. Despite being of headstrong ilk, there would be no devil-may-care fightback from the plucky librarian. She was already spent … and no one would ever lay their eyes on the manuscript she shouldered.

Feet pinned by duel metallic blades, her body lay spread-eagled with her midsection an open invitation. Sensing this, her tormentors exchanged a knowing and fatalistic look.

And then began to change again.

Bulbous heads of matted hair shredded apart then elongated, becoming questing limbs again in the process. Soon they were adjoined to each other, like fused twins of the womb reuniting for a second time in the physical world.

From this hybridization, a fresh body sprang, a thing of thorny distensions and rippling quicksilver extensions. With the silver serpent's head complete, one more final extremity was given birth: a driving, metallic tongue that grew to an unnatural length and sought out the sweet center of the sobbing girl on the sand.

***

During the night, Brandon Delgado had dreamed.

Typically, his nocturnal hours enabled for all kinds of fascinating theatrics of the mind, landscapes and scenarios perpetually inhabited by a parade of victims under the boot and heel of Hadley Grove's strong and able arm of the law: whores and miscreants; weak men of the geek tribe who could be bent and manipulated until the concept of a 'pecking order' was no longer just a colloquial term. But last night had been different. Last night, Brandon dreamed of one who was above the law.

Brandon dreamed of the disabled priest who swam through the arteries of his church like an obscene swamp-creature.

A priest who had (by a process Brandon did not fully comprehend) slowly come to assume the title of *boss*.

That in itself was hard to fathom because *nobody* on God's earth had ever come close to laying claim to being Brandon's *boss*. A higher-up on paper, sure. No problem there. Brandon could live with a title so long as he was the one calling all the shots – but a bona-fide, dyed-in-the-wool, ass-kissing *superior* who gave Brandon his marching orders? It was a miracle of the highest order. And the fact that it was a goddamn *priest* was probably the most surprising aspect of all.

Except he isn't really a priest.

161

Wasn't really a man, either, come to think of it. Though Brandon had recently attempted to cease thinking about that particular aspect altogether – because doing so made him itchy, and not in an *I'm-about-to-get-my-rocks-off* kind of way, either. No, itchy in the sense that his palms began to sweat and his balls shrunk inside their cocoon sacs of wrinkled flesh. Put simply: it didn't pay to dwell on such things

(that Malphas was some kind of hellish creature)

because they were ultimately things Brandon had no control over. What mattered – the *only* thing that mattered in this game of life – was self-preservation and having the means and opportunity to satisfy those *other* itches when they rose up (as they often did) from under the black cloud of his subconscious.

In his dream, Malphas had appeared … except it wasn't really Malphas. It was a black-caped wanderer-dude whose grey and dirty hair sprouted out from underneath a rawhide cowboy's brim like an ancient wig. But it was *also* Malphas, for they were one and the same creature. In lieu of human eyes, the wanderer-dude exhibited almond-shaped oculars of burnished silver that jittered and jived on a whisker-strewn face as old as time. Though the setting of the dream was familiar (inside the priest's church), almost none of it was. For *another* church had slipped over the veneer of this one: a nave of mottled silver stone and pews encrusted with filth. Atop the chancel, two brooding gargoyles leered down at Brandon with the wild abandon of mischievous monkeys. For the most part, the gargoyles were idle stone, their fanged rows of needle-point teeth glossy protuberances in the shell of rictus grins. Yet other times, they moved, jumping up and down in short and excited bursts of exaggerated simian agility, tusks and forked-tongues glistening with demonic spittle.

Brandon was seated in the front pew, his body as immovable and inviolate as someone in the throes of sleep paralysis. Above him, Malphas, aka the wanderer-dude, stared down at his dream-subject with what could be construed as unmasked antipathy. This was something Brandon did not take personally; the wanderer-dude *always* looked at the world with an expression of upmost contempt.

'I'm dreaming,' Brandon told his audience. Again he tried to move his arms; again he met nothing but resistance. 'You know, Malphas, if you want to talk with me ... have you ever considered simply picking up the phone? That's what they were invented for.'

At this, the gargoyles resumed their gibbering stationary dance, finding Brandon's statement the height of hilarity. And he supposed it *was* funny, in a way. Giving lip to something which had the power to not only enter his dreams but to snuff out his life. Malphas and his brother, Natal, however, also *needed* him. And this was something Brandon wouldn't let either of them forget, even in dreams.

Once the gargoyles ceased their clamoring, the wanderer-dude inched a few steps forward and whispered one little word, hoarse and low and full of portent. '*Samantha*,' he said.

Both in his dream and snoozing away in his king-sized bed, Brandon's shoulders jerked in a kind of lopsided resignation. 'Oh God. *Her* again?' he asked the apparition.

'I thought we'd discussed matters relating to that uppity bitch. I told you last time – my hands are tied in the matter. I can't touch her for now and neither should you.'

When the reply came back, it wasn't words the wanderer-dude conveyed this time but a tide of images, all of them concerning the uppity librarian-bitch. If Brandon Delgado wasn't a man accustomed to seasoned homicide, these images might have made him flinch. As it stood, both his experience with and appetite for carnage had fashioned a cocoon of protection against any atrocity, no matter how profane in the particulars.

Samantha's family would flinch though ... yessiree, Bob.

Spread-eagled on a beach and bereft of clothing, the uppity librarian-bitch had some kind of stakes protruding from her feet; hooks restraining her to the sand. Her blonde hair (hair Brandon had more than once envisaged running his fingers through) lay cradled in a web of dark seaweed, the tide and elements already having worked an assault of their own. While most of the librarian's skin lay intact and cooling to a shade of marble blue, something had taken place within the center of her ... something that Brandon was willing to bet had nothing to do with natural elements, whatsoever. Next to the rotting corpse, a black shoulder bag lay discarded and speckled with sand, seaweed, and dark splotches of what could only be Samantha's blood.

'Holy *shit*,' Brandon Delgado remarked in his New Hampshire drawl that came out as *sheet*. 'Looks like the earth just swallowed her up and spat her back out. What in the hell did you *do* to her?'

No immediate answer from the wanderer-dude. But (this being a dream), it wasn't long before he was given a reply by means of more imageries, these focused on Samantha donned in her uppity-bitch librarian glasses and engaged in the task of writing something with a black ballpoint biro. Which wasn't surprising, really. It was what all uppity –

'*Satchel*,' Malphas the wanderer-dude hissed, leaning over toward Brandon like some kind of dream goblin. This close, Brandon could make out the old dude's teeth: fossilized stumps of primeval mushroom stalks, their faces tattooed with stagnant patterns of purple decay.

And, ever so slowly, Brandon began to catch on to what was happening – why the mutant priest had summoned him via vision to his nether-church. Sheriff Brandon Delgado, being an errand boy and lackey to a supernatural power, was now required to go about more errands. Specifically, to help clean up a mess he'd taken no part in. Had, in fact, cautioned against.

'I do this for you, and you owe me bigtime,' Brandon said, knowing full well he had no latitude to request anything in any matter when it came to his masters.

Because when it came to his boss, Malphas the wanderer-dude, democratic deliberations simply did not figure into the equation.

***

Awakening from his nightmare at dawn, Brandon Delgado went about the business of the morning – which

entailed hightailing it down to the beach as swiftly as
possible in his unmarked sedan. Preferably before
somebody else came across Malphas's mess and all hell
broke loose. Not that it hadn't already to a degree.
Samantha Moffat lying fly-blown on the beach was only
the tip of an ice mountain whose madness was now
protruding above all of Hadley Grove. First had come
Brandon's attempts to cover up the disappearance of the
Bowthorpe girl (whose cries and visage he also dreamed
about, but that was another story); then had come the
arrival of the sly stranger, whose impeccable timing
somehow seemed connected to Madison's departure. If his
sermonizing superiors would just come clean and tell him
what they knew about this codswallop named Micha, tell
him *everything*, then fixing their goddamn collateral
damage wouldn't be such a pain in the ass.

But no … Malphas and Natal had to play the part of
dubious gatekeepers; concierges to the kind of agenda
Brandon had only a miniature grasp of.

*They want to open up portals to other worlds – that's
the only thing on their agenda that really matters to me.*

Or so Brandon kept telling himself. Providing him
ultimate cover to do as he pleased in Hadley Grove was one
thing, but when you got right down to the nitty-gritty, the
Sherriff continued to serve his masters because one of these
days (very soon if Malphas was to be believed) a massive
deluge of fire, brimstone, and crazy supernatural shit was
about to come waltzing into his town. And Brandon *did*
believe it. He believed it because he'd *seen* said crazy shit
up close and personal. Hell, he'd even been given a tour of

the place where it was all supposed to go down: the Hall of Portals, or whatever it was the mad priest had christened that limitless vat of stone. Of course, names didn't matter much – what *did* was what such a place could offer. Or, more accurately, *open*.

Portals into other worlds.

Worlds that would spill out onto this one; a storm of different universes populated by the different things that lived and breathed there, thereby ushering in (as promised by Malphas, himself), the only world that really mattered to a man like Brandon Delgado.

'A world where motherfucking Johnny Cash sings *Run On for a Long Time*,' Brandon said to himself, piloting his green Chevy sedan down a fog-shrouded bend that would eventually link him up with Esplanade Lane. 'That's the only kind of world I want to live in, by God.'

***

Samantha's body was exactly where the wanderer-dude had said it would be: splayed out like a beached dolphin on a jut of coast not far from the marina walkway.

More like a beached whale, he thought. *One whose innards have already blown out some.*

Through the plastic dashboard of his Chevy, a small digital clock proclaimed the time to be 6:15am. Good. It would be another two hours, at least, before the lazy pricks in town decided to rise and shine for their morning Cheerios. Enough time to get this uppity librarian-bitch loaded into the cargo trunk, he hoped. She would fit just fine. She would also reek … though Brandon thought he would be able to cope with that. Because in the past, he had survived just fine smelling a whole slew of things that would shame sulfur.

Like Vicky Rodale, for instance. Squirrelling that slut away in an abandoned refrigerator for three weeks sure emboldened her to a new kind of aroma.

Smiling at the thought, Brandon exited his car and began walking down to the beach. Vicky Rodale had been a cheerleader for a football team across state lines that nobody outside of Hicksville would ever know about. When Brandon had abducted her, she'd been wearing a blue-and-yellow cheerleader outfit, complete with pom-poms. After stowing her away in a disused refrigerator, her cheerleader outfit was no longer any recognizable color except black, the polyester fabric so enriched with blood even the crescent-hawk of her insignia had disappeared. On numerous occasions during their hours together, Vicky had tried to remove it – but Brandon would not oblige. Her outfit was perhaps the main reason he'd snatched her in the first place, pulling her skirt (followed by the rest of her) in through the cab of his cruiser after she'd made the grave mistake of wandering away from a set of bleachers at halftime to steal a smoke. From that moment until discovering her again weeks later … the uniform had never come off once. Of course, he'd never intended to forget about her at all. The refrigerator in the weedy lot far from his cabin had only been a temporary measure for Vicky, a commodity to be *put on ice* (ha ha) until she'd cooled her jets a little and Brandon could figure out what to do with her next.

But he *had* forgotten about her ... and coming across the fridge's isolated location again had given him the jolt of a lifetime. Preoccupied people did stupid things all the time: they couldn't recall where they'd left the family Dodge while out shopping; they sometimes forgot to flush the john when company was over. But leaving spritely Vicky Rodale to wither away like a dried apricot definitely took carelessness to a whole new level. Finding that fridge had been one thing; opening it was another. As Vicky's distended and decomposing body slithered out like a corpse from a coffin, Brandon had learned valuable lessons concerning carelessness he would take to the grave.

'She smelled so bad her teeth had plans to escape!' Brandon barked, and sniggered at the euphemism.

Upon reaching the librarian, his laughter abruptly died.

In his dream, vision, whatever you wanted to call it ... this had been a scene of carnage – but it was also riddled with the gin-glaze of reverie, something far away and barely tangible. Yet here, the full glory of Samantha's injuries were on display and, yes, accompanied by scent. Malphas's metallic rods (Brandon didn't quite know what they were but the name certainly fit), had been driven so deep into the earth and with such ferocity the sand around the librarian's feet had turned to glass. Her abdomen area – every organ and membrane sheathed in a film of gore – had been opened up like something on a dissecting table.

This was the calling card of Hadley Grove's Mercury Man – a predator whose savagery was becoming more violent by the month.

'Malphas, you son of a bitch …' the Sherriff uttered, and scratched his forehead in consternation.

Taking care of this uppity librarian-bitch was going to take a while. And – if the mercurial priest knew what was good for him – providing Brandon with a world where Johnny Cash serenaded *Run On for a Long Time* would be only a portion of the recompense due.

Chapter Twelve

During drunken binges (what Lila had once referred to as episodic cyclones), Micha could lose up to three days of life. Not all that uncommon for garden-variety drunks, of course – a period of missing time where both the brain and physical-self seemed to go on an extended hiatus from everything. One minute, you were roaring along good-naturedly on a kick-ass buzz; next, you wake up on a stranger's floor in a pool of drool. Or piss. Or even vomit-covered Rice Krispies. Once attaining an upright position again, consulting a calendar was literally a sobering experience. What happened to Monday and Tuesday? More importantly, what god-awful things *took place* during those days of absentia from reality?

Returning from Hadley Grove was similar in many ways … except awakening back in his own bed, Micha wasn't covered in any drool.

And no days had passed in the real world at all.

This was proving to be the most staggering part of the experience – something Micha had a hard time properly swallowing. Because *weeks* had gone by in the world of story and make-believe.

It's almost like a form of time-travel. Or being sucked into the fringes of a black hole where time is severely dilated.

Same clothes on the body; same haunted look in the eyes. The same juvenile posters adorned his bedroom walls – while the same shitty car sat parked in his driveway. It was Monday, June 14th, and it was like his time staying with Sara and her daughter in Hadley Grove had never taken place at all.

Only one thing was different.

The manuscript of *The Mercury Man* had grown again.

***

Micha showered and then ate. Afterward, he watched a few episodes of *South Park* from Lila's gift collection. This act, like all of the other boring ones, served as a weak attempt to acclimatize his body and mind back to the monotone reality of everyday living. While his food tasted uninspired, everything else was equally drab. Just how had his existence here in Concord ever seemed meaningful in any capacity? Sara's bar, while dispensing a poison that (while not always agreeing with him) was at least filled with the clamor and smells of *life* … of raucous footsteps navigating stairs; of happy humans breaking bread, laughing, and raising jugs, all while an artist known as *Prince* (never *formally known* in the fecund realm of 1985), sung about the desire to see *his* lover laughing inside a skein of purple-colored rain.

I want to be around people again? That doesn't sound right at all. Does this mean I'm cured of schizoid personality disorder?

Obviously not. Because the thought of being out *there* (that was, mingling in the world outside his window in the twenty-first century) filled Micha with a species of stoic dread somehow more acute than in the far-flung days of being undiagnosed. People in this world had never been overly kind, often lambasting him for the slightest infraction deviating from what they considered the norm. No children at your age? There was something wrong with you. Don't work fulltime? There's *definitely* something wrong with you. You spend your days doing *wha*t? Writing stories? Who the fuck does that in the modern age? No, there isn't something wrong with you, Micha – you're just cuckoo crazy, that's all.

That's just self-serving pity, Micha. Don't jive to that dance.

So what, exactly, had been the fundamental difference in Hadley Grove? Micha was still a freak there, too. He only had to cast his mind back to moustache man in the lineup for the Ferris wheel to ascertain that. And let's not forget the cops – namely one in particular – who'd been trying to get him alone since he'd first arrived in the dirty alleyway beside *The Grove Gourmet*. Was the major variance simply Sara Childs, the idealistic image of a dream girl, whose altruism (and kisses) had so far shielded him from the worst of Hadley Grove's looming threats?

There's only one real way to find out. I still have one friend in this world ... perhaps seeing him again can kill two birds with one stone.

***

That other bird was, of course, his manuscript. In the time to have elapsed since his most recent homecoming, simply picking up the new pages from the printer's tray and reading them had become a physical task his body seemed incapable of performing. Such an act would no doubt yield significant insights into the enigma that was the Mercury Man ... and yet he couldn't quite bring himself to do it. It was as if these revelations, once fully realized, might prohibit him from ever returning to Sara and Hadley Grove, altogether. A dreamer, once becoming conscious of the dream, invariably snaps awake upon the apprehension.

Consequently, one of Micha's options here was another set of eyes on the manuscript – an action he probably *should* have taken at the first occurrence of automatic ghost writing. Another published author (someone intimate with the mysterious machinations of writing prose and its frequently underrated effect on the human psyche) could feed Micha the bare bones of the story, in addition to being a soundboard for his philosophies regarding mental health.

Micha returned to Facebook and (relieved there were no more additional messages from Lila or anybody else) navigated to the personal page of local Concord scribe

Grayson Ross, another thirty-something writer who called the field of horror his home. Despite living over a twenty-minute drive away on the coast, Grayson would be more than happy to meet Micha somewhere in the inner-city after being emailed a Word copy of *The Mercury Man*. If, that was, Micha gravitated some urgency to the situation.

And promise that beer (specifically, the elixir of dark ale) would be in the equation.

***

'A personality disorder?' Grayson asked. 'You mean like the narcissistic jerk-wad who currently sits in the White House has going for him? That kind of thing?'

Micha laughed. 'Yes, I guess you could say that. Narcissism is a small part of it. Though a fragile part, thank God. I guess I wanted to ask … are you in any way surprised?'

Grayson and Micha were both seated and facing each other in a booth, overlooking three pool tables, two of which were manned by patrons. Above the subtle din of easy-listening music pumped through speakers at ground level, the snap and crack of billiard balls smashing up against each other was an ever-present hubbub. In front of the two writers sat a glass jug of Guinness beer, half-depleted, their chilled pints beside it with coasters underneath. *On Hindley* was a bar that encouraged cue-sports during the day (in addition to eating lunch), while advocating dancing after hours. Such was the owner's enthusiasm for the latter that all seating booths (in addition to the umbrella-donned tables on the street outside), were cordoned off or completely folded up, leaving a client of the establishment no choice but to stand and ultimately get their boogie shoes on.

Grayson said, 'That you've received a diagnosis? No, I'm not really surprised. You're an antisocial cunt.' His friend grinned, revealing large proportioned teeth with a small gap between the central incisors. 'But you're the *nicest* antisocial cunt I've ever had the pleasure of knowing, if that makes sense. So it's like you describe in your novel – this schizoid thing, is it something like Asperger's syndrome ... does it mean you're living on the spectrum?'

'Not quite,' Micha said, and adopted a small puzzled frown. More than anything, he was vaguely surprised there were references to SPD in *The Mercury Man*. 'Though there are similar dissociative traits. My final verdict from a head quack after all these years isn't really why I wanted to talk with you today. It's –'

'You want to know what I think of your new book?'

Both men reached down and grasped their respective pint glasses, Micha taking a small sip of his tan-colored head. Grayson, far less delicate, upended a third of his brew in three prolonged swallows before giving off a smack of appreciation ... and finishing off the whole process with a cupped belch. Grayson Ross (whose favorite living horror writer was Dan Simmons, and on occasion mimicked that author's distinctive style) wore a black designer shirt and black jeans; black Doc Martin boots and expensive spectacles completed the ensemble of a young intellectual who skated the fringes of being a modern hipster – though one bereft of any beard. Although not exactly pin-up material for any potential female suitor, Grayson Ross made up for any and all shortcomings with restrained charisma and a certain graceful style. Besides writing books, Grayson also illustrated, his aptitude in this area enough to secure him part-time employment at a local graphic design art school.

'Despite the fact your critiques give me a nervous twitch in my left eye,' Micha said purposefully. 'Yes, that's exactly what I need from you at the moment. To tell me what you think of *The Mercury Man* so far.'

'So far? Are you saying the finishing line isn't within sight? Reading, I didn't think this was a *should I go on with this story or not* kind of setup here. I figured I've been summoned into your presence to give you a personal lowdown on what I think should happen regarding the ending.'

Micha tried to stifle a sigh, but it was out before he knew it. Just how to navigate this landmine without divulging the fact that he, the supposed author here, had only skimmed part of the narrative? That he certainly didn't remember writing it … and that, in all essence, he had basically been *living it.*

By treading softly, came a voice, one that was unmistakably Lila's. *And tread softly with that beer, too, Micha. This isn't Hadley Grove, where the usual rules no longer apply. This is reality – and reality is a raw world where getting shitfaced can sometimes result in an attempt at taking your own life.*

'Not exactly,' Micha said. 'What's your initial reaction?'

'To the story as a whole? Well, it's certainly an interesting approach; I'm not usually a fan of metafiction. But I guess when it's done right, like those big Dark Tower books –'

'Meta?' Micha interrupted and (despite the warnings going off in his head), reached down and swallowed some more brew; no tan head this time.

'Well, you're writing about yourself, aren't you? I mean, you've changed the protagonist's name to Mason but kept the initials. You've changed a few other things, too, some of the nuts and bolts. But the meat and potatoes are all there.' Through his glasses, Grayson's eyes gleamed. 'Like my hackneyed use of synonyms there?'

'What do you mean by meat and potatoes?'

'Are you kidding? Umm ... let's see. He's a horror writer, there's that one. There's also the fact he fits your physical profile. And you've changed the love interest's name to Lani. Not exactly Lila, I'll grant you that, but it's pretty darn close. How is she, anyway? Lila? Are you guys still seeing each other?'

Micha knew erring on the side of truth here would be a wise course of action. 'No, not really. Not for a few weeks now.'

Grayson dipped his head in disappointment. 'Shame. I thought you two were really good together.'

'We were.'

Grayson's expression brightened. 'Though being single is definitely good for a more prolific daily word count, am I right? This I know from sad experience.'

So is having a personality disorder, Micha thought but did not say. Instead, he said, 'You got me. It didn't start out that way, of course. But it's a personal story, yes. And the protag's journey to Hadley Grove –'

'Is, now that I think about it, like a giant metaphor for your hero's personality disorder.'

A waitress, young, had wandered into their view, clad in a dark green apron and carrying a flat wooden tray. Though she smiled, she regarded both men with barely suppressed suspicion – or was it a simple form of jealousy, perhaps? Working tables while watching other people drink could never be anybody's idea of fun. 'Another?' she asked them, pointing at a jug soon to be depleted.

'Please,' Grayson said. 'We're discussing literature today – specifically, a work in progress. And if any subject needs a lubricant, it's that one.'

The waitress (Vicky her name tag proclaimed) arched her eyebrows in puzzlement and proceeded to collect their empty glasses. After she was gone, Grayson said, 'Gosh, if looks could kill. Doesn't anybody *read* anymore?' Tipping Micha a sly wink, he added, 'Did you catch her name tag? Vicky? The namesake of your poor cheerleader who got locked away in a refrigerator by one problematic police officer. Not exactly original, Micha, but I have to admit that part got under my skin a little. Brandon is one sick fuck.'

It took a few moments for Micha to process what his friend was alluding to: chapters of *The Mercury Man*, events that were fresh to him. Of course, the problematic

police officer was no new mystery here – but Brandon
Delgado's actions were. Just what had the sick fuck been
up to since his last visit to Sara's bar?

'He is a sick puppy, indeed,' Micha said, his tone
uncertain. 'But it's his relationship with the priest and his
motivations there that stump me. How they tie in together
when up until now, in the previous stories, Brandon
Delgado was pretty much a free agent.'

Grayson was looking at him aghast. 'Were you fucking
high when you wrote him? He's made a pact with the
bastard in exchange for immunity. He's also what you'd
call a lapdog and errand boy. Fucking Natal's brother,
Malphas, is also a piece of work. Swimming around in
those mercury conduits and producing golems from thin
air? It's patently creepy all right. And don't tell me how the
mercury thing ties into all of this yet … I want that to be a
surprise.'

There it was: pay dirt – a whole slew of massive
unknowns piled one atop the other. So many of them,
Micha's heart began to pound. *Golems*. And a brother
named Malphas. This was without question the floating
man Micha had briefly glimpsed Natal cradling inside the
greenhouse. One of them, in all probability, about the
business of producing animated beings. Which led to
something with almost a genuine certainty: the Mercury
Man had to *be* one of these animated beings.

Too much, too soon, he thought. *If only I was back in
Hadley Grove right now instead of –*

'Everything okay?' Grayson asked across the table.
'You look like someone just reached under the table and

grabbed your nuts.'

'I'm okay,' Micha replied, and sipped his drink. The beer was doing its work, rewiring neurons enough so that every thought he had was equipped with its own unique sticker of subtle merriment.

Including thoughts concerning Sara.

'What about the included love aspect? Is it at all believable? Is it something even important to the story?'

'I wouldn't say it's *believable*, no. But then again, I don't think it's supposed to be. Sara is Mason's wet dream, living her life inside another decade – someone who accepts all of his eccentricities and loves him anyway. And because he's so strange, from another world himself, they're like opposites attracting. I wouldn't say it's a monumentally important aspect, but it is kind of ... *sweet*. Most people in our generation have nostalgic memories of the Eighties, of being with someone they loved, of that first romance unchecked by all the pressures of being an adult. I think some readers will probably like hearing an echo of that.'

Only steps from their booth, the sound of half-a-dozen billiard balls being broken and dispersed brought Micha back. For the briefest of moments, he'd been sitting at the apex of a Ferris wheel again, cupping a small chin and leaning in to the soft curve of a smooth neck. A faint whiff of Sara's perfume, Christian Dior's *Poison*, co-mingled with a high-altitude wind direct from the ocean.

The sounds of the pool table had struck a chord with his friend. 'Time for a game?' he asked. 'It's on me.'

As Grayson slotted coins into the vacant machine and

manhandled a bunch of balls together with a triangle,
Micha downed his beer and poured himself another. Today,
for whatever reason, it was going down like medicine;
Lila's voice shoved aside and replaced with the hot coals of
being decisively drunk. Suddenly, he was beginning to like
his new book a hell of a lot more. Sure, Mason was kind of
unlikeable and not all that easy to relate to, but there was
some truth inside the story. And wasn't all good fiction
mired in the absolution of truth?'

In tandem, both men burped, and again (in tandem),
they broke into a gale of beer-addled laughter. 'Play for the
break?' Grayson said from his position at the foot of the
table. 'Man, let's do this quick before I'm too shitfaced to
kick your ass.'

With the small ritual of playing for the break decided
(Micha was victorious), they settled into the game, Grayson
pocketing smalls with the seasoned ability of a semi-pro.
Before long, he'd won, and they were on to a new game;
Micha saddled with bigger balls.

'What about the other characters?' Micha asked,
slurring the last part of his sentence and taking the time to
soften up his cue-tip with chalk. 'The other characters
making up the bulk of Hadley Grove?'

'You mean like that Penelope what's-her-face?' Here
Grayson screwed up a portion of his profile, closing one
eye in the process. 'We know fuck all about her. Basically,
you just shoved in her family to further the narrative.
Namely, having her little brat abducted and carted away to
a scary cottage in the woods. The scary cottage, of course,
being Malphas the pervert's church. And what was with her

just letting Mason out the door after their encounter with the silver serpent? I'm fairly fucking certain no one in real life would act *remotely* like that.'

That's because they're not from real life. They're from a story.

'The Bowthorpe family were carry-ons from my earlier novella, *Most of All*. You don't remember that one?'

'Course, I fuckin' remember it,' Grayson proclaimed. With every beer downed, just like Micha, his propensity to curse multiplied. 'That doesn't matter, though. Nobody but me ever reads your shit anyway.'

'True that. So very, very true.'

In the middle pocket, Micha downed the eight ball with a curving diagonal shot. 'Keep going?'

'Best of five, at least. In addition to more beer, we also need some decent music. What is this shit that they're playing now? Techno music during the day sounds unnatural.'

Grayson busied himself at a jukebox, making decisions, giving up, and extending his welcome with a smiling brunette barmaid beyond what was probably appropriate. Men, after a few in their system, all seemed to think they were Casanova. Which reminded him …

'So you think someone like Delgado has a weak spot?' he said as Grayson came back carrying another jug. 'Obviously, the freak isn't going to win the day and get his hands on Sara. That doesn't happen in books. How would you suggest I take him out of the equation?'

Again Grayson gave him a quizzical look – narrowing his brow in a manner that was almost comical. Questions of this type (discussing characters as if they were actors on a set) simply hadn't been asked before in quite this much detail. 'If I tell you how to do your job, you should pay me part of the proceeds – if you manage to sell it, that is. Of course, you can always do a me and self-publish the damn thing, thus guaranteeing you will receive absolutely bupkis for your efforts.'

Micha snatched his beer and drank deeply. He was getting hammered, all right. Going all the way up into a cyclone. 'That bad, huh?'

'*Worse*,' Grayson imparted. 'It's rotten. Don't get me wrong, I shift a few units in the aftermath of hitting the publish button. But after that, it's all downhill from there. I'm lucky if I move two copies a week. Why do we do it, Micha? Can you tell me that much? Why do we pump out so many words for such ill-begotten gain? Are we sadists? Is that it? Is there some part of us that actually *enjoys* this pain?'

Micha could only drink his beer in silence, his depressed look all the reply his friend needed. Because all writers in the current era knew the self-wounding pain of self-publishing … or publishing with anyone; which was fundamentally the same beast branded under a different name. Unless you already had an established base producing books through traditional means in the past, accruing royalty checks were slim. Playing the publishing game was akin to playing the lottery. Some independent authors were successful even while churning out sludge; others were regulated to the shadows while displaying feats of genuine class. It was simply the nature of any industry, not just the one where men and women sat down in front of laptops and typewriters and made up crap for the sake of entertainment.

At a thought, Grayson brightened. After lining up from a snookered shot, he said, 'So does getting branded on the nutcase spectrum entitle you to some kind of disability support? What about that gig you had at the movie store? Is that still a thing?'

If it was a subtle jab, there was enough alcohol in Micha's system to let it slide. 'No – my jobs never last more than a year, remember? I have a small amount of severance that was recently paid out. It'll tie me over for another month or two, but after that, I'll need to start looking for something else again. Listen, about Brandon –'

'He's easy to take out of the equation,' Grayson stated matter-of-factly. 'Because of that book that's now in his possession – the one Samantha was writing. And because his whole motivation, mental as it is, is wanting to live inside a world where Johnny Cash sings a fucking *Elvis* tune. Which is kind of hilarious. Since you're obviously talking about *our* world, aren't you? I heard that song just the other day. And if those weirdo priests creating golems are about the business of harvesting souls to fuel an interdimensional wormhole thingy, then one of the worlds they eventually open up will probably be *our* world, won't it? A kind of meta, metafiction. So I imagine your crazy-ass killing antagonist will probably get his wish, in a fashion, and become exiled somewhere. Nice name for their inter-dimensional wormhole machine, by the way. The Hall of Portals. Has a nice ring to it.'

There might be more Grayson said … but Micha didn't hear it. If he was going to remember any of this – the Hall of Portals, Delgado's newly acquired book and weird-ass motivation – copying some of it down before the beer got the better of him might go a long way to helping his quest. In Sara's world, he had kept a dossier of sorts, but most if not all of that information was now rendered moot. Better to start the slate again; perhaps even build up the sack to at least read a *portion* of *The Mercury Man*. Really, what was he scared of, anyway? Some kind of Nietzsche logic that staring into the abyss of those pages would somehow mean he was *also* being weighed and judged by some foreign abyss?

It's too late for all that, a voice whispered. Some UFO entity that was leagues away from Lila or anybody else he knew. *Something has already taken notice of you. A golem with a wide-brimmed hat and molten mercury for eyes. He knows you don't fit inside the story. He's marked you … and it's only a matter of time before he'll come for you personally.*

'Grayson,' Micha said, noticing his friend was now playing air guitar with his pool cue – the kind of act only the newly inebriated could carry out. 'I'm going to split. But thank you – thank you for everything. You have no idea how much you've helped me today.'

The air guitar abruptly stopped, Grayson's look of stoned mirth replaced by one of rejection. 'But you said best of five! That's what you said, *best of five*.'

'Another time,' Micha replied. 'And soon. But there's something really important at home I need to take care of.'

Schizoid

Exiting *On Hindley*, Micha expected another fusillade
of complaints. But his friend, ever the charmer, had already
resumed his tête-à-tête with the brunette behind the bar.

***

As it turned out, home wasn't his immediate
destination. With the beer coursing through Micha's
bloodstream like a serum amplifying his senses, the city
street outside took on the sudden look of something
hallucinogenic; a celebratory scene from Mardi Gras, the
sidewalks and pavement filled to the brim with people in
the first stages of getting their weekend high on. On the
road, itself, beefed-up cars of every stripe and predilection
slowly crept by, their occupants sizing Micha up with what
seemed like a lewd kind of invitation. Stunning girls were
everywhere, and rather than detour to a bus stop, Micha
decided to park his ass at another watering hole; one where
the music was guitar-orientated and grungier; where the
skirts were shorter and the lipstick a shade darker. If he
played his cards right, perhaps he could court somebody as
night fell. Such a thing wasn't outside the realm of
possibility now. After all …

*I'm a free man. At least in this world. Free of Lila, free
of anybody to answer to or bring me down. Hell, I could
even pony up for call girls if I so desired. Think of it as a
worthwhile activity in the interest of good mental health.
Even Halbrook would probably approve …*

There was a name he hadn't thought of in a while. Not
since his third return. Another appointment with the

designer-stubbled quack was only days away. And what would he tell the good doctor this time around? That he was 'technically' seeing an imaginary girl who existed within the scaffold of his imagination? That he had kissed this girl on the scaffolding of a rotating Ferris wheel? As likely as not, Halbrook could have him committed for such confessions … even before he found out about the mutant priest who conjured golems.

Forget about the doctor tonight; forget about everything ... including Hadley Grove.

Sage advice, and within minutes, Micha found exactly what he was looking for: a bar called *The World's End* which already had most of its clientele parked in the shade under umbrellas, almost every person smoking a rolled joint or tobacco. After buying another pint and finding an empty seat and table, not three minutes had passed before a blonde girl walking past took notice of him, saw the empty seat opposite, and without invitation decided to sit down. Though her phone was out during her journey from pavement to seat, her eyes were fixated on Micha, giving him a devilish lilt of a smile that was all unspoken solicitation.

'What time is it?' she asked him. The girl was older than Micha by at least five years, her attire understated but elegant. Plenty of makeup; an attractive face with large brown eyes, a button nose, and thinly-pressed lips.

Micha consulted his phone on the table. 'It's five: fifteen.'

'In the morning or at night?'

Micha laughed. 'You're serious? It's night. Does this

place look the same at five in morning?'

'Pretty much.' By physical appearance alone, Micha determined she potentially fell into the 'cougar' category. She said, 'I'm Mandy. I come here most Friday nights, and yes, it's still packed come dawn. Is it *really* night? Feels like I've been going for days.'

Mandy might have been telling the truth ... or not. Feigning a kind of amnesia could be a simple way to get the conversation started. Also without stating it, Mandy had just declared she was high on drugs – or possibly on a drunken bender. Both of which sounded appealing to Micha.

'Micha,' he said. Underneath the table, their legs brushed up against each other. Mandy made no effort to move hers away. 'I was here with a friend earlier but couldn't stand the thought of going home.'

'Are you wasted? You look a little wasted.'

There was enough light under their umbrella for Micha to see his face reflected back from the plate glass of his phone. Yes – those eyes were both rheumy and bloodshot.

'Guilty as charged,' he said. 'To be honest, I woke up this morning and thought: I'm going to get fucked up today. That happens sometimes.'

Mandy giggled, then proceeded to talk at length about her weekend so far, which had entailed dirt-bike racing somewhere in the hills with this guy she was sort-of-not-quite seeing. Through the spiel, Micha was able to glean she was also a mother to a teenage girl who was all grown up and didn't need her anymore. Then the subject returned to her on-again-off-again beau.

'Today he called me up for a threesome, and I just wasn't feeling it. Don't get me wrong. That kind of thing is fun when the right girl comes along, but I just wasn't in the mood. So here I am.'

It was the type of confession that didn't need to be rooted in complete accuracy. By stating she was bisexual and open to threesomes, Mandy was declaring to Micha her sometimes promiscuity.

'So what do you do?' she asked him, lighting up a cigarette from a packet filched from her bag. 'Are you a student from one of the universities?'

Again Micha laughed, happy strangers still thought of him as a young man. 'I'm almost thirty-five, believe it or not. My student years are long behind me. Though I guess you could say I'm a scholar, of sorts – that of the written word. I dabble in fiction. Specifically, tales of the macabre.'

'Really?' Though Mandy appeared dubious, her smile was still genuine. 'You write anything I might know of?'

'Not likely. But you can walk into any bookstore and order one of my titles. Listen, do you think we'll be kissing each other tonight?'

It was out of his mouth swiftly – but not surprisingly. While drunk, taking the forthright tact wasn't altogether unusual.

Mandy didn't reply at first, only quickened her batting leg under the table, increasing the frequency of her touch. After a protracted silence, she said simply, 'Only if you dance with me.'

**

Soon after, the first band of the evening took to the stage of *The World's End* … and Micha and Mandy took to the floor, threading their way through a curious knot of onlookers that included head bangers, goth-centric bystanders content to remain wholly immobile, and those who brandished their iPhones around like a torch-bearing mob of fanatics. The band (a four-piece Micha only caught partial glimpses of through a sea of heads) sounded like every *Tool* knock-off outfit rolled into one – albeit with an industrial synth-backing module the fourth member lorded over like a gothic monk. As the music built, so did Mandy's and Micha's gyrations; their perspiration accruing under clothes already slick with sweat. Every now and then, Mandy would caress his bulging front and flick him a seductive wink when their gazes met.

This isn't dancing, whispered a voice – an entirely new one in Micha's pantheon. Though he'd heard this voice in life, of course. It was Sara's. *Didn't I teach you anything? Everyone here, including you, is moving like a zombie.*

And all at once, Micha nearly crumpled. The dancefloor he'd experienced in Hadley Grove being super-imposed over this one like some twin-nightmare realm. Except the nightmare was *this* reality, the grungy here and now of the late 2010s where a girl he'd only just met continued to manhandle his genitals with every distorted power chord that carried across the floor. Beside him, another girl with bleached white hair and a tank top moved her midsection around like a penitent moving to the sounds of a pulpit, her eyelids cast at half-mast and a rueful, almost drugged smile stapled above her chin. In this half-stroboscopic light, the girl's countenance appeared macabre … as were the faces of every other mover and shaker on the floor.

Leave, came Sara's voice. *Get out while you still can.*

Too late. Mandy turned toward him, catching his chin in her palm and pulling his face forward. Toward her lips; toward a mouth tasting of peach champagne and cigarettes. Despite his initial intention of moving away, Micha reciprocated, a base reaction of hormones and recent unfulfilled desires. Again Mandy's hand returned to his erection, prodding, pushing, taking the time to slide down its shaft and then cupping the underside of his balls. With every pliant stroke, her tongue would lunge in accordance, lingering while fully extended and then sucking his own tongue back inside again. Giddy moments went by as she kissed in imitation of the fellatio act, moving her jowls together with the same momentum she would if his cock was located between her teeth. For a moment, everything (the band, the other patrons, the ever-present notion of life in Hadley Grove) was all but eclipsed as Mandy's motions brought on the whisper of orgasm. Having gone so long without even a rumor of that particular ecstasy, the sudden thought of fucking this woman in a prolonged, all-night manner – of licking between her cunt, buttocks, and naval; of sampling every fleshy part of her – brought Micha within a hair's breadth of ejaculation. Then, just as suddenly as it had arrived, the feeling dissipated: the potential to climax only something of a clinical gag-reflex, his body going through mechanical motions simply because it could. In the wake created, he felt himself sag against Mandy's breasts; felt his stomach clench and his balls retract.

Sensing rejection, Mandy retreated, questionable frown lines deepening her brow. Banalities were issued, inquiring to his health; wanting to know if he was going to throw up. Wanting to know if she should escort him away from the melee of sound and sweat.

In lieu of a reply, Micha could only maneuver her aside, gently, hoping to find a physical sanctum where the air was cooler and cleaner; a place bereft of leering smiles and macabre faces, all of them belonging to an era he no longer felt remotely a part of.

***

Minutes later, Micha was back on the main thoroughfare, navigating people drunker than he. The cacophony of sound they produced, like lamentations on a radio, increased his nausea and addled his sight. Concord's neon lights and crowded gossamer threads elongated and congealed into one fecund mass that finally caused him to trip over a footpath and belly-flop into a hot morass of garbage cans. No more than a drifting malcontent to others, people parted as though he carried a plague, shouting insults and obscenities at seeing him laid low; just another drunk who had had his fill for the night. With any luck, the intoxicated young man would sleep it off before the police arrived and decided to haul him off inside one of their strobing paddy wagons …

Chapter Thirteen

Malphas Purson had seen everything of the human tribe: the rise of townships in the Americas and their inevitable downfall. He'd borne witness to secret lives over the span of generations, men and women who had sold their souls for a glimpse of Hell only to run cowering when the Purson brothers had procured it for them. He'd seen fathers rape daughters and mothers drown their sons like a clowder of kittens. He'd observed the birth of potential messiahs and subsequently their executions when humanity, deceived at yet another failed second coming, took out their disillusionment with guillotines and gallows. All of their family shortcomings; all of their despair. Every appetite that could be siphoned and made manifest with the powers bequeathed to them. Put simply: there was nothing in humanity's menagerie of fears that Malphas had not encountered.

Until this child, perhaps.

Although the brothers' new acquisition, Madison Bowthorpe, was supposed to be off limits for now, Malphas had not been able to resist visiting the girl on occasion: physically (she was locked away in a small vestibule Natal had fashioned into a bedroom), and other times when the girl was prone to dream. While such alchemy had never been overly difficult, cracking the girl's defenses had been. Madison remained stoic in the face of her adversity and resolute at building walls not easily breached. Not only that, she appeared reconciled to the fate the brothers had assigned her. Or knew of another entirely. A timeline that did not involve harvesting her soul.

'You're mad,' Natal said to him. 'Little girls are not made to prophesy. Nor do they have any angelic potential. This human child will be no different from countless others we've feasted on.'

To divulge more would be to give away he had been snooping in her dreams so Malphas held his tongue during their exchange. Visiting Madison the next night, however, had given his insights a different dimension. The girl not only had a pulse on her future, but she seemed to know of other things taking place inside her little town.

'Have you found him yet, Malphas?' the girl asked.

Malphas was harnessed in one of his retrofitted wheelchairs – a contraption equipped with a footbath containing a skein of mercury solution. Enough to see him through extended visits away from the pools.

Their prisoner stood garbed in new clothes – a simple red dress that Natal had acquired from one of their donation drives. As always, her bob of brown hair was well

196

scrubbed, her pallor healthy; Natal seeing all basic amenities were accounted for.

'Found who, Madison?' Malphas replied. Though inwardly, he knew. They both did.

'Your ... what did you call him once? Your *wildcard*.'

In his wheelchair, Malphas twitched. Having the girl privy to secret things was ample evidence she was destined as a final ingredient for the Hall of Portals (as the shade Orobas had alluded). Hearing her espouse wisdom with the eloquence of an adult gave him ample pause.

Instead of replying straight away, the priest surveyed her little room ... a place containing dozens of wooden shelves and one slim cot. On the shelves sat a wide array of different dolls, though not of any type one would find in the ordinary bedroom of a ten-year-old child. Far from it. These were ancient, rune-inscribed puppets infused with bourgeoning talismanic power – every individual one a mock facsimile of the human anatomy. It could be said their purpose were twofold: to provoke disquiet in the girl, while the influence contained within the runes did the subtle work of fattening the stuff of her soul.

So far, the dolls had unequivocally failed to disquiet Madison.

'We know where he is, yes,' Malphas said. *Go on, say it*, an idle voice in his head quipped. *But you're afraid of another confrontation.* 'He'll be taken care of when the time is right. Tell me, child, if you know so much – perhaps you could see fit to enlighten me *how* you know of this ... problematic wildcard.'

'You forget,' Madison replied. 'He came into our

house. That's how you found me, wasn't it? He spent some time with my mommy, my sister, and me before you decided to take me away.'

Below, in his footbath, malformed feet more akin to flippers began to itch. An illusion, of course: phantom sensation no invocation neither he nor Natal possessed had been able to quell. Madison, seeming to sense his discomfort, approved of it with a smile. He said, 'Do you think it was by chance you came across him when you did? Just as I was about to snatch him away also? He wasn't with your family very long, was he? How much can you know about a person in such a short space of time?'

'I know,' Madison said. 'That he scares you more than a little bit. Both you *and* your brother. You should be scared, too. Because having a creator in the story is not something that's ever happened.'

A creator?

Despite not having the physical wherewithal to blanch, Malphas felt blood drain from his face. Just what ambiguities was the runt alluding to now? Inside Madison's dreams, he had taken the form of dragons, wolves, and on one occasion the nomadic Wanderer. He'd chased her through labyrinthine streets of her own making, licking her heels and spitting fire at her feet. Even the silver serpent of many talons had failed to properly capture any suitable amount of fear in the child. Perhaps, if he just reached across right now and …

Again, the girl seemed to sense his intentions. She said, 'If you hurt me, Malphas, won't your brother be mad with you?'

'Please,' Malphas said. 'Tell me what you mean by *creator*?'

More of that silent smile. Then, in a voice so low he had to strain forward to hear it, the girl whispered, 'Creator of *portals*.'

Malphas leaned back. 'Take a look around you, child. Do *those* …' He pointed at her wall of dolls. 'Seem like a joke to you? Even now, their influence is inside you like a poison, priming you for something you cannot comprehend. This isn't one of your picture books or fairy tales – this is a real world, and real monsters have come to show you suffering. My brother provides you with comfort, but you are completely helpless. As lost as a little girl wandering through the woods and looking for Grandmother's house.'

To this, Madison said nothing; merely regarded the dolls with a curious yet detached attention. Taking a small step back, she collided with the edge of her cot then primly sat down, both hands clasped as though coddling something small.

Far away, Malphas could hear the distant chime of a Carillon bell; Natal readying himself for another morning of ablutions. Afterward, a baptism was scheduled to take place inside the Nave for a newborn – a boy new to their congregation. For this, Malphas wanted to be present, an unseen spectator floating inside the glasshouse. With Delgado having properly taken care of the librarian this morning, there would be more time to meditate on upcoming events that didn't include the girl; a tide of happenings that would see his silver serpent given free rein in a way nobody could possibly predict.

And nothing (not the girl's vague opacities, nor even the shade of Orobas, himself) would stop him from completing this task.

***

For Natal, serving two gods had a price attached. Of course, worshipping the Nazarene acted as a complete subterfuge. But years of uttering his namesake did not come without some recompense for a family whose progeny began in Hell. Though the God of Jehovah (and all his prophets) had been exiled from earth for untold millennia, dallying daily with the rites and passages of a onetime enemy had the potential to corrode even the most stalwart heart. There had been a time, not long after their birth, when Orobas would have shied away from a depiction of the Christos, his infernal cells recalling the battles fought with the failed deity. Soon, however, Orobas realized that with their enemy no longer present (presumably dead), they were free to make a mockery of his once powerful name. Humans, with their limited lifespans, gravitated toward gods like flailing wolf cubs loosened from a mother's teat.

They're orphaned from their creator, Orobas Purson had once imparted. *Incomplete and hollow – forever damned to wander in a wilderness unreconciled to their greater whole. This divide is where the forces of Hell thrive and take their sustenance.*

As a mere child, Natal had asked his father if their kind

consumed the people who lived below – ate them as humans ate the livestock who girdled their paddocks and pastures. Not a creature wont to laugh, Daddy Orobas had done just that, holding his bellicose belly with one ring-studded hand and stroking the head of his offspring with the other.

Just the right question, young Natal – and one I've been waiting for you to ask. Gather around and let me tell you what it means to harvest a human soul …

That long ago day (when Hadley Grove had been no more than one wide Main Street with a smattering of farmhouses

(and before they fought back)

had entailed the first of what would be many lessons concerning the human herd. Although the child Natal had (initially) found the concept of harvesting men and women to be unappetizing, the tide had soon changed when both he and Malphas had begun displaying the early stages of hunting skills: the ability to change their physical forms at will, and on occasion, to make other forms appear from *nothing.*

Is it magic? Natal had asked his father. *Is what we do some kind of magic, Daddy?*

It's no more magic than the tiger who can see properly in the dark – or the spider who casts its silken net. We are simply born of different stock, Natal, having been around for a lot longer than those who live below. And though we look very much the same on top, humans are as different from us as day is to night.

More questions followed, a whole slew of them –

though only one of import was answered on that particular day. Others were revealed during the fullness of time. *But where do we come from, Daddy?*

Daddy Orobas had spoken at length about a place called Hell, a region humans thought existed below them; somewhere only accessible in the realm of dead things. While it was true that such a place existed, humans had misunderstood the mythology: Hell was a place in the very geography of the stars, a physical land in the gulfs between them. And their kind, indeed, came from that region, their ancestors crossing the vast expanses eons ago with massive bodies fat with many wings and many eyes. Here, on this resting place known as earth, sustenance was abundant, and the creatures from Hell could live and breed, knowing they had found a home. But they must never lose sight of their *true* home in the divide between the stars – where the father of all creation resided, the chief of chiefs – where they would one day return.

So you have a Daddy, too, Daddy?

The Devil is a father to all, Orobas confided. The oldest of all sentient beings in the entire cosmos. And the Devil must be both revered and worshipped, for one day you will be judged according to your deeds on earth. Take from it, and rape from it, my children – do what thou wilt according to the desires of your flesh and spirit. The meat of this world, the souls of mammalian men and women, were put here for both our nourishment and amusement. Gorge on them, torment them; your rewards will be great when returned to the realm of Hell.

Almost two centuries later, the lessons of Daddy

Orobas were still pertinent. The land of the Americas, a province ripe with spiritual plague during the building of its new frontier, had been the perfect cradle for the exiled tribes of Hell to make their home. Always watching from the shadows, their kind had observed the humans undergo vast changes (their technologies; their living standards). While the humans evolved, so did the methodology for harvesting them. As mere babes, a single reaped soul could provender their flesh for seasons, but as the decades passed and their own bodies atrophied into dissolution, more flesh was required. Thus Orobas had commissioned his cathedral where, under the fallacy of caring and communion, he and his family could assimilate with a bourgeoning new civilization; they would live amongst their quarry and ensure they never went hungry.

And Orobas was free to continue his great work ...

This work, the study of Hell's invocations, consumed their father for the better part of a century; the bulk of his labors taking place in the catacombs below. As his findings progressed, Orobas began to build even more additional rooms underneath the cathedral – workshops acting as voluminous incubators for exploration. Orobas discovered that Hell, while being a dominion far removed from the earth, could nonetheless be *broached* by small degrees, its borders accessed and sampled by harnessing the knowledge possessed by far-removed ancestors. Books were compiled, and through the knowledge contained within them, experiments were performed. While all creatures of Hell held natural power, these abilities could be enhanced further still. Orobas learned the proper petitions to make their cathedral one giant magnet – not only for the dead, but a lure for other worlds existing beyond the borders of this one. Like open wounds on the canvas of a body, schisms appeared throughout the cathedral as the work progressed, rents in the fabric of space-time. And through these fissures, Orobas had snatched glimpses of different beings equipped with appetites and abilities to rival Hell's own; towering, many-limbed things so vast their cities were like inverted thunderclaps containing no sky.

It's my dream, Orobas had told his sons. *To open up the divide permanently; to peel back the layers until all worlds everywhere are connected to one another.*

For this, Orobas would need to construct the ultimate machine – one powered by the properties of the dead; one that would split the canvas of the universe when put into motion; Pandora's Box, where Hell and the earth could become one. Shortly thereafter, the Hall of Portals was christened, an engineering project to outlive its creator. Consigned to be its custodians after their pater's return to the void, Natal and Malphas were also charged with feeding the machine until …

'Until Pandora's Box is finally opened,' Natal said, straightening his cassock and brought wholly back into the present by his reflection in the ovoid mirror. Yes, this deception played havoc with his mind, all right. It made him prone to brooding about their plight far too often, contemplating among the hallways like some lost adjutant when there were Clarion bells to be wrung and pressing duties to perform. And yet, was it really any wonder given the circumstances? His brother, for all of his special abilities, had things far easier than he. Siphoned away, a mutant freak, immune from having to deal with the creatures who paraded through their doors. Even now, those creatures brought their children to be blessed, completely oblivious that one of their own waited in the wings. It had to be this way, of course – *had* to be. Malphas was disabled *because* of them. Once, they had ignored the sheep, and that blatant disregard had sent the sheep into raptures of revenge.

Up to the church, they had travelled from Hadley Grove below, an endless procession led by a war veteran bearing pitchforks and pales of mercury to drown them in. Ready to deal out justice and do away with the demons on the hill who had a penchant for unnatural misdeeds, including snatching away infants under the cloth and collar of night …

Chapter Fourteen

Micha tasted bitumen and felt sharp pebbles in his mouth which caused him to splutter. Beyond his eyelids there was only white, stabbing sunshine … which slowly took on an amorphous shape: an outline of grimy walls, the side of a group of buildings he'd seen once before far away from home.

I'm back.

The revelation was enough to jolt him into full wakefulness. Pushing the bulk of his torso upright by the elbows, Micha hissed in pain when the right one grazed the asphalt. It was physical pain: regular, sweet, and altogether harmless. Nothing like the all-encompassing grey agony of a drinking-jag aftermath. Which meant …

'Hangovers don't carry over,' Micha croaked. 'I guess that's something to be thankful for.'

'*You* again.'

Turning toward the voice's owner, Micha was not

entirely surprised to see the proprietor of *The Grove Gourmet* staring down at him through the wire-mesh of her snot-green doorway. Harriet Wilson, wife of Edward, did not carry the look of a woman surprised to see him, either. Also noticeable on her expression: a lack of the reserved sympathy she had shown him last time. Her jutting cigarette, like some kind of elongated tooth, emitted a curl of blue smoke.

'Me again,' Micha said, and craned his neck to see beyond her. 'Say, where's your husband this time, Harriet? Placing a wager down at Mybookie, I'll bet? Or maybe knocking back a few frosty ones with that new waitress you hired last spring?'

The words were tumbling out, and their effects were immediate and compelling. Harriet's cigarette, liberated from lips parted by surprise, toppled to the ground in a slow-motion arc. Her eyebrows furrowed. Through the mesh, she regarded him with a species of suspicious disdain.

'How did you –'

'Know about that? I know all about your husband's philandering, Harriett. And a good deal about you, too. Say, that cat you backed over last winter? Did you ever end up telling the owners across the road that *you* were the one who did it? Poor thing was smooshed up pretty good, wasn't he? You know little Maria cried for a whole week after her Socks went missing … and she never even *saw* what the poor thing looked like afterward.'

Kept mostly under lock and key until now, Micha's sheer frustration with his predicament was boiling over.

Sure, awakening inside your own horror novel had a novelty element attached … at first. Yet did other souls have to contend with this crap on a weekly, ongoing basis? Or was Micha Stephen Tudor the first writer in the history of the world to make an enduring habit of it? Bereft of hangover or not, he suddenly felt very sick.

And a make-believe character of mine is currently in the line of fire.

Over Harriet Wilson's shoulder, Micha could hear the chitter-chatter of a dozen morning patrons, all of them entitled American halfwits; just a bunch of average Joes drinking their Joe, hitching up their stone-washed denims and moaning about the goddamn democrats trying to obstruct their beloved tax cuts …

No cowboy golem this time; I should at least be thankful for that.

As the realization dawned, so did the revelations brought to light by a friend in the world he'd left behind. Natal Purson wasn't alone; he had a creepy brother living with him up at the church. Sherriff Brandon Delgado was in possession of an enlightening manuscript, filched from the author. Murderous golems were running riot in Hadley Grove, and the granddaddy of them all was some kind of silver-limbed creature one would normally expect to see in the pages of a comic book …

From her snot-green doorway, Harriet Wilson's look of crazed suspicion grew. She said, 'Mister, I don't know who you are, but if you don't get out of here now I'm going to call the police.'

'You do that. And be sure to tell Brandon Delgado

when you speak to him that he doesn't need to stalk me anymore ... because pretty soon I'll be coming for *him*.'

The retort felt hollow; the entreaties of a schoolyard bully. But that was just fine, because Harriet Wilson was retreating back inside her snot-green doorway again. For a moment, Micha's last conscious memory of Concord came flooding back: of keeling over, blind-ass drunk in a stew of rotting garbage, the strange girl's taste still hot on his tongue.

It wasn't cheating. Those things don't apply when you're skipping flagrantly between worlds ...

Then why did he feel a sliver of guilt?

He didn't know; however, there was little choice but to return to Delta Bronze. If Hadley Grove truly was in the grip of a horror novel, then act three, or the climax, was about to commence. Antagonists would be sharpening their claws, while supporting characters would have a bullseye on their back. And while it was true Micha's protagonists had saved the day in all heretofore stories, *The Mercury Man* had never really been planned as that kind of a story.

It was going to be the kind of story where the whole town went up in flames, he thought, and began walking back toward Main Street. *The kind of story where the monsters have their day.*

Which meant trying a completely different tact concerning his role here.

One that involved circumnavigating the tropes.

One that involved becoming its author again.

***

Snaked with tinsel and glitter, freshly hung Christmas decorations garlanded Delta Bronze's street awning. Even the windows had sprouted fresh opaque designs, the one closest to Micha featuring Santa Claus getting hammered by the dregs of a large beer barrel. Stenciled above him were the words *WE'RE OPEN EVERY DAY THIS HOLIDAY SEASON*! Somehow, during the furor of both falling in love and evading a sadistic Sherriff, Micha had almost forgotten Christmas – and an annual float parade – loomed just around the corner. On the shopfront window next door (a shoe store called *The Ivy Room*), someone had pasted numerous flyers proclaiming the big event. Beyond caring if his actions appeared suspicious, Micha walked over, ripped one off, and studied it with the same absorption a drunk might have given to a rendition of Santa Claus in his cups.

Floats; parades. They were joyful events where the whole town came out to play. In horror fiction, these events could often be counted on for scenes of massive, climatic carnage. If you needed your story to go out with a bang, that was. According to the flyers, December 15th would see Main Street cordoned off and closed down. In place of regular traffic, decorated novelty platforms built into flatbed trucks would run the gamut of Main Street, instead. Could this be the event where Natal and his Mercury Man put on a final show for the people of Hadley Grove?

You don't know – that's the hell of it. Because you never had an inkling of the ending.

Breaking his reverie, Sara's jukebox suddenly ratcheted up, licks of bass making the windows shudder.

Through them, Micha could make out Bing Crosby and David Bowie doing *The Little Drummer Boy/Peace on Earth* duet. Its abrupt timbre, like a mournful callback to an even sweeter era, caused him to drop the flyer. Slowly, it seesawed to the footpath in an erratic arc before finally settling on the surface of a shallow puddle. Santa's visage, this one far more abstemious than his plastered counterpart, appeared to *wink* at Micha as a caul of water clouded over the surface.

It was a small thing, seemingly having no mystical import … but it was enough to get Micha moving again, off the sidewalk and through the front doors of a bar he now called home.

***

Alexa, the sole occupant behind the bar, grinned up at him as he came inside. 'You're in trouble,' she said.

'I am?'

Sara's daughter was garbed in more specialized attire: black all over, the stamp of hospitality workers the world over.

'Mom had you rostered for a shift last night, but yet again, you were a no-show.'

Yet again? His last memories of Hadley Grove entailed returning from Magic Mountain … or some time thereabouts. How much more time had elapsed since? Only a day or two, surely. Enough time for someone to hang up the Christmas decorations, at least.

'And I'm here to put in a personal apology.' He

nodded toward the stairway. 'Is your mom in this morning?'

'Just a minute.'

Alexa finished with opening ministrations, setting up the register float and adding to a garnish center. Despite her age, Alexa moved with the confident stride of someone well-versed in barkeep. Again, Micha couldn't help but parallel this decade with the one he belonged to. In his, having a kid work this environment would flirt the fringes of mistreatment. Here in '85, however, the boss's daughter was simply willing to roll up her sleeves for the business.

Tasks complete, Alexa disappeared up the stairway, calling her mother as she went. On the jukebox, Crosbie and Bowie had given way to Springsteen – the Boss's own version of Santa shenanigans.

When Sara came down the stairs, she was alone.

And before she could speak, Micha said, 'We need to go for a drive.'

***

In the passenger seat of her Ford Escort, Micha talked while Sara drove.

'When was the last time you left Hadley Grove?' he asked her. 'Can you remember the last time you and Alexa left town?'

'What do you mean? Left? Like, on a vacation?'

'I mean drove past the city limits. When was the last time you followed Terry Peak all the way past the town sign and saw it in your review mirror?'

'This is silly, Micha. Probably last winter, I think. We were going to get a Christmas tree and …'

'Do you remember coming back with the tree?'

Micha could see Sara thinking, cogs and gears at work.

'You didn't get a tree from the Mulder Farm that day, did you? And it wasn't because of a snow threat – it was simply deciding to make do with the plastic one you guys had stowed away in the attic. Alexa had been grouchy that day, not feeling altogether well, and she had asked if you could turn around and go back home. And you did. You drove back home and forgot all about that tree. You never left Hadley Grove at all.'

These incidents were lifted from some of the early chapters of *The Mercury Man*, mundane snippets of Sara's life. Judging from her confused look, he had touched on something.

'Micha, how on earth could you possibly know any of that? And what does it have to *do* with anything? Where are you taking us?'

'Keep going. We'll be there soon.'

This far north, bungalows bled into sparse farmhouses, their fronts set so far back only driveways and the occasional swing-set gave any evidence of human occupation. Water towers stood sentinel in between vacant pieces of land. Studding endless fence lines were clumps of small trees, their gnarled branches extending fingers and claws into the sky. Nobody Sara knew lived out here, of course. Nobody except …

'Delgado's cabin isn't that far away.' Looking down, Micha realized he was pinching his kneecaps hard enough to hurt. 'Down one of these side roads. Though I can't for the life of me tell you exactly which one. Some authors draw physical maps of the towns they create, but I never drew one for Hadley Grove. Which was pretty damn stupid, now that I think about it. I could've –'

Sara's Escort came to a sudden zigzagging stop, the forward momentum enough to produce a squealing from the brake pads. In tandem, they both flopped forward, Micha's forehead almost grazing the glove box. Entrails of smoke eddied above the hood.

'No further,' Sara said. 'Until you tell me what's really going on. Because unless you've planted some kind of snooping device in my car or have a window into my mind, there isn't any way you could've known about the Christmas tree.'

Micha could see Sara's perplexity hovered around this secret knowledge, yes. But there was another part she was grappling with: trying to pinpoint the last time she'd left Hadley Grove. Surely there had been visits to interstate relatives back home? Holidays? Sara was struggling because in Micha's stories each character led a self-contained life, seldom if ever leaving town while their narratives played out.

He said, 'Sara, I know you have absolutely no reason to trust me or believe the things I'm about to tell you – I simply haven't been in your life long enough. But please believe me that being with you these past few weeks are all the reason I need to trust *you*. What we shared on the Ferris wheel –'

'Meant something,' she finished. 'And you're right, I

don't have any reason to trust you at all. You waltzed into my bar like a common bum and then proceeded to … *seduce* me. I know nothing about your past, or even if you are who you say you are. All I do know is there is something about you that compelled me to take you in.' She swiveled toward him, and in that mini-second, Micha shrank back. 'Do you have an explanation for *that*? Does it have something to do with what you're trying to tell me now? Because if it does, I'm willing to listen wholeheartedly.'

In his seat, Micha slumped back. He was making small inroads.

'Do you remember anybody else leaving town? Has Alexa ever taken a vacation to the Big Apple, where her mom was raised? Has she crossed the state line for a basketball game or –'

'Alexa hates sports. She prefers the guitar and drums.'

'Or a concert at the tri-county fair? How many of your barflies have you ever seen come back from the big smoke? Your ex-husband is from out of town … but has he ever come back or contacted you for any reason?'

Lay off the questions. Coming clean with the truth about your identity is one thing, but if you make this seem like an interrogation, hating yourself will be the least of your worries.

'You get my point,' he said. 'It's difficult to remember. But trying to recall if people leave town or not is really just the tip of the iceberg. Have you ever once pondered to yourself how is it that a serial killer – or someone approximating one – is operating right here in

Hadley Grove … yet why haven't the state police or the FBI come barreling in with their white vans and questions? Why isn't there a manhunt? Where are the journalists and the assholes who write about true crime?'

Sara's expression changed. She was looking at him with something approaching amusement. And he suddenly realized why: *Micha Tudor* was an asshole who wrote about crime … or so he had professed during their first encounter. All at once, he felt galvanized under the glare of his own suspicious shortcomings. Here was a complete stranger who had wandered into town, shoeless. And this stranger, for whatever reason, had decided to *stay* in town even though a giant Duracell bunny was bouncing around and abducting children. If Micha wasn't the author of this story – a strange dynamic that saw him pass GO and collect two hundred dollars every time something prickly came up – then Brandon Delgado would have hauled his ass into a cage chapters ago.

Micha also felt the ghost of a smile forming, and he let it hang there.

'It *is* a peculiar town,' Sara said. 'I'll grant you that. But I'm still not sure what you're –'

'Stories,' Micha stated. A thread suddenly dangled, and he seized upon it before it could float away. 'You like them, too, don't you? Small-town horror stories. I've seen your shelves by the fireplace. There's a book by Stephen King tucked away, one by Robert McCammon, and another paperback called *Ghost Story* by a guy named Peter Straub.

That's your *library*, Lila's voice declared. *Pulled from your own subconscious into this fantasy world …*

'What are you getting at?' Sara asked … and Micha could see those cogs turning again, holding each of his words up for closer scrutiny. Did she see the parallels yet?

'I'm not sure if you've read those titles, but I haphazard a guess you know how some of them go. The small towns in horror stories are caught inside a web of monsters, some supernatural; some all too human. Sometimes the cast is huge; sometimes it's small. The monsters can exist under the sewers to devour unwary children … or they can run a shop that sells dreams. Maybe it's a deranged maniac who walks around in plain sight. Brought under their influence, the characters must band together to bring the monster low. Mostly they do, and become greater people for their efforts … even in the face of enormous personal loss.'

He knew he was in danger of rambling, but there was no stopping this juggernaut now. And though Micha had a sudden urge to reach over and touch Sara, he resisted.

'The stories can sometimes carry a message or a theme. Most of the time, a town in a horror novel is like a giant canvas for the author's imagination, where he or she can be given free rein to make up terrible yet beautiful monsters … or give a character the opportunity to play out dreams.'

'Micha … are you trying to tell me my town is nothing but a *story*? I honestly can't believe we're having this conversation.'

You're taking an enormous risk here. Lila's voice again. *You know that, don't you?*

He did. Because Sara's world wasn't real – only a

dream within a dream. And did *knowing* this kill the dream? Did apprehending a hologram suddenly dissolve it? Adam and Eve, eating from the tree of knowledge, the first casualties of such a graphing with ultimate truth.

Not looking at him, Sara said, 'I guess next you'll tell me that falling in love is one of those dreams?'

He didn't answer at first, only kept his eyes trained forward. Though dozens of replies were almost forthcoming – *I know how crazy this all sounds. Please, just hear me out.*

Though he chose none of them. Instead, Micha simply settled for a fatalistic call to arms.

'Let me prove it to you,' he said.

***

Though no ominous music played as they approached Delgado's cabin, Micha was sure he detected something in the air … a vibration like the strings of a harpsichord, plucked so tenderly they were at the behest of bones in lieu of fingers. Beside him and piloting the Escort, Sara had gone silent, staring out through the front windshield as though anticipating a storm.

'Keep going?' she asked.

'Keep going.'

Initially not knowing which road led to the Sherriff's house, canvassing a third had been enough to sell Micha on the first. Angular and unpaved, it led down into a small firmament of close-knit shrubbery, a sight he now recalled with startling clarity from a passage in *The Taste Lands*.

Once cleared of these, the road rose up again into a space cleared entirely of vegetation.

Delgado's own handiwork, Micha mused. *Like a lot of psychopaths, he likes to keep his environment clean.*

One minute later a brooding two-story log cabin emerged. Ringed on both sides by a rough semicircle of cypresses, this particular bungalow looked every inch something out of a Sam Raimi production.

Only the monster here doesn't live within the pages of the Necronomicon ...

'He's at work, isn't he?' Micha asked. 'Please tell me he's on duty.'

'No sign of his cruiser. No sign of his Chevy, either.'

'We still can't risk being seen. Park behind those bushes over there. That should give us enough cover.'

The Escort came to a rest, crunching gravel producing a sound like static. For a few moments, Micha simply stared at the cabin, noting the mirrored glass of the front windows resembled eyes. In the vacuum created by the silence, another sound crept through the car's windows ... one Micha had been counting on.

'There. Do you hear that?'

Sara listened. And heard. 'It sounds like wind chimes. Coming from under the porch?'

'They are wind chimes, but they're not exactly standard. You could say Brandon had them custom made.'

This event had taken place inside Micha's novella *Most of All.* In that story, Delgado's character had removed the spine of an earlier victim, Kate Deering. Deciding to use it for another application far removed from its original purpose as a central nervous system, he had gone on to fashion wind chimes after gut-wrapping the bones. Thereafter, a musical elegy was achieved, a fitting epilogue of funeral sounds after the short-lived cacophony of screams.

Still staring at the porch, Micha explained all of this.

Sara said, 'I'm hearing the tinkling of bones? Micha, despite everything I know about Brandon, that can't possibly be true.'

They exited the car. Making headway toward the porch, Micha had trouble blinking let alone looking away, the cabin's windows pinning him with the sun's glare like headlights.

Walking, Micha said, 'A dog used to guard this property, a Blue Heeler mutt named Cyclops. If Cyclops were still around, we wouldn't be striding in so casually.'

Sara stopped mid-stride, eyeing him with the same scrutiny she favored him in the car. 'You knew Cyclops?'

'Delgado told people the dog died from a liver infection, canine hepatitis. But the truth is a little more sordid. Cyclops died from an infection, all right – but it had nothing to do with his liver. He was wounded when a victim named Ben Barrow tried to escape. Ben … he was a prisoner inside Brandon's basement for a while.'

Micha stated all this matter-of-factly, off-hand, as if quoting passages from *Most of All*. But the moment was lent gravitas by knowing that soon they would both be *entering* said basement – a homemade dungeon of begrimed light and shadow where the good Sherriff had been practicing a hundred different depravities since first donning his badge.

***

The front door was open, as Micha had known it would be. Nobody in Hadley Grove – and that included psychopaths, it seemed – kept their doors locked during the day. Walking inside, Sara made a face at her surroundings: equal parts disgust and awkward fascination.

'I can smell him,' she said, stepping further into a living space wrapped in oblongs of sunshine. 'Like cheap aftershave and dog hair.'

Micha's first impression was one of normalcy: bear-skin rugs mounted on walls; a giant quilt-adorned duvet centered in the middle. Tallboys were arranged around the perimeter, each festooned with regular fracas like candles and keepsakes, some sporting ovoid mirrors. A kitchen area took up the greater portion of the cabin's eastern flank, complete with hanging pots and pans and a small jungle of creeper vines. Looking at it all, anyone would be forgiven for thinking this was the dwelling of a regular Joe six-pack, bereft a woman's touch. Then Micha spied a brass handle poking out of floorboards by a tallboy.

Sara's hand halted his progress as he walked toward it. 'This is breaking and entering, Micha. Breaking and entering into a *cop's* house. If we're caught, Brandon will probably do a lot more than just arrest us.'

Although it was on his tongue to give Sara a spiel about proof, Micha simply removed her hand and kept walking. Upon reaching the brass handle, he bent down for a closer inspection.

There was no need to touch it to ascertain it was part of a trapdoor … one that opened up Delgado's hidden wonderland like a chamber into the dark recesses of his mind. Seeing it, Sara let out a small hiccup of something like fright. Then she crept forward and joined Micha on his knees, staring at the creases of the trapdoor with a frown.

She murmured. 'A story …'

Reaching down, Micha pulled on the handle.

***

Dusty sunlight pervaded this part of the cabin, the source: a cross-section of windows built into a segment of the ceiling. Outside these, Micha spied a small sliver of grass and sky. If someone stood on the other side, both feet would be visible through the glass. For a full minute, he simply gawked at everything, seeing it all laid out verbatim from his imagination.

Beneath the windows stood a row of meat hooks, their blades gleaming. Front and center in the middle sat a wooden chair, its mammoth size more in keeping with an electric one. Fixed in the corners were tables, their surfaces bulging with an assortment of clamps, blades, and sex toys. On a far wall hung a television unit; beside it, a tripod mounted camcorder. The floor – what was essentially cement – had been covered with a translucent plastic, the material stretched so tight it was almost invisible. Not for the first time, Micha pondered his chosen genre to write in … and wondered why. Why would any sane individual want to inhabit this territory? It wasn't fun. Hell, it didn't even straddle the fringes of fun when you were up close and staring it in the face. No, this was …

'Obscene,' he said, barely aware he'd spoken until he felt Sara's hand gently touch his back.

If I ever get out of this, I should start penning romances. Mills and Boon dime-store trash. Hunks and dames getting it on for impractical love and a shag. Because let's face it … anything has got to be better than writing about a bat-shit crazy cop who gets his jollies from all this.

Sara was pinching him, her grip painful. 'Okay, I believe you about Brandon. Hell, I'll believe anything you say to me at this point. But please … *please* can we get out of here?'

'Not just yet.'

The tables contained drawers, and it was over to them Micha went. Here, the smell of the house's owner was more acute – masculine odors one would associate with an alpha male. Though lurking underneath it all was another scent, the suggestion of terror; a miasma of dirty flesh and screams. He passed the chair and the camera; Micha rifled through the first of the drawers, feeling tainted by their touch yet compelled to see this through.

Again he felt Sara touch his back, any misgivings she may have harbored concerning his sanity suddenly eroded by a drawer full of Delgado's Polaroid snaps – hundreds of them. They were lewd, grotesque, and everything in between. As he plundered through their bulk, Micha had to remind himself there was a reason Delgado's lair – while terrifying – also felt generic.

The dude lives in a two-dimensional environment you've partially cribbed from a hundred other books ...

That might be, but knowing this failed to take away any of Micha's core unease, which was exacerbated by photos of Delgado posing with dead people. After lingering on some of the worst offenders – in one a badly decomposing woman had been dressed in one of his police uniforms – Micha moved on to the next drawer, and then the one after. On his third inspection, he encountered some slight resistance from the contents inside. Pressured, the drawer came fully open to uncover exactly what he'd come here for.

Her voice just above a cracked whisper, Sara asked, 'What is it?'

Micha said nothing ... only studied the pages, hundreds of them bound together with twine. While the front page bore the insignia of both title and author in two centered and neatly typed lines, all corresponding pages appeared handwritten, containing a type of elegant and rotund scrawl Micha had always associated with the opposite sex.

'It's a book ... a kind of journal. Hopefully one that can shed some light on how this story ends.'

'By Samantha Moffat,' Sara said, mouthing the words stenciled on the front. 'I know her. She's local. One of our librarians. She's –'

'Dead,' Micha said. 'She's dead.'

Sara seemed poised to say more but fell silent at the sound of tires crunching on gravel.

A large car had pulled into the driveway.

***

Someone's been sleeping in my bed.

The words of a fairytale bear came to Brandon as he entered through the front door, every fiber of his being screaming that something was terribly amiss. Although the house *appeared* the same as when he'd left it hours earlier, his instinct insisted that it wasn't. In Brandon's absence, someone had paid him a visit.

Someone had been sleeping in his bed.

In the fairytale, the culprit was still in residence, she of the golden locks who had decided to take a nap after taking her fill of porridge. Being discovered by a family of talking bears, the bitch had bolted before they'd had an opportunity to lay their paws into her.

No one lay sleeping in Brandon's four-poster bed.

And yet ...

The air remained fragrant with a whiff of perfume ...

'Hello?' Brandon called out. He then stilled his breathing, listening for the subtle shift of a body, the low murmur of a voice.

There was nothing.

He called out again, this time shouting, adding the expletive threat that if he found anybody hiding, he would rip out their eyeballs and piss on their brain.

Silence again.

Not for the first time, Brandon wished Cyclops was still alive and wagging his tail every time his master returned to the manor. Although Cyclops had been prone to taking a large steaming dump on the shag rug during his time away, it had been a small price to pay when taking into consideration the peace of mind the mutt provided. He recalled Ben Barrow, a feisty young escapee, had been the one to make damn sure Cyclops would never take one of his famous shits again. Not on this side of doggy heaven, at least.

Just to be safe, Brandon called out one final time, then slapped his keys on a tallboy and walked over to the bed. There was nobody in town who would drive out here because everybody knew Brandon valued his privacy. And outside of an ungrateful brother who lived in Shitsville, Pennsylvania, no other family remained. Their mother Doreen, God rest her matriarchal soul, had perished in a house fire Brandon had started. So ... with no immediate well-wishers or kin to come calling, just who in the hell had paid him a visit today?

There's always the priest. Lord knows the wanderer-dude can come and go however the fuck he chooses.

There existed that possibility – but somehow Brandon doubted it. If the wanderer-dude needed his assistance, then the creepy old cunt could always be counted on to make an appearance in one of his dreams – exhibition complete with gibbering gargoyles. No, whoever chose to violate his sanctuary like this would be some kind of new threat; bona-fide stranger danger; someone who had taken it upon himself to trespass. There was also that subtle yet unmistakable whiff of *Jovian Musk* ...

Brandon's eyes travelled to the basement's trapdoor,

whose handle now faced due east.

'You can run,' Brandon whispered, and began walking toward his secret basement. 'But sooner or later the Sherriff will cut you down.'

Chapter Fifteen

Hands visibly shaking after their near-brush with Delgado, it was Micha's room they retreated to. Although a large part of Sara's anxiety stemmed from the basement discoveries, an even larger portion was derived from the psychological aftershock of Micha's addled revelations: admissions that would be deemed ridiculous no matter who was delivering them.

He's completely insane was, of course, Sara's first natural reaction. But inner voices soon raised a chorus of dissent, giving rise to pertinent questions.

But how does he know everything about me? Hundreds of small details he couldn't know otherwise unless ...

Unless what? Unless Hadley Grove was the setting for a novel he was writing?

The concept was preposterous; laughable, as utterly outlandish as any tall story she'd ever heard.

And yet, why do I feel as if he's telling a sliver of

truth?

Their new prize, recently filched from a torture dungeon, was likely to make that sliver grow.

'He stole it from her,' Micha said. Her guest had taken to pacing the length of the room before gravitating back to his bed, a process he'd repeated at least three times. 'Probably just before he killed her.'

'You can't know that Sam's dead. There could be a perfectly legitimate reason she hasn't called into work.'

Earlier they had verified this – Sara placing a call to the library and briefly chatting with Mr. Benford concerning Samantha's welfare.

'At the very least, Delgado paid her a visit. And do you think she just willingly handed over her property to him? No. You saw what he is … what he's capable of doing.'

'Why don't we just call the police?' she asked, then winced. 'The *other* police … the state ones. Just tell them to take a trip up to Brandon's cabin in the woods.' She grimaced again. 'That's if he hasn't figured out we were there by now.'

The look Micha gave her in return was all the reply Sara needed. There would be no calling the police, no calling anybody. Micha truly believed he was living inside a dream. Did this mean he also thought of her as a dream? Did he think of her daughter as one? Were they all just doing and saying things contiguous to characters in a novel? For a moment, any goodwill

(or feelings, let's just call them feelings)

she harbored for this man almost collapsed under the weight of his ludicrous beliefs.

Micha walked over to her, brandishing Samantha's manuscript like a talisman. Without saying anything, she took it. Then they proceeded to the small desk in the corner, Sara lifting away the title page.

The desk was ancient, as were the two chairs underneath it – secondhand claptrap that stank of age.

But more than adequate for the task at hand.

***

Once upon a time, two souls as old as Hell came to Hadley Grove.

Beginning this narrative with the opening sentence of an epistle might seem ill-fitting, but that's exactly where Hadley Grove finds itself now: at the start of an idealized story whose threads can be traced back to the dark fairytales of old.

That these souls continue to thrive, hiding in plain sight, is not only a testament to their wickedness but also to the sheer naivety of our people who have a long history of being fooled when the Devil decides to dress in God's robes and utter his sacred creeds.

First, let me do away with any penchant for subtlety and get straight to the heart of whom I implicate: Father Natal Purson and his brother, Father Malphas Purson. According to records, both received their ordination as deacons in the calendar year of 1921, some two years after a ribbon-cutting ceremony heralded the completion of their church, a building brought into being by their breaking away from the Assemblies of God. At the time, Hadley

Grove was no more than an industrial sawmill community, its population bordering 700 souls. This places the brothers somewhere in the age bracket of 120 or thereabouts.

Which begs the question: how have they gone about their business without anybody raising an alarm concerning their inability to age at a protracted rate? Are there older residents still living in Hadley Grove who can illuminate this mystery?

***

Micha had gone pale, his Adam's-apple clenching with every page turned. Sara said, 'When you came into the bar that first day looking completely lost, I mentioned Natal's church on the hill. Do you remember? You looked like someone had walked over your grave.'

'I did?'

'You're wearing that same look now.'

'I've always known about Natal. I just had no idea there was a brother. Reading this, it's like finding out the Devil had family somewhere in the shadows, and the teacher at Sunday School simply never mentioned it.'

They read some more, Sara handing Micha each page when she was done. Samantha, interviewing the residents (many of whom were now regulated to nursing homes and hospices), began to glean a greater picture of Natal and Malphas more in keeping with her opening monologue.

Though missing persons were commonplace in all counties during the period before the onset of the great depression, Hadley Grove was no ordinary county.

In Hadley Grove, people were wont to vanish.

***

Randolph Snider, who worked at the sawmill after leaving school at the age of thirteen, remembers vividly when suspicion first began to fall on Natal and Malphas. In aggregation with missing persons, strange things had also begun roaming the streets after dark ... things not altogether human.

'Like giants,' Randolph recalls. 'That's what I remember most about them – their height. Nine, sometimes eleven feet tall. But you also remember other things, how they were just sort of outlines, not really people. And their skin was bright, almost silver. Sometimes you would see only one at night, ambling down Main Street and eying the houses. Other times, two of them would congregate on the bandstand, sort of hunched over each other. At the mill, people speculated the sightings meant there might be something funny in our water ... or maybe things were wandering into our world just before Judgement Day. But the sightings increased, and gave away where they sprung from. Where they likely made their home.'

Here I stopped my little cassette recorder, going over Randolph's words multiple times. Tall beings at least eight feet tall and everyone – those who lived seaside to those who farmed – catching sight of something.

'It was the church,' Randolph declared, his huge spectacles magnifying eyes partially opaque. 'After dark, things covered the grounds of the church, lighting up the

232

*bluffs like spaceships landed from the sky. All sorts of
strange things. At first some of us were too scared to admit
what we'd seen, but people soon began talking when some
of the missing started to return.'*

'Return?' I asked the old man. *'The vanished people?'*

*'Some of them did, yes. Except they weren't the same
people. They had markings on their bodies, kind of like
scars or sealed-up portions. As if they had been opened up
and operated on.'*

***

Randolph's tale, like something from HG Wells,
became more outlandish with the telling. With the return of
the disappeared – only shadows of their former selves and
having no memory of their time away – activity from the
church began to escalate. In addition to ominous lights,
sound also became a constant: the din of creatures not
germane to this world.

*'It was like the priests had a laboratory up there inside
their church. That's what some of us thought ... we thought
they were performing experiments.'*

***

The meagre population of Hadley Grove, those with
enough courage to speak up in the face of ridicule, would
finally harangue the local authorities, though their pleas fell
on deaf ears. It was as if, knowing their midnight pursuits
would eventually draw fire, the priests had made some kind

of pact with the law.

***

'Even knowing what we knew, that whatever was going on up there was far from holy, Natal and Malphas still maintained a small company of devoted followers. Outcasts for the most part; those who would travel by cart up Terry Peak Road every Sunday morning for one of Natal's closed-door sermons.'

***

Disappearances began again shortly after, and this time, death was in the offing. On the beach, bodies were washing up, bloated, dissected and missing limbs. Three of them from the same family over the course of a month. Samantha, the intrepid chronicler, had moved onto fresh witnesses for her narrative, one of whom spoke of the wild weather and terrible storms to batter the coast of Hadley Grove during the winter of 1922. Though freakish squalls had always been a persistent dirge so close to the Atlantic, nothing could account for the ferocity of hurricanes that would decimate entire homes and lay waste to the fishing trade. Breakwaters installed years previous would fail under the assault, causing widespread flooding and the loss of seasonal livestock. With calamities increasing, so did the peoples' need to find a culprit.

***

'Witch hunt is a term that is used loosely these days, everyone from presidents to peasants expending the noun as a way to deflect culpability, but Hadley Grove soon created its own version of one – a sweeping worm of widespread paranoia that left no one unscathed.'

***

Except it wasn't paranoia, of course. The town of Hadley Grove was right to point their fingers at the brothers on the hill, condemnation eventually gravitated into full-scale mob mentality. When Hadley Grove *did* get together as one (their meetings taking place inside the town's other church on Trinity Avenue) talk no longer focused on God at all, but rather His nemesis.

And what they were going to do about Natal and Malphas Purson.

***

Loretta Hardin, once a teacher at Trinity Boys School, recalls how one person took to the podium during these meetings and soon became their leader by default. Martin Wexler, a man who had fought in the first war as a medic, had returned from the battlefields of Egypt, missing a hand but equipped with certain knowledge passed to him from natives in that part of the world. Evil, he proclaimed from a raised dais above the heads of some one hundred citizens, was truly everywhere, and during skirmishes by the Suez Canal, he'd seen men possessed of demons and witnessed their atrocities – heinous crimes taking place outside the theatre of war. These men, he said, had eyes like liquid silver. And they spoke with guttural voices like the bleating of goats, uttering unholy blasphemies against the God of Jehovah while giving praise to all that was profane. Bullets, Martin declared, did not bring them low. Nor did holy water filched from the Nile and blessed by local ecclesiastics. Impervious to physical harm, word soon travelled that battalions of the enemy were attempting to recruit them as soldiers, harnessing their rage by throwing them into the midst of battle. Once again, a plague scourged the byzantine streets of Egypt, demons guised in human form. In order to fight them, a radical countermeasure had to arise ... or the waters of the great Suez Canal would begin to run red with the blood of both sides.

***

Trying to imagine all this taking place only streets from where they sat – a one-handed war veteran named Wexler shouting his stories to a fearful populace – wasn't overly difficult. Not for Micha, who knew Hadley Grove more intimately than anybody should ... and neither for Sara, who had lived within its confines long enough to know the town's lineage lay blanketed in feudal superstition. What made Samantha's account so unsettling (at least for Micha), was learning about parts of a story he'd never so much as made notes about, even in the side margins of a manuscript. These were the great concealed acts, a whole fountain of appendixes that could turn *The Mercury Man* into a trilogy of films.

Peter Jackson would love it, Micha thought. *Act II could be called The Desolation of Samantha Moffatt. Or was the origin story of the priests a prequel?*

'Something funny?' Sara asked.

They returned to the story. To the town, Martin Wexlar asserted that while Natal and Malphas were not *possessed* of demons, they must certainly be of their ilk. For how else to account for the half-man things who roamed their streets at night, the strange lights, and most of all the missing and the dead? Simply put, they were spawns of Satan, concealing their hellish work under false pretenses.

***

Martin's radical countermeasure came from archaic Egyptian ministers who had been practicing their principles for so long they were more akin to alchemists or soothsayers. For them, demons inhabiting the flesh of man was nothing new upon the earth – something that had been dealt with by the church since the crucifixion of the Christos. In doing so, they had developed many ways to oppose them – rites involving the elements of earth and alchemical processes designed to banish the demon within.

Loretta continued: 'It was here that our would-be savior first made mention of the element called mercury, a chemical property that, when used in accordance to guidelines, could render the forces of evil impotent. Mercury, he said, was like divine fire from God that all demons and soldiers of Satan found reprehensible ... a scourge left over from the old myths which saw a werewolf killed by the silver contained within a bullet.

When confronted by this element, evil could be hermitically sealed.

And sometimes, killed outright.

***

Martin Wexler then divulged to his audience that if Hadley Grove were to defeat Natal and Malphas, a similar strategy would have to be employed – one that involved a complicated exorcism performed with the element of mercury.

By exposing the demons to it, they would be assigning them to a long passage of sleep.

Or potentially, the grave.

***

'Our dog has been summoned, has he not?'

Malphas, hoisting himself from wheelchair to floor, glared up at his brother. 'In a manner of speaking, yes. He's summoned himself.'

Natal looked puzzled. 'No parlor tricks to get him here? No theatrics?'

'They were not needed. Delgado has something important to tell us.'

On his elbows, Malphas positioned himself against the lip of a mercury pool then slid in, a sigh of contentment escaping his lips. Seeing him thus, naked and paddling, a subtle look of distaste crossed Natal's features.

Malphas, his eyes closed to contented slits, regarded his brother. 'Don't look so appalled. Father's shade, for all its protracted power, cannot stymie your arthritis forever. One day you'll join me in here.'

'No,' Natal agreed. 'It cannot. But a belated human harvest certainly could.'

Malphas guffawed, a rare sound on any occasion. 'I suspect you are right there. And do much more aside. Tell me, brother, how is Madison keeping? Does she still talk in riddles?'

Folding and depositing his brother's wheelchair into a small closet, Natal said, 'Spare me your feigned ignorance, Malphas. You know full well how she is keeping. And better than I, no doubt. Though with her hour very close at hand, what she says or doesn't say is of little importance to me. As it shouldn't be to you, either. Leave her be, Malphas. And let her enjoy what little time she has left.'

In reply, a curt and knowing smile played across the old man's lips. Then, buoyed up on his belly, Malphas pushed himself through whirlpools of mercury until he was facing one of the wall divisions, an arched passageway of current.

'Let's get this over with then,' he said. 'We shouldn't keep him waiting. God knows dogs can be venomous shits when provoked.'

'That,' said Natal absently. 'Is why we employed him.'

***

239

As was habit when visiting the church, Brandon
Delgado chose to park his Chevy far from the wrought-iron
gates foreshadowing the driveway. Once the car was locked
and secure, he would take the rest of the journey on foot.
Although the reason he kept doing this was somewhat of a
mystery

*(I'm not letting my baby near this fucking hornet's
nest)*

it seemed safer to not question a base instinct. Call it
thinking ahead. Call it insurance against what was coming.
If Brandon ever needed to make a quick getaway, somehow
the thought of fleeing on foot trumped every other method
of escape.

Then why even go up there? a voice demanded; a voice
that sounded suspiciously like every gum-chewing whore
he'd ever played with. *Why enter the one place where you
might have to make a hasty escape?*

Because when you make a deal with the Devil, there
was little fucking choice.

This late, the wrought-iron gates proved difficult to see
in the murk, but soon Brandon was upon them, striding
assuredly up the concrete veldt and hearing an echo of his
boots scrape across the asphalt. Lined on both sides of the
private road were planted shrubberies, strident hedgerows
with the stark outline of a maze. The gates, themselves,
were wide open, twin alms having the charm of giant fangs
and just as wholly embracing.

Brandon tensed, coming to a stop. The shadows of the
church were visible, needle-like abutments trained against a
darkening sky. Somewhere – in the catacombs below or the

attics above – two hyenas lorded over a young girl and waited for him.

It's not too late to go back. Get back inside your Chevy and blow this fucking town for good – before it blows itself up for good. Something you know is only days away from happening.

Yes, he did know that. Because Hadley Grove was like a big barrel of gunpowder long past its expiry date. Very soon, it would implode – most likely taking lives

(and opening up other worlds)

in the process. Of course, Hadley Grove's Chief of Police might have immunity in the matter ... but when in past instances had demons (being biblical or otherwise) ever honored their agreements? More often than not, they welshed.

Another voice suddenly spoke up, this one so close and personable Brandon felt his balls retract.

Betray us, Sherriff, and we'll string those balls up from the top of those gates!

Teetering for a moment, Brandon stumbled, throwing paranoid glances over his shoulder and up the driveway.

Politely make your way to the side entrance of the building. We have many things to discuss.

A sudden picture sprung to mind, one so startlingly rich it was more akin to a vision: being in the grip of the wanderer-dude's weather-beaten hands; the wanderer-dude effortlessly placing his ass onto one of the black pikes of the wrought-iron gate, there to be pinioned until he bled his innards out.

That's right, said the voice. *You'll be hanging up there like a bug on the end of a stick ... or like the librarian-bitch on the beach. A message to any would-be Judas Iscariots who think betraying us might be in their best interest. Keep walking, Sherriff. And don't look back.*

Facing forward, Brandon Delgado began walking again.

This time, he did not look back.

***

For their place of palaver, Natal had chosen an antechamber not far from the Hall of Portals, a room arranged with large rectangular stones. The stones were archetypal to a spiral, a most ancient religious symbol, diminishing circles indicating order from chaos, chaos from order. Long ago, Orobas had used the chamber for his own fieldwork, using the fat stones to disembowel livings things on their smooth surfaces.

Malphas asked, 'Do you know what these slabs remind me of, Natal?'

Natal did not answer at first, preferring to keep his gaze trained on the stairs.

'Sarcophagi. Do you think if we cracked one open, we'd find anything inside? I can't imagine Daddy kept them here purely for laboratory purposes.'

'Why don't you?' Natal asked his brother. 'Crack one open, that is? In all our years together, there has never been anything preventing you from doing this.'

Malphas turned around. Except it wasn't, Natal noted, Malphas the old man. For the occasion he wore the garb of a golem, a medium-sized centaur crowned with the head of a baboon. Or perhaps it was a different beast; Natal could never be altogether certain. Capricious creations from the mind of Malphas were as ever changing as a season in Hell.

Natal said, 'You'll frighten him.'

'That,' Malphas replied through his baboon mouth. 'Is entirely the point.'

***

As the voice urged, Brandon entered the church through one of the side doors, an arched stonewall ingress equipped with a brass ring. Swinging inward, its hinges emitted a timeworn basso creak. Had he ever come this way before? It seemed unlikely. Because the building had a habit of changing guises as often as the priests who employed him. Windows and doors that were here one day were gone the next. Subtle changes, to be sure … but changes all the same.

A meagre amount of light came from the beginnings of a staircase, its ruddy glow suggestive of fire. The staircase twisted in a gothic spiral. Walking in, Brandon took the risers slowly, running fingers over an alabaster handrail. Soon the light augmented, creating a cavalcade wall of flamed-wrapped shadow.

Suddenly he imagined one of Malphas's gibbering gargoyles at the bottom, a real-life companion to the dream minions. In the dream world they posed no threat … but this wasn't that world. Clearly, Brandon remembered their black scales and even blacker eyes attached to paper-thin skulls; their see-through wingspans and tumors mushrooming across them.

Malphas getting into my fucking head. Don't let –

The stairs ceased. In lieu of gargoyles, Brandon found himself standing in a room full of stone coffins.

***

'Sherriff!' the creature on Natal's left said. 'So nice of you to finally join us!'

Arriving, Brandon's plan had been to just unload; tell the brothers how Micha and his bitch had violated his sanctuary; how they had been *sleeping in his bed* and needed to die. Yesterday, if it could be arranged.

Yet once again in their presence, he was unable to speak.

Malphas, having forsaken his human condition, was presently some kind of horse-baboon atrocity, the head a pink oval encased in tussocks of sprouting fur. Natal – while still having the semblance of a man – appeared taller and gaunter, his bald crown of a head rising out of a black cassock like a parody of the grim reaper himself.

Two grinning jackals, Brandon thought.

'Something's …' He stopped, cleared his throat and had to begin again. The baboon thing was Malphas, all right. Those silver eyes didn't lie. 'Something's happened. The owner of the bar –'

'Sara?' said Natal. 'Yes, we know something of Sara. What has she done?'

'She's been inside my house. Both her and her …

fugitive.'

'Is that right?' the baboon asked. When speaking, portions of its large incisors came into view. 'When did this happen?'

'Earlier today. This afternoon, as a matter of fact. I recognized her perfume, *Jovian Musk*. Later I found evidence where their car was parked. They … found my basement. And they *stole* something.'

'You made the right decision to inform us,' Natal said.

Only now did Brandon notice the lack of any fire, what he'd originally attributed to the light source. The stone slabs, arranged in overarching spirals, seemed to emit their own brand of wan illumination.

'So …' he asked. 'May I take them out of the equation? Both of them?'

'Sherriff,' the baboon said. 'You've always been free to carry out whatever justice you feel is appropriate in Hadley Grove.'

'They found my *basement*,' he reiterated, as though this crime was on par with the many others to have occurred there.

'And you're sure it was them?' asked Natal.

'Who else *would* it be?' Indignation, his own police-issued brand of it, was a dam threatening to burst. 'They were trying to get some dirt on me …. and they *stole* something.'

'*Stole* something,' Natal parroted. 'And just what *was* that something?'

In his fury coming here, Brandon had regulated the librarian-bitch's manuscript to the back of his mind. What

Matthew Tait

the trespassers had stolen seemed infinitely less important than what they had *done*: waltzed into his goddamn territory like a couple of hardboiled gumshoes. The audacity of this brazen act was mind-numbing …

'Sherriff, there is enough information within those pages not only to waylay our mission but to bring attention to yourself. How does that sit with you? The prospect of one day sharing a cell with the very vermin you helped to put away?'

Not well, he thought. But there were other things going off in his head now, a tsunami of them.

'You talk of a mission,' he said. 'You promised me the harvest of Hadley Grove. I just thought … what does it matter what anybody knows? Those rats down there, they have no idea what's coming when –'

But Brandon did not finish. Because Malphas was changing yet again; his stallion physique bleeding from human, to horse, then back to human again. Through the motion, Brandon bore witness to a quick succession of mammalian anatomies, each as capricious as the last. Among it all, like a private bogeyman, were glimpses of the wanderer-dude.

But he's not the end game here …

When the Mercury Man finally emerged, Brandon took a step back, shielding himself against a terrible nimbus of bright heat and quicksilver limbs.

***

Martin Wexler, armed with a small army, sought

*vengeance against the perpetrators of evil on one freezing
night in the winter of 1922. Numbering close to one
hundred souls from Hadley Grove – people who had lost
loved ones – fortified with stacks of Bibles and pails of
mercury (the modern equivalent of holy water, sometimes
called Azogue by the Egyptian priests of old), they walked
in a procession up to the church.*

*Loretta said, 'Some of us wore necklaces of the stuff,
and some carried it in pouches. When bringing the batches
into being, Martin had siphoned portions into his devotion
candles so its potency constantly surrounded us. Needless
to say, there were people in our group who succumbed to
the element's natural poison after becoming exposed, and
they died in an agony of muscle atrophy and spastic
tremors. Of course – it was all in God's plan according to
Wexler; soldiers of God had to make sacrifices when going
into combat against the Devil.'*

*And not everyone would make it to the top, either.
Harried by sleet and their own mounting terror, some of
the faithful simply turned around and abandoned the troupe
altogether, desperate to see another sunrise before the
demons caught wind of them. At this stage, Loretta
described a kind of cult mentality had pervaded the group,
and Wexler saw defectors as treasonous in the eyes of God.*

*'Two were bludgeoned to death; I remember an old
man being shot. By the time our carriages rolled up to
those big wrought-iron gates we were all clutching our
rosaries and feeling as terrified as sin. We'd made it,
though. And that seemed like a small miracle in itself. No
contrived evil by the brothers had interrupted our journey*

to the summit.'

What would happen next – the storming of the church and the swift confrontation of Natal and Malphas – would become an event only witnessed by a handful. But when Loretta recounts her version, tears cloud her eyes, as if the occasion were only yesterday; the gulf of years between now and then only something manufactured by the generations to come after.

'The priests had no idea we were coming ... I believe that's the only way we were able to get in. When Wexler and those closest to him broke down the door and shuffled in, there was nothing to greet us. The Nave was lit by a million candles flickering under the wind we brought in. I'm not sure what most of us were expecting – at least at first – but it wasn't a beautiful church that put our own to shame. Almost the entire west wall was filled with stained glass, stunning friezes depicting our Lord and Savior in his many martyred acts of grace. And the tabernacle ... it rose out of the floor like a little building, full of archways and spires and a stairway leading up to it.

'There must have been moments when some of us were having second thoughts – I know I was. Maybe we had somehow misunderstood Malphas and Natal from the very beginning. Or maybe other forces were at work in Hadley Grove we simply didn't comprehend. But then we began to hear sounds as if coming from the earth, itself – terrible things not caused by any natural wind. Wexler didn't hear at first; he was too busy being flustered and accounting for the mercury cargo.'

Loretta went on to describe reverberations like

machinery. And living sounds, too; roars and screams like a thousand foul things in copulation.

'If our small group was scared before, that was nothing compared to how we all felt hearing that. Fear of execution be damned, some bolted back through the front doors. Wexler wasn't scared, though. He was grinning from ear-to-ear like he'd just discovered gold. Our enemy was now in sight – or hearing distance – proof positive our journey here was a righteous one. Down below came the sounds of Hell, and down below we would all travel.

Led from the Nave, we walked through passageways carrying our caches of mercury and flinching at every sound. After trudging for a while, the passageways became a warren of tunnels, makeshift things hewn from the earth and containing niches for the dead.'

***

Seemingly impervious to the Mercury Man's strange energy, Natal had simply motioned himself a few steps to the right.

In a shifting state of mutability, the golem's eyes glowed like hot embers, each one rotating as though untethered from its primal meat. Underneath the eyes were an arrangement of teeth, their tips serrated like points of chiseled ice. Jostling limbs flailed at a void of air suddenly turned scorching.

Natal said, 'Due to this unfortunate event, our arrangements have changed. Tomorrow night, you'll escort Sara Childs and guest up to the church. You will then chaperon them into the Hall of Portals.'

'The Hall of *Portals*,' Brandon said, aghast. 'So the harvest is going ahead then?'

Golem aside, Brandon could hardly suppress his delight. Had fucking things up on his end likely given the brothers an impetus to move their timetable forward? All the way to *tomorrow night*? For a fleeting moment, he could suddenly see Johnny Cash riding the flotsam and jetsam of other dimensions and beckoning Brandon's company.

Choosing to ignore the question, Natal said, 'If you do not do your level best to meet this demand, we will be unhappy. And you don't want to see either Malphas or I unhappy, do you, Sherriff?'

'No,' said Brandon, though he barely comprehended the inquiry. In front of him, the Mercury Man's stalactite teeth and molten eyes were hypnotizing with their intent. For possibly the first time ever, Brandon brooded seriously on just how these two fuckers had come to be – Tweedledum and Tweedledee lording over his town like magical parasites, both hell-bent on sucking the life out of it.

'Good!' Natal said, clapping both of his hands together in mock theatrics. 'After sunset, Sherriff. Admission to the Nave by the back entrance this time.'

At this, Brandon expected Malphas to cease his own theatrics … but the Mercury Man only continued to grow, its spiked forearms snapping at the concentric slabs of stone like something in the paroxysms of a temper tantrum.

Schizoid

***

'What those walls contained – ghosts, the spirits of the dead – both those names seem apt. Some, contained within makeshift mausoleums, howled at the group as we passed, their agony plain. Whatever purpose the priests had kept them for – as pets, perhaps – seeing new faces below threw them into a violent frenzy. Wexler, leading the front, told us to ignore the creatures. They were damned as well, he said; demons in spirit form who would deceive us just as the brothers had deceived us from the first. While most listened, some of the mothers among us stayed behind, convinced their missing children were contained within those walls. And who could blame them? This was the first living proof we had seen of life beyond the grave.

'The brothers ... we could sense them before they came into view. I remember trying to stop but was pressed forward by the bodies behind me. Then open space replaced the passageways, a vast tract of it, and we were greeted with a wall of stone taller than anything built in the world above.'

***

'Loretta must be dead by now,' Micha said.

This put her age somewhere in the nineties at the time the librarian had siphoned this story. Had any of them, seeing what they'd seen inside the bowels of the church, gone on to live ordinary lives in the aftermath?

Sarah, standing up from her ratty chair, appeared sheepish and resigned. She said, 'And there's no one alive who can vouch for any of this. Whatever things Malphas and Natal were capable of back then, they're amplified somehow. Because that creature of theirs now walks around in broad daylight with complete impunity.'

Here was a puzzle almost a century in the making. The alchemical element Wexler and his entourage felt certain would waylay the demons had instead done something different: given them an evolutionary nudge and perhaps transmuted parts of their anatomical make-up.

As if the fabled kryptonite, Superman's perpetual weakness, had never faired as his Achilles heel. Rather, the element would become an arbiter for a wellspring of herculean strength.

***

'*Near the foot of the wall, two tiny figures were standing on a raised platform. They were Malphas and Natal, of course; their cassocked forms facing away from our group and staring up at something I have no name for. Blackened shadows, smudges in the air, like giant doorways. And the priests were looking up at it ... as if communicating with it. Even from so far away, I could sense that. Hypnotized by the shadows, the brothers were oblivious to us as we crossed the remaining distance.*

'*Wexler never hesitated – the man had come more than prepared. And not only with his holy mercury, either; but the hallowed epistles taught to him by Egyptian priests who presided over battlefields. Our approach didn't rouse the brothers ... but those words did. At first only a shocked*

Malphas turned around – Malphas looking young and almost handsome. And he was smiling, too. Then he flinched backward, falling over, completely covered in a corrosive silver while vapor surrounded him like a cloud. Natal was next, but the other priest had seen his imminent danger, sidestepping the bulk of Wexler's projectile before it could find his skin. By now, the others had rushed forward with their own munitions, hoping to pin the brothers while they were down, but whatever loomed above us chose that moment to intervene.

'I looked up and saw reptilian eyes bearing down, fixing us with a dragon's gaze.'

***

Looking up from the manuscript, Micha let out a long sigh, one that sounded despondent even to his own ears. 'I'm not sure anybody would believe this, even if Samantha had gone on to complete it. It all just sounds like …'

'Like a story?' Sara offered, and smiled.

Through the walls came the raucous bray of blue-collar laughter, the sounds of a tavern filling up. For now, the story of the Mercury Man would have to be abandoned.

Because even during the big reveals of a horror novel, Micha thought. *The show goes on.*

He asked, 'Isn't Mary Lamont playing tonight?'

Sara's dimple perked into being. 'She is. Her band will be on in an hour or so'

Micha stood up, offered her his arm. 'Then how about we dance?'

Chapter Sixteen

Micha was awoken by a doorbell, the sound a piercing shriek that seemed to flood his whole brain. For moments he simply lay inert, struggling to recall exactly where he was ... or even *who* he was. By degrees, his name came back – a good start. Slowly a few other things followed

(I like to read and drive a crappy car)

and then the doorbell interjected again, even more penetrating and prolonged than before.

The bastard has his finger pressed down on the bell, he thought randomly. And on the heels of this: *My apartment in Concord has a bell ...*

Concord. A place that now felt as far removed from reality as one of his stories. A place where he was all alone in the world and shitty things often happened.

That goddamn sound – if only he could place his hands around the throat of the culprit behind the door. He would squeeze until ...

Could be Lila – and you don't want to choke her.
No, he did not. Because he loved Lila, right?
It's Sara you love.

Rapidly, memories of his other life surfaced, every one of them; of living inside a complete fabrication and yet feeling more alive than ever before. Because in that particular world, another person genuinely cared for him.

And incessant doorbells did not come with the dawn.

'I'm coming,' he croaked, only just managing to get the words out … and then coming to the slow realization he wasn't lying in bed. In fact, he was *far* from his bed, having somehow migrated to the bathtub during the time his consciousness had been AWOL. He was still fully clothed, thank God, but there was a dampness suffusing his trousers and torso he didn't much care for. That area was slightly slimy around the edges … and even a touch smelly.

It seems your concerns back in Hadley Grove were warranted, Micha, old chum. I believe you may have pissed your pants.

Managing to bring himself forward in the tub was a herculean task, every muscle in his lower abdomen screaming in agitated protest. Again the doorbell sounded, and this time there was a voice added on like a severe exclamation point. Though there was no making out the words, Micha recognized the voice in a heartbeat: a throaty growl like background radio static drifting through an open window every day of his life since moving into the street.

'Gerald,' he muttered, gritting his teeth and pushing himself into an upright position. 'You old prick.'

Gerald Caron had been his immediate neighbor going

on five years – the one he had disclosed to Sara brandished a cane and often chased people down the street; those unlucky souls who had committed the grave crime of dispensing junk mail into letterboxes that clearly proclaimed leaflets, brochures, and junk did not figure into its inventory. Gerald was an absolute, died-in-the-wool asshole who sounded like a pissed-off mob boss and tried to make life a living hell for anybody under fifty. Even at the best of times, Micha tried diligently to avoid the man in any capacity – yet the belligerent prick had an uncanny way of turning up at the *worst* possible times. Like today, for instance.

'I'm coming,' Micha croaked, knowing he couldn't be heard but also knowing the man on his doorstep wouldn't leave until he had an audience.

Legs still throbbing, he managed to maneuver himself out of the tub and was struck by an arc of outside light through the louvered windows that made his eyes sting. No hangover, but returning to the world after time spent in Hadley Grove definitely had the subtext of one. In the bedroom, he quickly changed into a fresh pair of tracksuit pants, wincing at both the task and the smell coming off his body. Soon, a shower would be in the offing, roughly five hours of it if the hot water managed to hold out that long.

Underneath the veranda, Gerald's asthmatic wheeze of a voice was now loud enough for Micha to make out some of his words. *Not leaving* and *little piss-head* were among them.

Micha was halfway to the door when, from the corner of his eye, he spied the fat rectangle of his manuscript sitting in its tray underneath the laptop.

Time enough to register that once again *The Mercury Man* had grown in size.

***

'And so he wakes,' the old man standing on his doorstep said. 'Thought you were probably in a fucking coma.'

Bleary-eyed yet somewhat lucid, Micha regarded his visitor with unconcealed disdain. Though pushing sixty, Gerald still had the portly frame of a retired bouncer. He also had a head completely devoid of hair which gleamed as though recently oiled. 'What the hell is your problem, Gerald? You better make this quick.'

'Besides the fact you smell like a brewery, I'll tell you what my problem is, asshole. Your trash bins out back – you haven't put them on the curb for *weeks*. And they're starting to stink up not just my yard, but the whole fucking neighborhood.'

'Bullshit.'

On any other day, Micha would navigate his neighbor's words like a man crossing a tract of land filled with unexploded bombs. Not today, though. Today, any and all diplomatic negotiations had ceased. For years, he had towed the line with this ass-hat, purely in the interest of keeping the peace. But such brazen acts of restraint – those things never outlined in any *Neighbors Handbook* – always had their limits.

'Open the door properly,' Gerald spat. In his right

hand, he brandished the custom eagle-topped cane he always carried, thrusting its bottom outward toward Micha's door. 'Were you born in a fucking tent?'

Micha made a half-hearted effort to kick the end of the cane. 'What the hell does that even *mean*, Gerald? Are ridiculous catch phrases parceled out with your medication? Because every time you show your face, you excrete one as if I'm supposed to understand what the hell you're talking about.'

A brief moment of righteous triumph poked through Micha's malaise, but it was gone before he could grasp it properly. Gerald, his eyebrows narrowed, leaned in almost conspiratorially and proceeded to sniff. Coke-bottle reading glasses reflected his bald pate. 'You've been on the piss again, haven't you? Don't think everybody around here doesn't know what you get up to, because we do. '

'And what do *you* do?' Micha replied. 'You smoke one joint after the other from dusk 'til dawn.'

'Why you little –'

'Do you really think,' Micha motioned his arms around to the silent and sleepy street outside, 'that I really give a shit what anybody around here thinks of me? Not a single one of you knows how to send an email or, I'll wager, even knows what that *is*.'

To this, his neighbor had fallen deathly silent. Though his face had reddened considerably at the sides, steam from his ears imminent.

'Gerald, with the amount you smoke – both weed *and* cigarettes, I figure you only have about seven years to live. Ten, tops. Soon, you'll be dead. And absolutely no one on this street is going to miss you. In fact, do you know what I *really* think?' He tipped Gerald a wink. 'I think on the day that happens, they'll all get together and throw a party.'

Now Gerald's cane rose up, every inch of the man intending to strike him. His complexion, ruddy, had turned a boiler-plate red.

Micha quickly slammed the door before Gerald's cane found him.

***

In past instances of feuding with Gerald, the man had not gone quietly. Once, Micha was pushed to call the police when the old crank had refused to leave, proceeding to amble down the side of his driveway, seeking a window and more confrontation. On this occasion, there was only a heavy silence ... punctuated by the sound of slippers walking slowly off the tiled porch.

Micha let out a relieved sigh.

He had fought back, yes – but that didn't mean Gerald had been cowed. Right this moment, he was no doubt plotting some kind of revenge.

Could have been worse. Could've been an old man from Mississippi with allegations of plagiarism ...

Micha smiled, fond memories of Stephen King's novella *Secret Window, Secret Garden* coming back with clarity. He'd only been a teenager when first reading that story in the collection *Four Past Midnight*, in one instance skipping school so he could be at home with the dog-eared paperback. And such a decent movie had been made from the story, too; Johnny Depp eating up the camera with every frame. Good-old Steve King, writing about writing. It was a motif all writers seem to take a stab at, eventually. Metafiction working as the ultimate psychoanalysis. No need to pay a quack when ...

Therapy. I'm involved in my own therapy. With a quack named Halbrook.

Walking back to his bedroom, Micha winced, sure in the knowledge he had missed an appointment, perhaps several. Halbrook was potentially the only person worried about his world, ruminating about another possible suicide attempt. After some fruitless minutes spent ransacking his belongings for both wallet and phone (a small tower of denim jeans was often their resting place, and this occasion proved no different), Micha sat stonily silent on the edge of his bed, waiting for those blessed bars of power to come into being.

Tuesday, June 18th, just past 9am in the morning.

His meeting with Grayson had taken place exactly four days ago.

Almost one hundred hours had transpired since then, time lost to a completely different kind of cyclone. Halbrook would not be missing him.

Micha's last conscious memories were of diving headfirst into a hot stew of garbage, drunker than the last lord of creation. How the hell he had gotten home in one piece was anybody's guess. Perhaps he somehow managed to call an Uber; or he simply walked the entire distance, trailing strings of vomit along the way. There was no real way to know for sure. Unless ...

From across the bedroom, the manuscript called out to him. The manuscript fresh with added scenes and fat with new information.

Getting up from his bed, Micha walked over to it.

This time, for whatever reason, he felt none of the erstwhile superstitious anxiety that gripped him before. For better or for worse, the time had come to finally get into the meat of his story.

The Mercury Man, after all, was almost done.

***

For the task, Micha discovered some leftover beers in the fridge, a surplus detritus from his last jag. Coming home, he must have made one of his famous customary walking detours into a drive-thru liquor store … the only ones open after a certain hour. With nobody around to perform an intervention, to ask: *Hey, Micha, how about you laying off the drinks for the night?* he then set about devouring a can, then another; each sip interrupted with a constant and blessed belching.

Belching feels like an old friend, he thought cryptically.

Thoughts swimming, Micha dove headfirst into the manuscript, splaying out the used copy pages in a bourgeoning semi-circle around the living room carpet.

I'll be damned. It's here. Every inch of it is here.

Mason, having palavered with a fellow writer concerning his new book, proceeded to get shitfaced and almost puked on a random girl – all of this taking place *after* their tongues had joined together in a moment of wanton desire. Thereafter, it was back to the mean streets of Hadley Grove again, whereby this other version of his dynamic-self led a charge of sweet-talk, staving off the big bad Sherriff, everybody's favorite Johnny Cash fan and all round nutball, Mr. Brandon Delgado. Reading, problems became apparent immediately – everything from technical aspects to spelling errors.

'You would think,' Micha told his empty living room. 'That supernatural ghost writing would have immunity from spelling errors.'

Not so. They crowded the paragraphs like dead flies, and in some sections, small droplets of spattered blood had dried to maroon stains, as if whoever had authored these words had a terrible case of whooping cough or pneumonia.

You authored them. This time it was Lila's voice, coming through loud and clear. *Nobody has been living here except you.*

Despite the errors, the story soon picked up, although some gaping continuity overlaps became evident. Alexa, the daughter bequeathed with moxie and barely a presence, had almost fallen victim to the Mercury Man during a sighting. Why then, did this revelation only poke its snout through in the latter stages … long after Micha's protagonist was firmly embedded in the action? Better to have the admission disclosed earlier, a tangible tether bringing both Sara and her man closer together.

'Foreshadowing,' Micha mumbled, and cracked open another canned beer. 'Grayson would tell you this goddamn book needs more foreshadowing.'

And then something else reared up in the story, expected but somehow unexpected, head-butting its damned self into the chapters with all the rude aplomb of someone entering an occupied toilet stall before knocking.

The Mercury Man contained Samantha Moffat's journal.

The same one revealing the origins of the demonic priests.

Micha had sworn off including journals into his fiction years ago, when Lila had referred to one inside *The Midnight Mare* as 'the boring-ass part' of the story. Personally, he didn't see a problem with their inclusion, and habitually enjoyed reading them in some of the horror novels penned by friends, Grayson included. But readers seemed to fucking *hate* them, often glossing over the italicized text as if the words were of no import whatsoever … even if they *were* divulging pertinent plot points.

And then came what was perhaps the biggest surprise of all: little Madison Bowthorpe, the abducted girl put on ice, had turned into some kind of magical child-sage. Somehow, she had become aware of Micha's place in the story and admitted as much to one of her captors. Which was downright silly, in the scheme of things. How had she come by such power? Did her character dream of Micha, as he did of her? Was her new-found knowledge of the author some kind of McGuffin to save her life? And if *she* knew, then Malphas and Natal probably did, too.

No wonder they haven't taken you out of the equation, yet. It says right here they're scared of you …

Finally, the big reveal of what these brothers were:

demons sired from Hell, a place between the stars. So it turned out they were Lovecraftian after all, their forefathers flying through the gulfs of space on tenebrous wings the size of skyscrapers. Though this revelation hardly surprised him, the origin of Malphas's deformities did. Having been scalded by Wexlar's supposed holy water, the mercury had gone to work inside the demon's system, splicing and bonding itself with an alien anatomy not designed for such an incursion.

He retains powers ... but now needs liquid mercury to survive.

Malphas Purson had the supernatural ability to create monstrous golems out of thin air, and one of those golems just happened to be a *fiend* composed of liquid mercury whose mission seemed to be frightening, abducting, and sometimes butchering people with its large silvery appendages. As absurd as it sounded to Micha (and it sounded *wholly* absurd), the Mercury Man was really nothing more than a souped-up revenge monster unleashed upon the citizens of Hadley Grove for Wexler's crimes. Some of them; hell, *many* of them, were perhaps direct descendants of his original posse. Malphas had been scarred and disfigured ... and that scar now roamed the streets as a kind of engram gifted with a corporeal body.

As expected, the final written chapters closed around a reading of Samantha's journal, the hero and Sara hunched over the pages like lovers sharing gospels by candlelight.

Although *The Mercury Man* was a hefty manuscript, it was still bereft around thirty pages or so from being a *true* novel.

The end game, while hinted at, hadn't quiet played out properly.

A showdown at the church would be the final stanza in Micha Tudor's metafiction horror novel.

***

What would be Micha's final appointment with Halbrook took place two days later, as originally scheduled. The doctor, unaware of recent events surrounding his patient, grinned at Micha as if their last session had occurred only recently.

'You've lost weight,' Halbrook told him. 'Where's that belly gone? How have you been, anyway?'

Micha proceeded to give the good doctor another curtailed version of events. After a day out with his friend, Grayson, he'd fallen (headfirst this time) off the wagon, drinking well into the night and days following that meeting.

'Seems to be something I just cannot learn. Why can't I stop at four or five? The impetus that drives one to binge drink … all these years later, and I still haven't really figured out the how and why of it.'

'Like a switch,' Halbrook ventured. 'Like a switch is thrown in your head?'

Micha was surprised at his own inability to conjure that particular metaphor in the past. 'Yes!' he cried, and laughed. 'God, yes. That sums it up rather perfectly. One minute, you're rollicking along in life just dandy – hell, even the *thought* of going into a liquor shop is somehow repulsive to me – then *whammo*. A switch is thrown, and I could lap up all the dark ale in the universe.'

'Is that what you drank this time around? Dark ale?'

Micha nodded. 'At the beginning, at least. Afterward, it was anything goes. I bought some regular beers on the way home. Yesterday, I discovered a few empties of four and five dollar red wine. *Yuck.* Back in the day, we used to call that stuff the two-buck chuck.'

Halbrook, who had probably never drunk a bottle of anything under fifty dollars in his life, simply nodded in return. Then he said, 'But the … How did you term it? The cyclone is over for you now? Tell me … what happened on this particular occasion? Do you have some recollection of those days?'

Here it is – time to fess up.

'Yes,' he replied in a voice that was barely audible. Confessions were always a bitch, it seemed. 'I returned to Hadley Grove.'

Though Halbrook raised an eyebrow, he didn't seem overly surprised.

'This time, I didn't pick up right where I left off, either. Something's changed in that regard. Events occurred when I was not present, and vice versa in *this* world. It's like … whoever is writing this story only needs me there for certain scenes – certain *important* scenes. And the rest of the time, a lot of stuff happens that I don't even know about.'

'Such as?'

'Things to other characters. There's a whole second story going on I'm not quite aware of. One that isn't my own.'

'So you're actually interacting with these characters you've created? Living a kind of life?'

Micha thought about Sara's green eyes – the hot taste of her mouth. While schizoids were certainly wont to demonstrate an exclusive internal fantasy world, did his experience jive with that criterion at all anymore?

'I am,' Micha admitted. 'And before you say anything, I do realize that booze can do remarkable things to the average person's psyche. Hallucinations, psychotic breaks with reality. Hell, making first contact with aliens. I mean, how many times do you see that? The stark-raving bum on the street holding up a sign and gibbering about space beings and ass-probes? The truth is, I've weighed and considered all of these things, and I am willing to accept it's all just a fever dream. But this doesn't take away the fact that it's happening and feels every bit as real as me sitting here, talking to you.'

'Did you have an opportunity to go through some of that literature I gave you regarding SPD?'

'Some of it. Most of the stuff I just Googled.'

'Then you might have read individuals with schizoid personality disorder can have brief psychotic episodes, particularly if tired or nervous, and these are often of atypical visual hallucinations, nihilistic thoughts; strange scenes, auditory hallucinations and even paranoid delusions.'

'That bad, huh?'

Halbrook grinned with such jocularity Micha felt certain nothing on earth was ever *that bad*. 'The good news is they're brief, and often don't directly impact your real life.'

'Doc,' Micha pointed out. 'I lost days this time.'

'Which I believe was a direct result of you falling off the wagon again, my friend. You're definitely okay now. Do you think you'll be able to stay completely sober for the foreseeable future? Is there anybody you can call for support when triggers come into play? I can refer you to a DASSA program here in Concord if that's an area you find lacking.'

Micha thought about his one friend in the real world; he thought about his church-going family in Hicksville who preferred, on the whole, to keep him out of their thoughts entirely. Ironically, only Sara Childs seemed to offer the kind of support he'd been so desperately craving his whole life …

And she wasn't even real.

Instead of saying these things, Micha turned on his own smile, one so cunning and rehearsed it shared league with the doctor's own.

'Don't worry about me, doc. The cyclone's over for now. And the story is almost finished.'

***

Though there was a certain cathartic release leaving Halbrook's office, Micha knew he needed liberating of a different kind. Returning home, he decided to call (Skype, never the phone) Grayson Ross, hoping his friend's hermetical lifestyle was in effect late on a Friday.

Grayson answered on the fourth ring. 'There you are,' he said, wiping his spectacles on a t-shirt to better see the screen. 'Thought you'd fallen off the face of the earth. You know *I* don't really give a shit, but some of your social media buddies were a bit worried.'

'Oh, come on – without me you'd be dead inside. How did you pull up the other night?'

Grayson looked confused for a moment, then his vision cleared as their last encounter returned. 'It wasn't *business time* with that barmaid if that's what you mean, but I managed to get someone's phone number later on with the aid of a certain app called Tinder.'

'Have you called her yet?'

'Of course I haven't! What about you? You were swaying a bit when you left the bar. Manage to get home in one piece?'

More or less, Micha thought. *I did manage to stagger into another world, Grayson – but I found my way back again.*

'All good. Listen, the reason I called …'

For a moment he drew a blank, struggling to find the best possible route to take … or perhaps the right order of words to make his case. Behind his friend, Micha could see Grayson's posters, a geeky multitude of them, filling up his walls. There was a large *Evil Dead* poster (subtitled *Dead by Dawn* with a malevolent and protruding skull); there was one for a Dean Koontz book, *Midnight*, which displayed fog-shrouded ranks of serried homes strafed by an ominous and purple twilight. *Moonlight Cove*, Micha thought, now recalling the narrative of the book. *God, that town isn't all that far removed from –*

'Micha? You called about your book again, didn't you?'

'I'm that transparent?'

'Not to anyone but me.'

'Grayson, I need to know. What would it take ... what would have to happen in *The Mercury Man* for our hero to be where he needs to be? For him to end up *living* in Hadley Grove.'

'*Living* in Hadley Grove? So you're talking about the stock phrase happily-ever-after?'

'Not exactly. Well ... kind of. I mean, there would be a price to pay, of course.'

His words to Sara in the car suddenly floated back: *The characters must band together to unwit an enemy and bring it low. Most of the time, they do, and become greater people for their efforts. Even in the face of enormous personal loss ...*'

Good Christ ... he'd actually said that? It sounded pretty pretentious – but it was, of course, true in tales of fiction. Sometimes the good guys got what they wanted, but there was always – *always* – a price to pay.

'Grayson?'

'Just a minute – I'm thinking. You want Mason to live permanently inside the world of his novel ... although not necessarily defeat the demons?' Grayson drew in a thoughtful breath, chewing his lower lip in study. 'In that case, I think he would have to make some kind of purely unselfish sacrifice – perhaps even die, so-to-speak, so that someone else can live.'

'Sacrifice?'

'Yes, a sacrifice. Maybe even a species of martyrdom.'

And there it was – a kind of *Deuce Ex Machina* served up on a steaming plate of the obvious. A purely unselfish act on his part would mitigate if not entirely waylay his shortcomings as a character. Could it potentially redeem him? Probably not. But it would definitely go a long way to giving him something like an arc, at least in the eyes of any story gods. So far, in the saga that was Hadley Grove, Micha Tudor hadn't done much of anything to justify a happily-ever-after or a perpetual stay in town; no reckless acts of confrontation or devil-may-care heroics had been breached. He was, when you got right down to the creative nitty-gritty, just a stupid lovesick writer in a world where he could barely justify his own existence.

But if I … did something unselfish? Grayson's sacrifice …

'Dude … are you okay?' Grayson was looking at him through the laptop's monitor with questioning eyebrows and genuine concern. 'You went spacey there all of a sudden.'

'I'm fine,' Micha said. 'Grayson, I need to thank you again.'

'For what?'

'For getting me out of this log-jam. You know what, if this thing ever does get published, I probably *will* have to give you part of the proceeds. Or better yet …' Micha grinned. 'How about a dedication?'

'Ha-ha. Listen, it was really only a suggestion. I can't tell you how to end your own book, Micha. Anyway, didn't you once tell me you believed the old chestnut of *it is the tale and not he who tells it*? That you're basically an automaton when writing? Even if *you* don't know, you're subconscious does, and everything will roll out as easily as tears or laughter. It's a pretty good little book, Micha – a bit Steve King-esque without the weight. In the second edit, just give it some more urgency and pace.' Grayson leaned back in his desk chair, sliding a casual hand through his hair. 'First things first, though.'

'What?'

'Finish that sucker and knock it out of the park.'

***

As Micha made preparations for bed, there was a sense of finality about the ritual.

You've had this feeling once before, remember? That afternoon you decided to die.

But was it the same? On that occasion, he'd gone through similar acts: cleaning the house from top to bottom, making sure his stomach was halfway empty and that he smelled sanitary. Arrangements to leave everything behind. To leave the *world*.

It's not the fucking same. That was a conscious decision to die. I'm not making the same decision. This is about ...

'It's about not coming back,' he breathed out loud to his empty house. 'It's about never returning, that's all. Same result, don't you think?'

No answer from the sarcastic inner monologue.

Planning aside, there had never been any kind of goodbye note or farewell message that previous juncture. Should he make one now? Would Lila or anybody in his family be expecting one?

Not if things work out how you intend, if you succeed.

And if he didn't succeed?

This time it was Lila's reply again; Lila adopting her knowing yet critical voice that was equal parts loving and grave. *You* will *succeed. And do you know how I know, Micha Tudor? I know because you're the writer – you've* always *been the writer – and at the end of the day it's the writer who has the final say.*

Alone in his room, Micha smiled wryly.

He made his way to bed.

Slipping beneath the covers, he reached out and clapped once, extinguishing the sound-sensitive lamp. In complete darkness, Micha burrowed deeper beneath the comforters … and his wry smile did not fade.

Chapter Seventeen

Something's changed in that regard, he'd told
Halbrook when describing the physical properties of
jaunting from one world to another – the time now elapsing
between. *It's like ... whoever is writing this story only
needs me there for certain scenes.*

Opening his eyes, Micha was confronted with a sight
(while not wholly unexpected), was not quite anticipated,
either. Immediately in front, a small melee of cheering and
sweaty bodies gyrated, their catcalls and wolf-whistles
directed toward a stage of music and sound. For a short-
lived moment, he thought he was back beside Mandy; she
of the champagne breath, addled hour displacement, and
questing tongue. Then the revelers' characteristics became
more focused, revealing a cavalcade spectacle of permed
hairdos, sweatshirts worn off one shoulder, and fluorescent
leg warmers. The music blaring from the stage was loud
and familiar, a wall of bass mainlined with honky-tonk

hooks.

Why it's Mary Lamont, Micha thought in dumb wonder. *Complete with her backing band, I see.*

Four of them, including Mary, were swaggering underneath a halo of spotlights, smiling faces sheened with runnels of perspiration. On bass, there was the beautiful and blonde, Britney Tingay, a character who had spoken no more than three words of dialogue in three different books. And behind her on drums, his large forehead sheathed in a terrific corona of red bandana, was Eric Soudas, a young adept whose christened nickname among friends was *Captain Cymbals.* Rhythm guitar duties were currently helmed by Shannon Brigham, a twenty-something mother-of-two who was strumming the kind of Les Paul Gibson Micha had only ever *dreamed* about owning in the world he came from.

And that's the beautiful thing about fiction, ladies and gentleman: you can make up any old beautiful thing, and just for a fleeting moment on the page, it's every bit as real and tangible as stone.

Leaning back, Micha felt a hand. Turning around, there was Sara, *his* Sara, appearing every bit as sweaty and luminous as the rest of this giant entourage. She took his hand gently, guiding him through the throng of patrons, hoping to catch the attention of her staff with wild gesticulating hands. A number finished, the crowd went wild, and Mary Lamont chatted briefly with her audience, telling them about taking the drive into New Hampshire, about what it was like sharing a van with bandmates whose personal hygiene was sometimes questionable. Wild applause followed, all of it superseded by a riotous species of laughter only the newly inebriated could summon.

On the mahogany bar top, a colander glass filled with ice cubes skidded in Micha's direction. With a flourish, Sara picked it up and proffered it. 'It's a *double* screwdriver,' she said amiably, then winked. 'I tipped Rachel off earlier about our preferences.'

Micha took the drink but stopped short of raising the glass. 'What should we drink to tonight, do you think?'

Laden with a straw, her own glass appeared. 'Ever the gentleman. How about …' here she lifted the liquor, clinked it against Micha's glass. 'How about we raise a toast to surviving *The Horror of Hadley Grove*?'

Despite the serious pronouncement (and their predicament), Micha managed to produce a lopsided grin. 'So you don't think I'm completely nuts about this story thing, huh?'

'Well, I *did* read somewhere that pretty much all writers are crazy.'

'Now *that's* something I'll drink to.'

As they did so, Micha grimaced at the acidic tang. 'Sara … there's some more I need to tell you. Before we go any –'

Mary and her band chose that moment to launch into another song, this one complete with a familiar melody; familiar because he recalled writing the lyrics himself, the song an inclusion into one of the Hadley Grove novellas.

Century's gone …
Nobody's here because …

The curtain went down ...
It feels so wrong.

Sara was looking at him with wide eyes, her expression glazed yet expectant. 'What is it? What's wrong?'

Mid-chorus, the song came to a crashing conclusion. Without missing a beat, Mary's band took up the reigns of another, mellower tune ... a blues dirge, dark and hauntingly familiar.

I know what's happening here ...

He did. Mary's band wasn't just siphoning songs from his subconscious; they were playing its greatest hits. And what background song was perhaps Hadley Grove's main theme this far into the story?

You can run on for a long time, Mary sang into her microphone, now looking directly into Micha's eyes across a sea of heads. *Run on for a long time. Sooner or later, God is gonna cut you down.*

Across the width of the stage, multicolored dance lights were evenly placed, and their illumination was abruptly eclipsed by another pulsating light broadcast through the windows behind them, this one the color of confrontation and coming from a police cruiser.

***

Standing inside the open driver's side door of his cruiser, Brandon watched as the trespassers exited Delta Bronze; he watched as they closed the door behind them and stepped onto the footpath.

From the tavern, nobody else followed them … and that was good.

'Slowly now,' Brandon said. 'Ever so slowly, put your hands out where I can see them.'

Driving here, Brandon did not have the slightest presentiment how his unannounced arrival would pan out. He needn't have worried.

Because he wasn't alone in tonight's endeavors.

'Sherriff,' said the man who (up until now) Brandon had never laid eyes upon. 'There's no need to wave that thing around. We're prepared to come with you quietly.'

Brandon absently looked down at the revolver clenched in his right fist. As the two came closer, he said, 'You know, it's a very good thing you and I have not so much as exchanged a single word until now.'

'And why do you say that, Sherriff?'

'Because you have the kind of monkey face my mother used to call woebegone. Faggots like you shouldn't be breathing air or walking the earth.'

In his experience (and Brandon's experience was vast), such utterances usually put a suspect on edge – even the hardened ones. But Micha and his bride only stared back casually as though privy to a world of secrets he could only guess at.

'Get in trespassers,' he said, stepping aside and opening the backdoor of the cruiser in the process. 'Mind the upholstery, though. You two lovebirds look sweaty as fuck.'

Inside, the cruiser had been retrofitted, subtle adjustments made; the space between driver and rear passengers fitted with bulletproof glass and certain other oddments. If Clyde and his bride decided to get any ideas, these oddments could put them into a world of pain. Again with that eerie nonchalance defying expectation, the trespassers hunkered down; Sara quickly ducked forward, depriving Brandon any opportunity to give her a shove.

The woebegone wasn't as cooperative.

Standing close enough that Brandon could reach out and smack him, he asked, 'Did the scars on your shaft ever heal, officer?'

If you do not do your level best to meet these demands, came the voice of his masters, *we will be unhappy.*

'What?'

'On the horizontal tissue of your dick, did the scars ever heal?'

For a moment, everything (the still-strobing parked cruiser, the gun held tautly in his hand) was eclipsed in a hot minute of piercing memory: of being no more than twelve and wincing in agony as his mother rubbed the nub of his penis with sandpaper. The memory was so long ago now – and so long buried – that Brandon had often been dubious it had ever occurred. But now a banquet of emotions were in the offing: guilt, shame, and the hot, searing torment of recall.

'It was a punishment,' Micha was saying. 'Punishment for ferreting away your sister's panties on occasion. Secretly, though, you *enjoyed* the experience of it a little, didn't you? Once the shame had mellowed, that is. You got to do something the big kids did long *before* they did. And you had the scars to prove it, too. Little white lines like the top of a doughnut running the length of your five inch manhood.'

'Quiet,' Brandon said, and discovered he had no more than this. His thoughts (usually a coherent wall of hardened stone) had suddenly taken a freefall nosedive. Just how anybody – least of all the skinny fuck standing beside him – could possibly *know* such a thing defied belief. Brandon had borne witness to the miraculous before, of course; he could even now smell its clammy wind on Main Street. But this was far out of the loop of what constituted miraculous. This was –

'The abused becomes the abuser, right?' said Micha Tudor. 'Mommy issues all the way for a pervert like you.'

An unconscious action, Brandon's left fist flew out. With claw-like fingers, he gripped the trespasser's windpipe. He proceeded to squeeze, more memories of his mother

(remember the time she put steel pegs around it?)

trying to intrude as he did so.

Then, as swiftly as it had arrived, the rage subsided. Brought about by the night air, which seemed to contain an unseen presence in addition to a rising breeze.

If you do not do your level best to meet these demands, we will be unhappy.

'All right,' Brandon said, dropping his hand in mock surrender. 'All right. You win.'

The air quieted. The breeze calmed.

Brandon looked at Micha Tudor, hoping the trespasser saw in his gaze every bit of malice afforded it. His masters had authority here, yes; but Brandon would personally intervene when and if they chose to let their guard down, even for a moment.

***

From inside the vehicle, both driver and passengers watched as the streets of Hadley Grove came alive with wonders and terrors.

Having only been in possession of the librarian's manuscript for a short time, Brandon Delgado had not been exposed to the world contained within those pages: a world of midnight apparitions and strange alchemy. Had he been aware, Loretta Hardin's descriptions and everything seen through the windshield would have immediate parallels.

Slowing down somewhat so that the cruiser's eagle eye headlights could pick out the anomaly, Brandon said, 'Jesus Christ, would you look at that.'

Revealed in the beams: a staggering entity of life; a thing composed of juxtaposed flesh. Acting as a burden as it ambled along, its back supported a giant growth like a tumescent cancer. Devoid of anything but one spheroid eye, a misshapen face blinked back at them in league with its slow footfalls.

Brandon floored the accelerator.

In the houses, living rooms and bedrooms were animated with their own aggressive activity – stuttering flashes like distant ball lightning. Within some, hoarse screaming could be heard as occupants inside battled whatever was producing the illumination. Although not knowing for sure, Brandon was willing to bet some citizens had their own version of the ambling giant to contend with.

Finally pulling onto Terry Peak Road, the sky abruptly changed color; the above firmament ablaze with mottled greens and reds. From out of the clouds, like some kind of celestial birth, creatures the size of dogs with bat-like wingspans took flight, honing in on houses but leaving their moving vehicle unscathed. In the storm drains, glistening wet apparitions addled with eyes were briefly illumed by the passing headlights.

Brandon hit the gas even harder, all the while swerving to avoid fresh horrors sprung from the shadows.

'Do you *see* all this?' he shouted at his passengers. 'This is just a *taste* of what Malphas has planned for this shitty town. Has planned for *you*. Tonight, by God, you're going to wish you'd never stepped foot inside my home.'

When the church came into view, natural thunder rolled across the horizon, bringing with it the seeds of a storm whose reverberations would be felt in Hadley Grove for years to come.

***

One sentence beat a litany inside Sara's head:

Micha was telling the truth all along. Micha was telling the truth all along.

In the deepest chasms of her heart, she'd believed him, of course – but it had taken coming face-to-face with the miraculous to fully cement the notion. Delgado's cabin hadn't quite been enough; neither had Samantha's manuscript or even the lifelong perception, sometimes all-pervading, that something was terribly wrong with Hadley Grove.

The final arbiter had come in the form of monsters.

They slunk in culverts and pooled in alleyways; they filled the homes of Hadley Grove in the form of a peristaltic light so bright it left a burning afterimage when she looked away. Which led to the thought: was every home now being invaded by one of Malphas's mercury incarnations?

Was Alexa currently screaming for her mother or perhaps even fighting for her life?

The Sherriff was speaking, 'This is just a *taste* of what Malphas has planned for this shitty town. Has planned for *you*. Tonight, by God, you're going to wish you'd never stepped foot inside my home.'

The cruiser lurched, and with the momentum, they rounded Terry Peak's final bend. Doing so granted them a new view filling up every portion of the front windshield: a cathedral's overbearing arches created the impression of something gone to seed; of something haunted. Once upon a time, its reputation was one of amusement more than anything else, Natal broadcasting antiquated sermons from a raised dais. Now Sara saw it exactly for what it was: a nightmare structure brought into being by forces she had only a rudimentary understanding of.

They came from the stars, a voice whispered. A voice that sounded like a dead woman's. Loretta Hardin's, perhaps. *They came from the stars to feed.*

Sara shuddered and felt Micha's hand grip her own. He'd sensed her discomfort, as he'd sensed and known so much about this story already. Was he the author here, as his confessions alluded? Or was he only a passenger like herself, drawn crudely into someone else's vision? If he was an architect, then she hoped this part of the story had already been previsualized and fleshed out; they were merely going about the motions to a victorious finale.

Opening of their own accord, the gates widened, welcoming inside Brandon Delgado and his captured entourage.

***

In preceding stories featuring the church, Micha had never taken great pains to describe its architecture, preferring instead to let Natal's character be the main focal point when highlighting Hadley Grove's adversarial element. Now, descending upon the building, he wished to Christ he had.

Knowing its proper layout sure would come in handy.

Despite the late hour, an opaque luminosity played over every brick and corner. In addition to flying buttresses and pointed arches, the front façade had ribbed vaults, groups of colonnettes, and lancet-shaped openings. Wheel windows sat above richly carved tympana enclosed by bands of archivolt molding. Jutting shafts of odd bulbous enlargements shared space with strange five-ringed arrangements. Malphas and Natal's church, despite being a lair for demonic souls, had an undeniable beauty.

Because the Devil's voice is sweet to hear, Micha thought absently.

'We're here,' Delgado announced, as if Micha and his companion were blind to what they were seeing. 'Don't forget that I have a gun. When we get out, it will be trained on you.'

For a short period, they travelled through an extended driveway hugging the church like an accompanying moat, tall shrubs and conical saplings blocking out anything visible beyond them. The closer they got, the more their driver began to exhibit visible signs of anxiety.

'You never come this far, do you?' Micha remarked, recalling fresh portions of *The Mercury Man*. 'This far is like a point of no return. You're terrified of them. Tell me something, is all of this really worth the price of admission? What the fuck are you going to do if Johnny Cash is dead in *all* worlds?'

'Shut up!' Delgado roared from the front seat. 'Just shut your goddamn trap. I don't know who the fuck you are, or how you know anything, but when we're finished with you, you're going to be singing hallelujah out of your asshole *and* your prick. *That's* the kind of world coming for *you*. Both of you get out of this car now and walk slowly toward that door.'

Still holding Sara's hand, Micha obliged the Sherriff.

***

Compared to the rest of the church, the door in question was nondescript – an ordinary door. With the promised gun trained on their backs, Micha and Sara walked through first, Delgado trailing behind. Dim light revealed a small antechamber that broached into a carpeted hallway. Following it, a ribbed ceiling gave way to their inevitable destination, the Nave.

Micha toured here once before, as a kind of wandering spirit after drinking his cocktail of death. During that sojourn, Natal's church wasn't too far removed from countless others built during the medieval epochs of human history. Natal had even been present, bathing his brother in a greenhouse pool of mercury solution.

Micha looked upon a central aisle vastly transformed.

Over every inch of available space ran a silken molten-like webbing. What sprung to mind immediately were dozens of films with a similar motif: the lair of a monster slimed with its evil residue. In film, such aesthetic existed as a visual prop. What Micha saw here was an engineered tapestry existing for a malign purpose.

Sara said, 'Those are … *people*.'

They stopped to watch the scene: bladders of life trapped inside the webbing. Some sat in the pews like a macabre audience, while others hung from the ceiling. Inside a translucent casing, humanoid forms writhed in an agony of their own making; the more they moved, the more the bladders seem to cultivate themselves. As Micha observed, faces writhed against the organic surface, lips pulled taunt in a feral smile within a framework of floating hair.

Delgado swallowed, trying to contain his distaste. 'Keep going,' he said.

'You're okay with all this?' Sara asked. 'Are you really?'

'What do I care? Coming up here, each and every one of them got what they deserved.'

Passing close to a bladder, Micha saw what the man meant: they were indeed people – remnants of the priest's flock.

Visible through amber liquid, a woman's high-heeled shoe floated. Next to it, still enshrouded in a black dress, a torso lay buoyant. Smaller bladders lay embedded in the main aisle, their minor contents foreshadowing their previous physical selves as children. And in some cases, infants. Whatever metamorphosis was currently taking place had rendered them unrecognizable, a return to the prenatal womb. Beyond these lesser spawns, a scattering of parent ones lay plastered to the walls of the greenhouse.

'They're not here,' he whispered. 'Not this late in the narrative.'

'*What* did you say?' Micha winced as Delgado's gun punched into his back.

'Nothing.'

'Then keep moving. We've still got a ways to go.'

Past a web-shrouded chancel and into a final corridor, they walked, inching closer to the larger bladders as they did so.

They're chrysalis, Micha thought, watching a debris field of human sediment inside its oval sphere. *That's what I'm looking at, a roomful of human cocoons.*

***

Although Samantha's manuscript had provided ample

description of the corridor they negotiated, the years had reconditioned the walls enough for Micha to feel completely lost. Of course, it wasn't merely the years at work. Below, decades of intensive labor begun by Orobas was coming to fruition. The stone walls were bleeding, an amalgamation of steaming mercury and crimson material with the consistency of sap.

When the dead entered their path, Micha was not surprised.

Though their captor clearly was.

'Jesus Christ,' the Sherriff said, peering at a sarcophagus lining the wall. He seemed poised to say something else; something of greater import but could only repeat the phrase.

Though the coffins lay lidless, some sort of invisible barrier tethered something inside. Pressing a glistering face against the unseen wall, a male spirit favored Delgado with a scowl equal parts hunger and hatred. Draping its anatomy, cobs of spirit-stuff shared space with contrails of meat, a flower of viscera like a petticoat. Despite its state (or perhaps because of it), the sarcophagus was in the process of splitting apart, fissures appearing like vines. More dead, already unshackled and sniffing in growing agitation, had begun to throng the corridor as luminous silver faces, gliding over coffins like sharks. Sensing their desperation, Delgado motioned his prisoners forward with a wave of his weapon.

He's rattled, Micha thought. *Now would be a good time to –*

No, Micha. That's not the way this story ends.

No authorship to the voice. Not one he recognized, anyway. Of course, it didn't matter – because the statement was true. Horror novels like *The Mercury Man* did not end with the hero cold-cocking his rival and running away with the girl …

They ended in blood.

Chapter Eighteen

Born into the realm of earth, Natal Purson had nevertheless retained memories of Hell; that unfathomable place between the stars his species called home. Likening these recollections to race memories, Orobas had been proud of his son's skillful art of remembrance; the young demon on occasion describing a megalopolis of titanic black ships traversing a sea of profound suffering. Though such recollections weren't without sporadic embellishment, Natal had (for the most part) characterized a diagram of Hell not far removed from the real thing. When the task had fallen to him to build upon the Hall of Portals, those very same race memories had served as stimuli in the architectural process.

Built and conceived as a gateway to many worlds, the Hall of Portals took its main inspiration from one.

Hell.

Stitched together to form partitioned bulwarks, a

bleeding profundity of flesh attached to flesh formed walls with no discernible arrangement, an insult to the Homo sapiens' creator, the God of Jehovah. Where a human head began, rib sections and torsos overlapped. Serving as a bridge to these, inverted and glistering viscera met a conurbation of arms and hands, an organization suggestive of invented deities. There were stacked breasts and stretched pubis regions; there were steaming invertebrate and reversed organ systems. Hundreds of eyes, all seemingly alive, had been sewed together to form jostling sections of life like piles of refuse on a saltwater sea. No longer void, breathtaking to its architects, the Hall of Portals was more a vast labyrinth of roofless rooms serving the soon-to-be-opened schisms.

***

At the center of the growing mass, they stood; Malphas and Natal both donned in their finest cassocks. Only steps away from the false priests, Madison Bowthorpe lay unconscious on a slab of stone. Her complexion was pale, almost white, the center of her body rising and falling with a steady beat of breath.

Natal inquired of his brother, 'Malphas?'

'Yes, brother?'

For tonight's final harvest, the maladies afflicting his sibling had weakened somewhat, granting Malphas the provisional ability to stand. Though seeing him thus could be disconcerting, Natal was, nonetheless, overcome with a willful pride. Their journey had been long; their battles hard fought. Tonight, their suffering would be for *something*.

'I know you come here for private mediations in addition to speaking with Father's shade. The truth is, only he had a proper grasp of the power at our fingertips. Only he knew its secret machinations. Has this ever made you feel ill at ease?'

Malphas stifled an annoyed expression. 'It is natural to feel nervous when we are so close to seeing a life's work realized.'

For a while neither spoke, only stared at the unmoving girl. Finally Natal said, 'Do you think our wildcard is the final ingredient instead of this girl?'

'We've discussed this.'

'But where does her knowledge come from? What if she's in league with what's coming through?'

'I suppose we'll soon find out. Look, Delgado has arrived.'

Natal followed the direction of his brother's silver eyes, now trained on the thin stone bridge serving as the only conduit to the world above.

***

Brandon came to another halt, all coherent thought suddenly lost in a conflagration of sight.

Like Micha Tudor, he had travelled to this place once before; he even knew its secret name. But trying to reconcile *that* occasion with this one was like trying to compare separate worlds.

An underground void had been replaced with a city.

No, not a city. This is a labyrinth.

Inside the labyrinth were many roofless rooms, each one cordoned off from the other by moving organic walls. Like buildings in a squall, they oscillated, completely raw and glistening with life. Though parts of the labyrinth were swabbed in shadow, Brandon could perceive each room was only a kind of conduit to the center of it all …

Titanic oblongs of blackened reality, shapes like welts in the fabric of space-time. Things Brandon could only assume were the physical portals he'd briefly glimpsed in his previous visit. Much like the dead parishioners spread about the Nave, they were graduating into something new.

Even my dreams haven't quite prepared me for this.

Prepared or not, this was exactly what he had signed up for.

It was time to come through with his end of the bargain.

Much as they had on the journey here, the woebegone and his mistress said nothing, hands clamped together like lovers on a tour of Hell.

'Not far to go now,' Brandon muttered, taking his first tentative steps into the labyrinth below.

***

The cocooned bodies had been bad.

This was worse.

Within the labyrinth, a progressive passageway presented itself, one whose walls were seemingly biological; a cavernous funhouse of gristle and meat. Now gripping Micha's hand so tightly her tendons showed, Sara resisted the urge to simply flee. Until now, the core of her resolve had come from those to have previously trodden this path: Loretta Hardin and her ilk, many of whom had gone on to wound the architects and survived to tell the tale. But now that path had changed, and there was nothing in the manuscript regarding it. Perhaps embracing story hour for Micha's sake had not been the wisest course to take. After all, did it guarantee she would ever see Alexa again?

In the stew of the walls, limbs had given way to a montage of children's faces, stripped of hair follicles yet completely hirsute with the meat binding them. Bereft of teeth, slickened gums greeted the newcomers in open expressions of malice.

Whatever the priests have planned for us – surely nothing can be worse than these walls ...

Sara peered over at Micha, briefly studying his eyes. Perhaps the sentiment of love she felt for him had always been there, despite the brevity of their time together. Perhaps it was no more than an illusory emotion written for her character – the obligatory romance.

Despite knowing this, she still recognized it as a fundamentally real thing.

So there would be no running away from what lay at the end of the passageway.

***

Before their final walk into the Hall of Portals, Malphas Purson had spent the entire day in rigorous preparation, his body immersed deep within the mercury pools – so deep that no daylight had penetrated from the skylights above. Lent power by the awakening machine below, Malphas proceeded to summon dozens of golems, an army of them, each one's birthing canal a river of light near the front gates. Having attained enough corporeal mass, the golems walked, slithered, and in some cases flew down into Hadley Grove. While some took their inspiration from the silver serpent, others were of a different order; beings whose prototypes had begun when the brothers were just babes. As Natal had taken inspiration from the topographical nature of Hell, so had Malphas from the creature's native realm. Among the golem army were flying brutes whose wings outweighed their bodies, and whose passage through the streets created a wake of suffering for any pedestrian unlucky enough to be caught in their path. Sentient things, more in league with the forgotten species of *this* world, roamed the alleyways like a troop of conspirators, their source of sustenance (by design) forever elusive. Having been stretched to the full limit of his abilities, Malphas had deigned to summon the greatest golem of them all, a beast whose mythic nickname had sprung from his greatest torment.

On this last night, the Mercury Man would not be confined to one avatar, one incarnation. There would be dozens of the creatures, each as formidable as the last, marauding through entire households. Drilled to slaughter only some, the silver serpents would proceed to terrorize the remainder; temporary harbingers before the deluge to come.

Next, Malphas had called out to his human congregation. Come up to the church, he implored them. Come and witness a great miracle performed by your presbyter, a singularity centuries in the making. Not all of them had come, but enough had – eager acolytes ready for a special kind of martyrdom where their physical bodies would undergo a vast upgrade. Soldiers, Natal christened them, ready to fight for their masters should any enemies attempt to thwart what was coming.

Enemies ...

Given access by the human dog, Delgado, the one they'd assumed to be the enemy was now close. Though thanks to the girl-child, their wildcard was not some great unknown; instead, he was the most pertinent player of all.

At the far tether of exhaustion, Malphas had vacated his pools, making haste toward the arteries where Madison lay. Every inch the enigma since her capture, he decided to induce paralysis, thus waylaying any ambition she may have been fostering of fighting back.

Humans, while easy to cow before a harvest, still carried within them an unpredictable fervor; a thing neither he nor his brother had anticipated before their near capture at the hands of Wexler's mob.

***

Party of five, Micha thought. *The gang's all here.*
Stepping into the world of Hadley Grove on that first

occasion, Micha had been confronted with a caped cowboy belonging to another time … if not another world. The same apparition was present again, standing tall beside another villain who – before now – had only ever existed in Micha's imagination.

Micha said, 'You're not as imposing as I'd hoped you'd be. I guess that one's on me. They say a story is only as strong as its villain. Maybe I was never good at writing villains.'

Natal Purson only grinned at this, open lips revealing tombstone teeth mottled with age.

In the space between them rested a slab of stone, contoured like a coffin. Lying atop was Madison Bowthorpe, twin to Bethany, daughter to Penelope, looking for all the world like a young adult version of Sleeping Beauty under the pall of her death enchantment.

In the air directly above, titanic smudges of shadow churned, black portals in a process of becoming.

Delgado's voice came from behind. 'I did everything you asked, didn't I? I brought them here. I even dealt with that fucking uppity librarian-*bitch*. All I ask now is for you to give me what's rightfully mine. What was *promised*.'

It was the caped cowboy who answered, not in words but the swift reorganization of its flesh. The outcome of this – like a measured special effect – brought about the disintegration of its garb into the original progenitor: a squat man riddled with scar tissue bearing a leathery countenance. Above the face sprouted a mane of grey hair trailing to his buttocks. Gimp legs and scarecrow arms grew out of a thin frame. During the metamorphosis, only

Malphas's silver eyes remained a constant.

'We thank you,' said Natal. 'But tell me, Sherriff. Did you *also* happen to bring the manuscript we requested? The one you foolishly lost to these two?'

Brandon's features dimpled with sudden pain and regret. For a brief moment, Micha almost felt sorry for him. *It's like watching the schoolyard bully stumped by a teacher,* he thought. *Psychopath or not, he's just as clueless as we are ...*

'In your haste, you forgot, didn't you? No matter. Perhaps you were right before. Perhaps soon everything will be irrevocably changed.'

Sara, who until now had remained quiet, suddenly moved toward Madison ... then halted when Natal raised a spindly arm. 'Don't let a mother's nascent instinct take over,' he said. 'You can't stop what's about to happen.'

'We know what you are. Samantha's book told us. You're a twisted species who gets their jollies from playing the Devil. But you're no more the Devil than you are priests. You're *pretenders* to that crown. A couple of daddy-less demons orphaned from home.'

'And you,' said Malphas, speaking for the first time. 'Are nothing but a plain character in a fictional story. That *is* what this man has told you, isn't it? That we're all just bit players in his apocryphal masterpiece?'

Sara blinked in surprise.

'That's right,' Malphas said, smiling and nodding. 'We know all about lover boy's antics. This child before us might be outwardly strong, but inside she's as frail as the rest of your species. The landscape of her mind, such fertile ground for secrets. Take a look around you, Sara. Do you have any idea what this place *really* is?'

Sara looked … and so did Micha. The labyrinth they'd emerged from was distant and fading, the walls of flesh having succumbed to a kind of entropy; the shadow structures, another type of entropy altogether, continued to grow. Studying them, there could be little doubt of their purpose: they were portals, schisms in reality, the background music to this whole sorry tale. Within their centers, blooming through a fascia of black, other colors were becoming prevalent, a torrent of indigo and blue colliding. Arcs of lightning, or some derivative of the same, crackled from their peripheries.

'Micha knows, don't you? I suspect he knows very well. This place is in its very given name – a hall composed of portals into other uncountable realities. You see, for any event, there are an infinite number of possible outcomes to that event, a universe populated with *immeasurable* outcomes. The structure of the universe has always been, essentially, a snake eating its own tail. Our father, Orobas, understood some of this, if only its rudimentary aspects, and so does your friend. This man fancies himself as a kind of deity in Hadley Grove, and he would be somewhat right. Because he found a way to *escape the snake.*'

'What in the hell are you *talking* about?' Delgado roared. 'There is only one thing I'm interested in. And I want it delivered. I want it delivered *now.*'

Dismissively, Malphas said, 'You'll get your precious world, Sherriff. And not just that one, but more besides. The key to unlocking it all is standing here with us now.'

The key? It took Micha a few moments to realize he'd spoken the words out loud as a question.

Malphas was nodding again. 'At first we thought it had to be the twins, their special nature. Our Father's only instruction for his creation was to keep feeding it; to keep it greased ... that all the souls harvested here would be fuel for the machine. But we knew it wasn't enough. Something has always been missing, keeping it stagnant. A final soul, a key to unlocking it all.

'You're appearance in Hadley Grove is no accident, Micha Tudor. Don't you *see*? You're the missing element ... the final key that the Hall of Portals requires.'

Confounded, Micha tried to produce a reply but could only swallow.

'I knew from the first time I caught scent of you in Hadley Grove that you come from another world. You come from a world where *we are the story you created*. That's what Madison was trying to tell me. You think none of this is real – or you invented it. And perhaps, in a way, you did. This late in the game, I don't think it matters very much, do you? Because that which can be imagined *is* real. How did you do it, though? That's what I really want to know. How did you create what has taken us human lifetimes to build?'

Despite the rambling nature of the demon's spiel, Micha felt cold realization dawn. Yes – he *had* travelled here from another world. And yes, it was a world of his own making. Could Malphas be right in some capacity? Had he, Micha Tudor, created a doorway between realities simply by dying at his own hand? Had he somehow tapped reservoirs of strength only available to souls crippled enough? Souls diagnosed with mental maladies nobody else could see, for instance, who lived in the dark spaces between isolation and despair …

Souls with personality disorders?

No, that was too easy, surely. He hadn't checked himself into Hadley Grove simply by being born weird or having an intimate brush with death … had he? Such a thing was too horror fiction in itself. But if not a tango with the hereafter, then what? What did any of this *mean*?

Delgado shouted, 'You think all this is a fucking *story*? Well that explains some things, doesn't it? Please, let me kill this fucker, Malphas. He doesn't belong here. He doesn't belong in *Hadley Grove*.'

'I can assure you, he does,' Natal said, picking up from his brother's narrative. 'Crossing over, he changed the course of the story and has a final part to play. Give yourself over to us, Micha Tudor, and be the final key to unlocking all of this.'

Overhead something boomed, ricocheted, then *cracked*. Undergoing birth pangs, the portals were producing sounds in league with weather phenomena.

That's just what this place is, Micha realized. *A kind of birthing canal. And that sound we all heard was a crowning head of imminent life.*

Abruptly, Micha asked, 'How do *you* do it? That's what *I* really want to know. You harvest the living to feed yourselves. And you feed this *thing*. You think I'm some kind of deity? I don't know anything. Nothing more than your lackey here. So tell me how it all works. Tell me how it works and maybe I can help you.'

Sara's grip, an anchor till now, suddenly let go. Confusion was on her face, writ large. Micha looked back tiredly, hoping to convey this wasn't any kind of betrayal or long-pondered ruse – only simple curiosity. If a way out of this remained, they needed to discover if any kind of kryptonite still existed ... one far removed from the superstitious theories of a one-handed war veteran.

'We're just a simple species with simple appetites,' Malphas said. 'And your kin play the role of livestock. Not you though, Micha. You've risen beyond such primitive mammalian shackles.' He paused, regarding his subject thoughtfully. 'But you *are* ignorant, aren't you? Very well. If you must know. See for yourself, then.'

As his brother had before him, Malphas raised one scarecrow arm. With the motion, Micha reeled backward, though kept his balance because it wasn't any kind of physical assault. More an assault on his senses, which were presently being crowded by an array of imageries pertinent to Hadley Grove.

Demons possessed of powers to produce life (golems), Malphas participated in what could be construed as hunting expeditions; his brother a smiling showman concealing what lurked beneath. Here Micha was given some insight into the harvesting process, humans escorted like cattle to the feet of a thing augmented with talon-like claws and wings unfurled like sails. Not all were devoured in every instance, however, and the fates of entire families were consigned to the ossuary below, animal trophies on display. Fast forward a generation or so, and the demons came to understand that with each soul interred, the once empty hallways of their church began to cultivate themselves, literal doorways coming into being.

These strange edifices were the first to appear, Malphas imparted, now speaking inside his head. *But soon more architecture began to spring up. Catacombs housing the dead began flowing with the epoxy of life, blood and bone, born into being by the harvested.*

They had come to the brothers' lair through such passageways, of course; mortar replaced with a flotsam of human flesh ...and Micha was beginning to see all of it anew. There was no great mystery here after all, only an uncomplicated and unvarnished truth.

'You don't have any *idea* how this works, do you? You're like children left to run a school in the absence of adults. Only your *father* had knowledge behind the science, and he's dead. You've just been feeding it scraps until it got fat and decided to come of age. You're not any great mystery at all. Why, you're just ... *children*. Two kids who have no idea how to spend what they inherited.'

'You're wrong,' said Natal. 'About one thing. Our father isn't dead. He was *never* dead.'

With the words came another deluge of sound. Micha looked up and observed the portals changing course, their underbellies no longer idle but gravitating downward toward the witnesses below. And something else had also changed; rather, something else had been *added*.

Suddenly it was Samantha Moffatt's words springing to mind, the last portion both he and Sara had read before abandoning the manuscript. A paragraph concerning

Loretta Hardin's glimpse of something above …
*I looked up and saw reptilian eyes bearing down,
fixing us with a dragon's gaze.*

***

Flapping its wings in the space between the portals,
Loretta's creature had returned.

A kind of recognition had also dawned on Sara.
Though she didn't speak. Simply looked aloft with her
mouth agape.

Micha, who knew the established lore because he'd
dreamt the story in another world, said, 'I think Daddy has
finally come home to roost.'

'What?'

'Orobas. Their father. He's returned.'

Delgado was retreating, back toward the route they'd
taken, his intentions of fleeing clear. Though even he
couldn't prevent his eyes from straying skyward.

'Of this development, we couldn't be certain,' said
Natal, raising his voice to be heard over a thunderous elegy.
'Though we suspected … and we hoped.'

As the winged creature lowered itself, so did the
portals, their outlines changing shape in the process.
Hexagonal one moment; trapezoidal the next. For the first
time, Micha caught sight of their nucleus beyond the
shifting of colors: there was a promise of sky.

Malphas shouted something, an issue of warning to his
escaping dog, but the words were drowned out in a tempest
of storm sounds. Beside him, Micha could feel Sara

pressing for escape, so he reached out and held her hand again, then her gaze, hoping to project a fortitude that coming from another world still held currency in this foul place full of demons.

***

With the body of a Chinese dragon and the elongated head of a hammerhead shark, the original form of Orobas Purson hovered only a short distance from the onlookers.

The portals had reached ground level, creating a makeshift ring around their intended target. Their surfaces, shimmering bands of rainbow arrangements, presently revealed scenery more than the sum of skies: mountains and oceans and back to mountains again, peaks presiding over by many-limbed leviathans.

Orobas took up the field of vision once again, the dragon-like body riding currents of air with the lithe motion of a roller-coaster.

Eyeing Micha, Malphas said, 'Your purpose is now. Go to our father. Once the key steps into the schism, his great work will be realized.'

But it wasn't Orobas Micha was suddenly interested in – it was Madison resting on her slab. In the furor of events she'd been largely forgotten, more a casual side note in the story than anything else.

This is it. I'm at the crossroad. Whatever I do next will determine how this plays out.

And how *did* he want this played out? He wanted Sara and Madison out of this dungeon alive, certainly. And he wanted the demons sent back to whatever fresh hell they'd sprouted from. His own life could be forfeit, of course; Grayson's sacrifice inviting in the prospect of a happily ever after.

Perhaps there was another way to achieve what he wanted.

The answer lies within the portals, came a young voice. Little Madison's, perhaps. *And Malphas's words.*

What had the false priest claimed only a short time ago?

For any event, there are an infinite number of possible outcomes to that event, a universe populated with immeasurable outcomes.

It was a notion theoretical physicists had postulated about for decades ... the existence of a multi (or Meta) universe. Though no evidence existed for this hypothetical realm, the collective dreams of man where enough to give the concept a certain kind of weight.

And Orobas's portals, only a short distance away, were gateways into many realities.

Including one where the demons were defeated.

Doing as Malphas instructed, Micha began walking toward the portals.

***

With the appearance of the flying dragon – like something out of fucking Lovecraft – Brandon Delgado had finally seen enough. He'd made foolish decisions his entire life, but hooking up with the wanderer-dude, aka Malphas, was perhaps the granddaddy of them all. Instead of burning his mother alive, it was feasible he should have listened to her. Doreen's dire warnings (that one day he'd be undone by falling in with the wrong crowd) were now prophetic.

Attaching pegs to his cock, notwithstanding, Doreen had been wise.

The thought led him to the man who knew this secret, Mr. Woebegone, himself, who was now the priests' promised child – or something. Having instructed him to move toward their precious portals, the asshole was doing just that. It seemed to appease the flying dragon, its roiling body making lazy serpentine patterns as it glided. If that creature was an entrée for whatever lay on the other side, then Brandon decided he wanted no part of it … Johnny Cash singing his favorite ditty be damned. What was that old saying? That it was better to reign in Hell than to serve in Heaven? Well, Brandon was no longer fit to serve.

Because he was the kind of man who could be king practically anywhere.

His journey back to a regular passageway was thankfully without incident – gone were the flesh and blood walls; gone, too, the ghosts. With his masters' attentions diverted, perhaps there was a chance he could slink away unharmed before the shit really hit the fan.

No such luck.

Waiting for him around a corner, freshly hatched and even more transformed, were the cocooned abominations. Though parts of their humanity remained intact – Brandon saw human heads dangling atop writhing carapaces – these were more in league with the flying monstrosity. Two at first, then three, scuttling on hind legs like giant crabs. Above the heads and sprouting from a wet sleeve of pink flesh, snout-like proboscis sampled the air in Brandon's general direction.

Perhaps Woebegone was right after all, he thought as the creatures advanced, seizing up his avenues of escape and blocking them. *Perhaps the whole world really is nothing but a fucking horror story.*

Inside his head, Brandon heard the mocking, self-satisfied laughter of his one-time master.

You can run on for a long time, Sherriff, Malphas gibbered. *But sooner or later the Devil is gonna cut you down.*

***

Away from the priests and approaching the portals, Micha was almost overcome by the absurdity of the moment. He'd traversed familiar territory countless times before … although always in the comfort of his desk chair in front of a laptop. The imagination was one thing; the veracity of life quite another. The more he advanced, the more the portals seemed to grow, fluttering curtains draping three-dimensional reality.

Somehow, I don't think any of the greats came this far, he thought. *Did Laymon or Lovecraft ever get this close to one of their dreams?*

Sara, perhaps sensing the gravity of the moment, had failed to follow him. The demons, in turn, had also stayed behind, having somehow arrived at the conclusion this was all part of their grand design. Father Orobas – the floating dragon – had also gone quiet, and Delgado had vanished with its arrival. All Micha had to do now was walk up to a schism, walk *through* it, and the universe would either open up or …

Cease to be.

A question surfaced, one proposed by Lila long ago, who could spar with the best of them when it came to matters of the metaphysical. *What would happen to the world if God stepped into his own design?* she'd asked once.

Is that what I'm doing? Stepping into the design?

Micha marched forward, only feet away from the surface of a portal.

***

What became instantly apparent: the act of stepping through would not be necessary.

Presented to Micha on the portal's surface, like an interface, was a startling array of imagery: stories within stories, worlds within worlds.

Micha witnessed a world where Hadley Grove had never met its antagonists, Natal and Malphas Purson. In that story, another would rise in their place: the spirit of a murdered child. Haunted by the wrongs dealt to him, the child would go on to haunt the town. And another, branching away from this probability, where Micha was bested by the Mercury Man. Samantha Moffat, witnessing

309

the crime, would partake of a different adventure, clashing with the priests and their silver serpent in lieu of Micha. One more, an ending where Hadley Grove was consumed in a sea of flames, the lithe form of Orobas residing over the carnage.

On and on the stories went, bleeding and bleeding, the spiral of outcomes and narratives infinite. One, Micha saw, even had its roots in *his* world, where a young writer

(his name is Tait something Matthew Tait)

presently composed Micha's metafictional horror story as though it were his own.

But where was the narrative he sought?

The one where Malphas and Natal were defeated, and his sacrifice guaranteed safety for Sara?

There.

Micha watched as the narrative expanded, a gamut of images rising up from the schism to greet him.

What now?

Not a voice in his head but a physical presence standing close by, Sara Childs said, 'I think … *we* step through.'

And together, they did just that.

Chapter Nineteen

From the Monitor.com
Fears for Missing Concord Writer.

Police are seeking the help of New Hampshire residents who may have information on the whereabouts of a local man whose disappearance remains unsolved.

Micha Tudor, 34, of Concord has been missing since June 28th. Micha was last accounted for around 9am that day, when a neighbor spoke briefly to him.

The 34-year-old had been prolific in the local indie-writing scene, his debut book *The Taste Lands* shortlisted for the World Fantasy Award.

His disappearance has caused concern among some friends and industry colleagues. Though recently separated from

Micha, ex-girlfriend Lila Owen has urged anyone knowing of his whereabouts to contact either the police or his family immediately. Lila also states 'he wouldn't have gone far' after unearthing a recently completed, unpublished manuscript at Micha's place of residence.

Police have been unable to confirm if Tudor posted a series of worrying Facebook posts in the lead up to his disappearance.

The Taste Lands, originally published in 2011, chronicles the downfall of a rock star and his subsequent isolation from the world.

Micha, also a columnist, regularly contributed to dark fiction review publications and in recent times wrote a review of the latest Stephen King film adaptation *It*.

Authorities are asking anyone who has seen, spoken with, or had contact with Micha Tudor since June 25th to please contact Trooper First Class Aaron Russell via New Hampshire State Police Troop C Dispatch at (703) 223 – 8494

Epilogue

She approaches the bandstand wearing faded blue-wash denims, the kind with rips through the front. In her left hand she held a picnic basket; in her right she carried a boom-box radio.

'Wearing black again on a day like this?' Sara asked. 'Really?'

'You know me,' Micha replied. 'I have to fit the profile.'

Further down from the bandstand was a bright knot of children tempting the breeze with a small armada of kites. Their cries, at once playful and energetic, echoed across the park and carried toward the couple.

Sara mounted the steps. 'The profile of an eccentric horror writer living in a small town?'

'You know it.'

Loaded with three fat batteries, Sara positioned the boom box off to the right, leaving plenty of empty concrete for the task at hand. 'Did you want a drink now or …?'

'Later. First things first.'

'No Dutch courage this time? Why, Micha Tudor, you've come a long way since the day I met you as a shoeless vagrant.'

Micha smiled at the memory, though it quickly evaporated. Sara, sensing his darkening mood, stepped over to him. 'Hey, The Horror of Hadley Grove is over, remember?'

'Yes,' Micha replied in a shaky voice. 'It's over.'

There was a silence, and their gazes traveled upward beyond the children and away from the park. On the oceanic bluffs, a church built like a cathedral sat entirely empty, an abandoned crime scene. Though its role in recent events surrounding the Mercury Man were well known, few spoke of it. Hadley Grove, like many towns, harbored secrets. And now everything – the deaths of the priests and the strange supernatural occurrences at night – everything will go down as just another story to be told under the glow of beach bonfires at night. Sheriff Delgado, missing since the events of that night, is widely rumored to have been the Mercury Man all along. With his disappearance, so too will vanish the tales of that mythical monster.

'Madison?' Sara asks. 'She remembers nothing?'

'Oh I think she remembers … some things.'

'Her mother …'

'Is just glad to have her back. Anyway, I have a feeling that for Madison Bowthorpe, things are only just beginning.'

'What do you mean?'

'Her story isn't over yet.

Sara eyeballed him. 'Just promise me you won't be the one telling it.'

Micha laughed. 'I won't be. My part playing author with Madison is done. Let someone else take up the mantle.'

Sara was thoughtful for a time. Finally she said, 'So ... happily ever after? It's not just a stock phrase anymore?'

Leaning forward, Micha kissed the tip of her nose. 'No, it isn't. In our story, it's the real deal. Now, shall we do this thing or not?'

Bending down, Sara pushed play on the boom box's tape deck. From the speakers, Belinda Carlisle sang about living your life; about being free.

For the verse, Micha and Sara both sang along.

When the chorus melted in, Sara fell into step, and they danced.

February 2017 – July 2018
Adelaide, Australia.

Matthew Tait

ABOUT THE AUTHOR

A vociferous horror columnist since 2005, Matthew Tait published his first collection of dark fiction in 2011. Since then, he has twice been nominated for the Australian Shadows Award. Described as writing 'the sort of horror Clive Barker must read on his days off,' Matthew's fiction often treads the line between the familiar and the fantastic.

www.ingramcontent.com/pod-product-compliance
Lightning Source LLC
Chambersburg PA
CBHW060359260626
47160CB00006B/2370